RECOLLECTIONS

OF THE

RESTLESS

Recollections of the Restless

Recollections of the Restless
Copyright © 2018 by B. Masashi Kunisaki

Cover Art 2018 by Justin Hauser

ISBN 9781983223686

For my two grandpas, Haruji and Leo.
One I met, one I didn't.

RECOLLECTIONS

OF THE

RESTLESS

Contents

Home. 9

protection. 12

meet Kat.. 14

meet Fred Briggs.. 21

it's your damn choice. 41

can't trust polite. 60

what's up. I'm Fred Briggs. 69

enso.. 80

living poor. 84

too fucking quiet. 92

Hi, I'm Kat Scindo 97

relate. 107

stumble.. 120

life of a raindrop. 135

miyamoto.. 137

build. 139

appreciate.. 154

life of Donnie. 167

Marco Scindo. 176

Death's relapse.. 186

the Major. 189

being found. 196

roadtrip. 202

thin air tastes better. 207

the Major's memoire. 209

distract. 216

vice. 229

wild. 234

those fucking deer. 254

amigos nuevos.. 256

edge. 263

dive. 270

digest. 288

adios. 291

fallout. 299

preserve. 309

reunion.. 318

burn. 328

detach. 331

realization. 341

continue. 351

Homecoming. 357

Home.

I wish I could say I wasn't lonely. Miles ahead, miles behind. Didn't know where I was going, but definitely not lost. A chase? An escape? Or was I just discontent? Bored? All that mattered was a direction. Forward. I had little, but I was grateful to have that.

I thought about my recent past. My heart tightened. A feeling unfamiliar to me so I fell back on something I was accustomed to.

I wrote.

> *A man looks back on his past. He finds shelter in the only home he knows. It sprawls ahead, beyond his weary eyes, and, as the colors bleed into a gradual dark hue, he finds comfort in the nothingness. He sees what others do not see. He walks where others do not walk. The sun-soaked*

rock faces offer a warmth without caveat, without judgment, without wish for restitution.

He breathes deeply, slowly. The warm air fills his lungs, lifting his spirits as hills crawl over the horizon ahead, then retreat beyond the horizon behind. His world is packed on his back, yet his past is what weighs him down.

In his exodus from the world he once knew, he came upon the world he was meant to love. With a guardian protecting his steps, the man walks forward into abyss.

I stood up and circled to the back of the car, opened the trunk. I took inventory. A couple jugs of water. Some beef jerky. Cheetos from a gas station. Some oranges plucked from a grove that I passed a couple days back. My pack. A weathered, black-and-grey Osprey internal frame pack. Light, but it contained most of my life. I grabbed the bottom, and dumped the contents on the floor of the trunk. Gave it a shake as I watched the contents spill out. The normal backpacking stuff: waterproof matches, kindling, toilet paper, first aid kit, flashlight and headlamp, a Gerber fixed-blade knife. My old tent and sleeping bag. A small bundle wrapped in a red bandana tumbled out of the pack. I knew my gear in and out, yet this bundle was still an unfamiliar addition.

I grabbed the bandana and unfolded it. A photo with a piece of paper clipped to the back lay in the bandana. There were charred edges, apparently saved from licking flames. I didn't spend the time to study the photo or the note. Not now. I thought about how that photo had reached me but couldn't dwell. It was too early for that.

Another item in that bundle. I held it still partially wrapped in the bandana. I looked out at the empty road, squeezing the handle. The wood grip was soothing, and the cold steel bit at my fingers. The steel began to warm, as if fusing to its new owner. It was small but I knew the power it had, and what it meant to be carrying this. I tucked it in my front jacket pocket and circled back to the open trunk. Repacked my gear. Neat, organized. It was easier when there wasn't much to organize.

I sat in the driver's seat, hanging my feet out of the car. I opened my notebook and stared at it. Thoughts of the recent past crept back. I closed it.

"Alright, time to go. Andiamo." I tossed the notebook on the back seat, pen in my front pocket. Stretched my back before ducking back into the car. 7AM. Good early start on the day. I took a long pull of whiskey from my flask, and took the first steps of the day down the road.

protection.

Again, on the road, I wrote:

Waddling along, an Armadillo journeys alone though the desert. He comes upon a Scorpion. Scorpion tries to sting and pinch the Armadillo, but the Armadillo curls up in his armor before the Scorpion can hurt him. Whew. That was close.

Armadillo continues through the desert, Sunset warming his skin. Purple Mountains rose in the west and stood tall, ever-balancing on the horizon.

Armadillo comes upon Snake. Snake befriends Armadillo, with smooth talk and gifts of fresh water. Armadillo is cautious, but loosens as Snake earns his trust. Without warning, Snake's eyes turn a treacherous red, and Snake lunges out, poisonous fangs slicing the air. Armadillo is barely able to curl up into his armor in time. But he does. Whew. That was close.

Armadillo continues through the desert. The setting sun spills watercolors across the sky: reds and oranges and pinks and purples.

Night falls. Armadillo grows cautious because his Armadillo eyes fail him in the dark. He decides to stop, and curls up in his armor for the night. Coyote comes upon the armored Armadillo. He bites, claws, scratches at Armadillo but cannot break through his Armadillo armor. Frustrated, Coyote leaves him be.

Terrified but grateful, Armadillo makes a decision then and there.

"The world is a scary place. I have traveled through this desert and everything is trying to kill me. From now on, I will make sure I am always armored. No one will ever get me in here."

And so, that's what Armadillo did. He traveled through the desert, rolling much faster than he could ever waddle. Coyote, Snake, and Scorpion never harmed him again. And Sunset and Purple Mountains never saw Armadillo again.

meet Kat.

I loved the road. My sole focus on my next step, no long-term plans. Life simple. Not easy, but simple. I sped through miles quicker than minutes, and my survival sat squarely in my own hands. It was sometimes a challenge, living like that. When your focus is boiled down to the struggle of living, you can't be bothered by the hardships of a distant future or of the past. What a relief.

Rumbled through the desert in my white '92 Grand Cherokee. Windows open, sun beating me down. I drove alone. Stopped when I wanted to, stopped when I had to. Progress slowed sometimes by one distraction or another but I continued forward. I knew the Pacific was somewhere ahead of me, and I wondered what I would do when we met.

I pulled into the outskirts of a coastal town, and selected the first bar that I came across to collect my thoughts and rest my road-weary feet. Alcohol and a club sandwich made up my short to-do list. I grabbed my map of California, my wallet, and my notebook before heading in the bar.

A girl, a young woman, sat alone at the bar. Tattered and dirty Chuck Taylors clung to her feet. Her backpack, scarred and stained from adventures passed, rested against her bar stool. As I walked up behind this apparent fellow vagabond, I noticed big, thick rimmed glasses hanging from her front pocket. I took the seat next to her. She continued to scan the bar's meager selection against the wall. Her face was scrunched and she squinted so intently, her eyes almost closed.

"Why don't you use these?" I motioned toward her glasses.

She turned her head toward me, and I saw her deep, dark eyes for the first time. Her face was clean compared to her worn Converse. She held my eye contact for a few moments before speaking. Sizing me up, I think. The corners of her mouth curled upward ever so slightly, almost imperceptibly. As she did so, she exuded an aura of calm. She spoke quiet.

"I choose not to wear these glasses because this world is not meant to be seen clearly."

That was Kat.

"Thirsty?" I asked.

"Sure."

"Two doubles of Jack, straight," I told the barkeep. He poured them, spilling some whiskey on the scratched and worn bar. The two of us clinked glasses and tossed them down. I looked at her face raised toward the ceiling, eyes closed. I could almost see the medicine flowing through her body, down to her legs to her toes and through her arms to the tips of her fingers. She exhaled, opened her eyes, and slammed the glass on the counter. She glanced at the barkeep and tapped the glass with two fingers. He obliged, and poured both of us another round.

We drank. We told stories. We laughed. We lowered some of our outer defensive walls, but neither of us would allow such a stranger see the real inner core. We both understood and enjoyed surface level interactions; there was no need to have existential conversations with every person you meet. We both could present ourselves to the world in friendly masks, never truly getting bare. Besides, it was fucking exhausting to get too deep.

As our third round warmed our stomachs, she began a story that she had clearly told hundreds of times. The cadence and rhythm of the story came as if engraved in a stonewall thousands of years ago.

"Have I told you the time I had a gun stuck in my face?" Of course not, idiot. I just met you. But she continued without pausing. "Well, I was ding-dong ditching back in high school, and this asshole retired cop pulls out a piece to try and scare me or some shit. I mean, it worked, but what a dick, right?"

I laughed and threw back the rest of my whiskey. She competitively matched me. I ordered refills.

"I had never seen a Glock that close before. Classic cop weapon, right? The square slide wrapped around a steel barrel that sat on top of a polymer grip which housed the magazine, which housed those bullets. Neatly inscribed on the side of the slide spelled 'GLOCK 17'".

She held up two fingers and a thumb, simulating a gun. She pointed her finger gun at my face.

"I would have wanted to take a closer look at it, were circumstances different. I would have asked to see it shoot, or maybe even ask for the chance to hold it myself. Not tonight, nope. Staring down the business end of that lethal weapon, and remember being enveloped by adrenaline. Like I swallowed a lead weight. I was kinda excited, too. Weird, right? I just felt so aware that I was alive.

"The man holding the gun was roughly 60 years old, wore a ragged tank top and jeans, stood 78 feet tall, and had eyes that each showed a different level of the fiery depths of hell. His raspy but deep voice slapped my ears, but I don't really remember what he said at first. He lifted the pistol so it was level with my forehead. The cold steel almost felt soothing against my sweating brow. Alright, man. I'm paying attention.

"'You know who you're talking to? I'm a fucking cop!'" Kat paused here to ask for a glass of water from the barkeep, and then continued her story.

"To show he was extra-tough, he swung the fucking gun from my head to his left, pointing to the street behind me. In that direction, my friend was hiding across the street in some bushes, listening to the entire exchange. For a second my fear reached a new height. I really didn't want anyone else to get involved. Turned out to be coincidence, though. My buddy stayed in the bush and watched everything.

It wasn't that I was afraid he was going to kill me on his own front lawn. Let's face it though, I just was not used to having a fucking gun stuck in my face. I was just not expecting this when I went out on that warm September night. This was also my first serious run-in with a man of the law, and I didn't know how to react. I got better at dealing with these kinda things. I got better at lying. Way better. Do you think I was going to stop causing trouble just because some old fuck didn't like me on his lawn?"

At this, Kat threw back her shot glass but it was already empty. She tried to play it off like she was just looking at her wrist.

"So he pulled a gun on you for ding-dong ditching?" I finally spoke up, realizing that I had been staring at her eyes as they scrunched, widened, and twitched with the ebbs and tides and emotions of the story.

"Yup," she replied flatly. "You know, ring the doorbell and run away? We were kids."

That was it. She stood up placed a few bills on the bar. She picked her pack up but the weight of the pack threw her alcohol-weakened sense of balance back onto the bar-stool. She paused, put her glasses on, and turned to head out of the bar.

"Adios, whatever-your-name-is," she called out, back turned to me.

"Leo." I was holding the remainder of my whiskey as I

watched her reach the door in the mirror behind the bar.

"Kat," she turned, and relayed a drunken smile and a friendly up-nod through the mirror.

I sat staring into the amber liquid in my glass.

Well, buddy. It's you and me tonight. Just the way we like it. The drink joined its compadres in my stomach. I reached in my jacket pocket and grabbed a few bills, placed them under the empty glass. The barkeep gave me an up-nod in appreciation as I stood. I returned it as I turned to leave the bar.

To my surprise, it was dark when I faced the real world outside of the bar. Must have lost track of time. Tonight, the whiskey pulled me toward sleep; I was a little too drunk to drive. Just a little. I moved my Jeep to the back corner of the parking lot of the bar where asphalt turned to unmaintained dirt. I unwrapped my sleeping bag in the back seat, laid down on top of it. Thoughts of Kat breezed through my whiskied mind, and I almost reached up front to grab my notebook to record my thoughts. But the gravity of sleep pinned me to my sleeping bag, and I was too weak to resist.

meet Fred Briggs.

The sun tried to rise before I did but failed by a few minutes. I woke with a slight headache so I fired up my propane backpacking stove and set some water to boil. Coffee was a cure to my current ail. I stretched and walked around the side of my Jeep. I grabbed my notebook from the front seat and the pen that rested in the center console.

I wrote.

> *"I have some unfortunate news," God said to Jack. "You will die in five years."*

> *"Shit, God…" Jack stammered, coming to grips with the news, kneading his brow with his thumb. "Is there anything I can do?"*

> *"Possibly. You will have to come back tomorrow and file an appeal for extension."*

> *Jack submitted his form. The next day, Jack stood in line until his number was finally called. It was his turn to speak with God. Jack stepped up, excited and hopeful to hear God's verdict.*
>
> *"I'm sorry, Jack, but your appeal has been denied. You can file another appeal tomorrow."*
>
> *Next day, Jack stood in line and filed his appeal. Denied.*
>
> *Next day, denied.*
>
> *Everyday for 4 years and 364 days, Jack applied. Denied.*
>
> *Until finally, the next day, Jack again applied for his extension. Jack, still hopeful, stepped up when his number was called.*
>
> *Denied.*
>
> *Jack died.*

Closed the notebook, tossed it on the front dash, returned to the stove where the water was heating up. I lifted the tin lid to check the progress. Not yet boiling but close enough. The headache was starting to increase its presence behind my right eye, and I needed that sweet brown liquid. I put two scoops of Kauai coffee in my French press, and poured in the hot water. I leaned in and inhaled the first fumes of coffee creation. The heavy smoothness entered me through my nose holes and calmed me. The to-do list of the day, the regrets from previous nights all slid away in a bliss of floating comfort. I imagine heroin users have a similar sensation but I would recommend coffee to them. I suppose they would recommend the same to me. After a few minutes, I pushed the plunger down on the French press and poured a cup. The warmth revitalized me as the whiskey of last night was drowned by the caffeine of the morning. I was ready to head on.

Sometime between pulling into that bar parking lot on the previous day and pulling out of the parking lot the next day, I felt the need to see the ocean. So west I headed. I cruised down a road bordered first by storefronts, then by residential homes, and eventually cleared out to reveal emerald stretches and rolling hills. Far off in the distance, I saw the deep blue of the Pacific. I continued forward.

Not five minutes out of town, gurgles and sputters crawled their way out from the engine bay. As I slowed to a stop, the gurgles and sputters slowed as well but thin white streams of smoke found their way out from underneath my hood. I knew it was coming. My dad hadn't put too many miles on the Jeep originally, but I had put it through its paces since the keys were put in my hands. Stopped on the shoulder of the road, I popped the hood and got out. I opened the hood to be greeted by a cloud of white steam and a metallic bite to my nostrils. I leaned in, hoping for an easy answer but my auto-knowledge was comprised of quick fixes and temporary solutions. My old man didn't get a chance to teach me much more than an oil change and a flat tire swap.

I walked the short walk back toward town past the residential neighborhood, and back toward the store-fronts. I took a right on Broad Street and a sign reading Sonrisa Automotive caught my eye. I stepped up to the paint-peeled door and went in. A radio played top 40, and young girl stood at the front desk. She tapped her fingers, gazing out the window as she thumbed, mindless, through her phone. I explained my situation to the phone-thumber, and she called back into the shop.

"Roberto! We need a tow for a Jeep!"

The tow truck pulled up front. I jumped in and navigated Roberto to my Jeep on the shoulder of the road. Our conversation was minimal; my mind was mulling over options as I thought about worse case scenarios and potential outcomes.

meet Fred Briggs.

* * * * *

They took my car into surgery. I grabbed a seat and a magazine in the waiting room, hoping for the best. I stared at the pages without reading. I stood and unconsciously started pacing. What am I going to do? What the fuck am I going to do if it's bad? Impatience engulfed me. I left the waiting room and walked over to the front desk. The receptionist, or anyone else, was nowhere to be seen. I saw a door that read "Employees Only." I heard electric wrenches and car lifts running so I assumed it was the garage. I looked around the storefront, and still no one there. I opened the door and stepped in.

I saw my Jeep at the far side of the garage, and strode casually toward it. Through travels, I had learned to blend in and act as if I knew what I was doing. There were a few mechanics with blue work shirts, busy diagnosing trucks, cars, and SUVs. As I approached mine, I saw a pair of legs poking out from underneath the engine bay.

"What the fuck..." The voice that came from beneath the Jeep but was not aimed at me. It was aimed at the world, at society, at the universal Creator, as if questioning how this car's condition came to be.

I felt I had the answer. "How's it going? Any luck down there?"

The feet stopped moving for a second, and I heard a sigh. The mechanic slid out just enough to see who was talking. The beard on his face could hide neither the axle grease smeared on his cheek nor his contempt for being interrupted. "Can I help you?"

"Think it's the coolant hose? Oh, must be the radiator, right?" I was offered snow to the cold stare of a polar bear. He closed his eyes and breathed in deep. When he opened them, he looked disappointed that I was still there.

"Listen, buddy, what's your name?"

"Leo. Leo Mas."

"Nice to meet you, Leo, but why don't you take a seat in the lounge, or grab a coffee or something."

"Yeah, I know what you're saying, but..."

"OK, let me focus on this for a few minutes. This isn't something you can fix with duct tape." That light jab was aimed at my patchwork holding together various parts of the car. Like I said, my mechanic knowledge was limited.

He softened the blow with a follow up, "I'll take good care of her, I'm sure she'll be fixed up in no time." A smile crept out from the beard, and I nodded and returned to the waiting room.

One hour went by. Then another. There are only so many times you can read People magazine before you want to jam your head through a glass coffee table. I took my angst outside to the afternoon sunlight. Caught a whiff of something on the air. I walked around the corner to the alley adjacent to the auto shop. A sweet, burning aroma wafted, and I followed my nose. Leaning against the brick alley wall was the mechanic that was working on my Jeep. Lifting a cigarette to his lips buried beneath the beard, he stared at his feet with a blank expression. He bore the blue work shirt uniform of all the other auto shop employees. I approached him, and he half-hid the cigarette behind his back. I got closer, and saw a white name patch sewn on his shirt. It read Freddy.

"Can I help you?" Freddy switched to customer service mode. A wide grin poked its way through his facial hair, revealing crooked but white teeth. His furrowed eyebrows sat on top of straining eyes as he tried to see me in the dark alley, but they relaxed as I got closer. "Ah, the Jeep guy. What's up, man?"

I returned the smile and pointed to his hand behind his back. "Got another one of those?"

Drawing a pack of American Spirits from his back pocket and a book of matches from his front, he handed the bundle to me. I pulled out a single. Struck the match and it sparked to life. Inhale. Exhale.

"You from around here?" Freddy asked as I returned his tobacco stuffs.

"No, just passing through."

"Yeah? Where you from?"

Before I had a chance to answer, a deep bellow boomed down the alley. "FRED! Need a hand over here!"

He didn't even look up. He took two more drags from his cigarette before putting it out on the bottom of his shoe.

"Thanks for the cigarette, Freddy," I offered as he turned toward the booming voice. He paused, turned, and stuck out a hand. I gave it a firm shake.

"No problem, Leo." He strode off.

I finished my cigarette alone in that alley, and headed back inside where hard plastic-leather chairs and the People magazine awaited me. I took the seat, but passed on the tabloid. Slouched back and closed my eyes, folding my hands on my chest. Funny how you don't realize how tired you are until you shut yourself off from the world. I don't even remember falling asleep.

A nudge to my boots and a voice awoke me. "Hey, bro! Leo!" Freddy's bearded face was level with mine. "You look fucking uncomfortable."

I sat up straight and stretched. I rubbed the knot that had formed in my neck. "I'll be alright. How's the car look?"

Freddy's grin glitched, and he took the seat across from me. He leaned forward, resting his elbows on his knees. It felt like I was in the waiting room of an ER, and a sick feeling clenched my gut.

"Well, it's not good. You're Jeep's going to need some work. A lot."

"How much are we looking at?"

"Well, I can tell she's seen some things. Have you been living on a beach or something?" He glanced at me sideways. "There's a good amount of corrosion. After all is said and done, at least two weeks in the shop, and hopefully that will get her back on the road."

"Wait, now, Freddy. No bullshit, how much is this going to cost me?" I was always wary of mechanics and their conniving ways, but I was hoping Freddy's apparent sincerity was genuine.

The smile vanished, and Freddy looked me straight in the eye. "If I were to guess, at least six grand. And that's just the minimum."

"Goddamn! I was just supposed to be passing through. I'm not sure if I can pull that off. Is there anything else I can do?" I had a few dollars saved but that cash wasn't meant to cover some auto repair bill. Not today.

Freddy looked down at his grease-and-dirt covered hands, and I stared at them too, hoping they would offer some unforeseen alternative. Nope.

Freddy broke the silence. "Listen, man. I'm off in ten. I just have to close up shop. We aren't going to fix it today anyway. Want to grab a beer on me?"

"Sure," was all I could muster in my frustration. I left my pack and duffle bag behind the counter after grabbing my wallet, notebook, and pen, as always.

Across the street stood a bar that sold pizza, or possibly a pizza place that sold booze. Either way, Freddy and I went over. The sign outside read "Fatte's Pizza", and inside echoed memories of every other pizza parlor that I had been in. Cheap beer fizzled in cheaper pitchers. Various muted sports games played on high-mounted TVs. Photos of Little League teams featuring smiling kids and proud father-coaches. Just like all the other pizza places.

But, we came for beer, so beer is what we got. Freddy ordered two glasses and a pitcher of Miller Light. We chose a table next to a window with the evening sun dimly shining in. Freddy slopped some beer into my glass before filling his own. I stared down at the white foam, at the bubbles popping. I tried to guess which individual bubble would pop next. None of my guesses were right.

"To a quick recovery!" Freddy's toast shook me from my trance. I looked up as he lifted his glass. I met his glass with mine.

"Cheers," I mumbled. I tipped the glass back and took a deep gulp. Refreshing. Before letting the glass leave my lips, I took another gulp. Equally refreshing. As I swallowed the brown elixir, I felt my worries melt away. So I finished off that pint, and placed the empty glass on the table. Before it hit the table, Freddy was refilling my glass, smile shining through his beard.

"Drink up - that beer isn't going to drink itself," Freddy tipped his glass back and gulped his own.

I took a more modest sip. I felt better. "Thanks for the beer, Freddy. I needed this."

"You kidding? This beer is shit. They should be paying

us for helping them get rid of it." He took a sip. "Also," he wiped some foam from his mustache, "My name is Fred, not Freddy. Fred Briggs."

"I just saw your name tag on your shirt, and assumed it was Freddy. Fred Britts?"

"No, Briggs."

"Briggs?"

"Yeah, damn it. Are you deaf? I said Fred Briggs! Now finish that beer, Leo!"

I couldn't help but smile. "Yes, sir, Fred Briggs." I finished off glass number two.

"So, why 'Freddy' on your shirt, if you go by Fred?"

For a split second, I caught a snag in the warmth that came from Fred Briggs. So quick, I hardly noticed it was there. But it was.

"Hold that thought, I'm going to order a pizza," Fred stood.

"How would you feel about another pitcher?" I felt obligated to contribute.

"Do it," he called out as he turned to talk to the cashier at the pizza counter. I strode back over to the bar and ordered another round of Miller Light.

We reconvened at the table with a filled pitcher. I filled our glasses. I reminded him of my question. "So, why 'Freddy', Fred Briggs?"

"This is my dad's shirt. Was my dad's shirt," he took a sip. "Dad's shirt, dad's shop. The old man went by 'Freddy', and was too cheap to buy me a new shirt. So he gave me one of his old ones. I was an independent teenager when I decided to drop the 'dy', but my pops didn't care. I got the 'Freddy' shirt."

Just then, the pizza came out. I didn't realize how hungry I was. I hadn't eaten anything all day, save for the dried up granola bar that I bought from a vending machine in the waiting room. The steam rose from that pizza and grabbed my stomach from my nose holes. I could have slammed my face in that pizza but I conceded to grab a slice and take voracious bites, burning my tongue and sending cheesy chunks down into my shirt.

Fred must have been hungry, too. We sat in silence as we wolfed down pizza and washed it down with beer. We didn't stop until all the beer and pizza was gone.

"Ah…" Fred Briggs leaned back, balancing his chair on two legs, and rubbing his full belly.

"That hit the spot." I felt like I could barely move. I had more beer than Fred Briggs; he kept filling mine to the top, even if I wasn't empty.

"So, what's your plan, Leo?"

The question sobered me. "I'll figure something out. Is there a hostel or a cheap motel in this town?"

"Sure there's some shitty motels here and there. But, if you want, I have an empty room at my place. You can crash there while we figure your car out."

I hated handouts. My gut instinct was to turn it down and find my own way. Some deep guilt persisted inside me, some vestigial reflex that herded me away from freebies. But, a welcoming soul and a real bed were too tempting.

"Are you sure? I'm fine with grabbing a room in a Motel 6 somewhere," I offered him a way out.

"Yeah, man. You just buy the booze, and we'll call it even for now."

"You have a preference?"

"I'm a whiskey man, but I don't really care."

"Whiskey it is."

Fred Briggs leaned forward so all four chair legs rested on the floor. We both stood and left. We returned to the shop, which was now closed up and quiet. Fred Briggs opened the front door and I walked in, grabbed my backpack, my duffle, and set them both by the curb.

"You ready?" Fred Briggs came up from behind and slapped me on the shoulder.

"Yeah. Thanks again, man."

"Alright, it's cool. Don't thank me again. Throw your shit in the back."

Fred Briggs pulled out a single key and pointed it across the street. Parked was a beautiful midnight black 1969 Chevelle. The sun reflected off the metallic paint. Fred Briggs opened the back door on the driver's side. The interior was less stunning. The front bucket seats were in decent condition with black leather stretched tight over them, but the dash was worn and cracked in places. The rear bench seat was definitely in need of some love. Yellow foam stuck out of places, and the leather was worn by butts and jeans. I tossed my packs on the worn seats and jumped into the passenger seat.

"Not bad, man." I complimented his car.

Fred Briggs beamed. "I'm restoring her myself. She

was my dad's car back in the day, but I got her when he passed away. We were going to restore her together, but the old fuck had to go and die. You haven't seen nothing yet." And with that Fred Briggs inserted the key in the ignition.

A twist of the wrist. A mechanical roar chased by a baritone throaty growl. The car vibrated and hummed with life. I looked at Fred Briggs and saw a wicked grin. He gripped the steering wheel and wrung his hands around the black stitched leather. I could not help but smile, too. It was strange how an inanimate, man-made beast could provoke such visceral emotions to the depths of a man's soul. He feathered the gas, and the Chevelle rumbled and barked, eager to leave its parking spot by the curb.

"That's a 454," Fred Briggs said not-so-modestly. "Popped an SS engine into her."

"Gorgeous." I didn't exactly know what an SS was, but I picked up that a 454 was worth bragging about.

He threw his baby into gear and pulled out onto the street.

"You ready?" Fred muttered under his breath as we pulled to a stop at an empty intersection.

I wasn't sure if he was talking to me or the car, but I

responded any way. "Fucking do it, man."

Before the words had left my throat, Fred Briggs punched the gas. We lurched forward. The squeal of tires slipping on hot asphalt filled the air. Felt the rear end slip out sideways, grasping, desperate for traction. Then, she found it. The acceleration put a hand on my chest and pushed me back into the black bucket seat. My palms started to sweat as we whizzed passed the world outside of our cockpit. The beastly woman screamed and crescendoed viscous. Finally, Fred Briggs toed the brakes until we came to a stop. The smell of melted rubber is one that only a select group of people enjoy and lavish over. It appeared that both Fred Briggs and I were in this group.

"Here we are," he said as the car stopped next to the curb in front of a house with a tall willow tree in front. It was an older house with an attached tin-roofed car-port. I opened the car door, distractedly. Crunch. We had parked close to the unusually high curb that bordered his lawn, and the Chevelle door was lodged in the grass and dirt. Instinctively, I pulled on the door handle to dislodge the door.

"WAIT, DON'T DO THAT!" he yelled. It was too late. No sooner had the words left his mouth than the door scraped clear of the lawn. "Fuck, man..."

I cracked the door open again and shimmied my way out of the car. I inspected the door to find the bottom was scraped and slightly bent where I had forced the door free. Fred Briggs circled around the back of the car, and stood next to me.

"Man..." He started to complain, then shrugged his shoulders. "Grab your shit and come on in." He headed for the front door.

An ache panged my gut. He clearly loved that car, and put some serious time into it. Within a few minutes of me sitting in his car, I already fucked it up. I went around to the driver's side to open the back door and grab my packs. I shuffled my feet inside as I scoured my mind to find a way to make it up to him.

"Ey, man, my bad about the car."

"Don't worry about it. It's just a door, you sorry-looking pansy!" Fred Briggs tossed me a brown bottle of beer, and I had to drop my duffle to catch it. I cracked it open and took a gulp.

"Nice place. You have this place to yourself?"

"Not exactly." Just then, I heard the back door open, and a brown dog with lighter brown spots bounded in the house. Looked to have some German Shepard swimming around in his genes, but he was without a doubt, a mutt. He was largish, at around 70 pounds, but judging by his mannerisms, he was just a pup. His eyes swung wildly between Fred Briggs and myself, and he bounded over to Fred to greet him.

"What's up, Donnie?" Fred Briggs smiled as Donnie licked his face. Putting hands on either side of Donnie's face, he bent down and kissed him on his furry forehead. Then Donnie turned toward me.

In two excited bounds, he was at my feet. He sniffed my legs a bit, probably smelling the road on my pants and clothes. He looked up to me, smiling, tongue lolling out of his mouth, tail wagging. I offered the back of my hand, testing the waters. Donnie licked my hand, and then up my wrist and forearm. I scratched him behind his ears and he closed his eyes, enjoying the attention. I grew up with dogs, and I thought I knew how to carry myself around them, but Donnie, big as he was, offered only love to me. Good dog.

I heard the back door slam again and I looked up. A girl walked in.

"Leo, this is..." Fred started but was interrupted.

"I'm Nicole." Nicole marched toward me with an

outstretched hand. She was a tiny girl, but her grip was even smaller. It was like handshaking an old sock.

"I'm Leo. Fred's working on my car for a few days, and he was nice enough to offer me a place to crash."

"Oh, how nice of Fred." She left the room.

Fred sighed. I would have asked but I already had an idea where that sigh came from.

"Nicole wasn't too happy about having a guest," Fred Briggs looked at me. He cracked his smile. "It's alright. She'll come around. She's probably just tired. I'm going to give Donnie a walk. Want to come?"

The three of us left the house into the twilight of the day.

it's your damn choice.

Those who argue against any truth in the cliché "Ignorance is bliss" have not spent adequate time with dogs.

Donnie bore no collar but Fred tied an old nylon rope around the pup's neck as a leash. Tongue rolling out the side of his mouth, Donnie ran about, exploring and sometimes straining against the limited range of the rope. He stopped and sniffed every flower, every fire hydrant, every shoe of passersby. Simplicity in detail.

Because of his size and eagerness to make new friends, he intimidated other people on their walks. Some even crossed the street to avoid us. How could they possibly misconstrue his enthusiasm and fascination at the world for aggression? Were they more fearful of his appearance or did they fear his energy?

We crossed the street, and headed down the residential

street. There was a long silence where I was hypnotized by Donnie's antics, until Fred broke the trance.

"Sorry about that, back there."

I turned to him with a quizzical look.

He sighed as he wrapped Donnie's rope leash a little tighter. We were approaching a busier intersection. "Nicole."

"Ah. She seemed cool. Who is she?" I had gotten a whiff of something brewing under the surface but I wanted to remain respectful of my host.

"Well, I guess we're a thing. Started as her renting out the spare bedroom but at some point, she ended up spending more time in mine."

We had left the residential neighborhood and were now passing a few small restaurants, a gas station, a laundromat. Finally, we stopped in front of a liquor store featuring a towering sign, a beacon to parched passersby. It was supposed to read "CORK 'N CASK" but with a few letters missing, it read "CO K 'N CA K."

"You going to make good on your deal or what?" Fred Briggs grinned and shoved me toward the door.

"I'll be back," and I walked in the store. As soon as I

it's your damn choice.

walked in, I heard a yell.

"HEY!! No homeless in my shop! What, you think I'm handing out free cardboard boxes?" The store clerk leaned against the counter, waving his hand in the air.

"No, man, I'm just trying to get..."

"BUDDY! I kid, I kid. What, you have no sense of humor?" He must have thought he was fucking hilarious because he burst out into a fit of laughter. I chuckled politely and continued inside.

Just like the thousands of other liquor stores that I had visited. A wall of glass bottles of various shapes and sizes were lined up behind the clerk.

"Ey, fucking hippy! Don't you steal nothing!" Again, a howl of laughter.

I strolled through the aisles of wine. Reds, whites, boxes, bottles, corks. Through the refrigerated shelves that held beers and sodas and Gatorade and chelada. I grabbed two cans of chelada and headed to the counter.

"Give me a fifth of Jack. Actually, give me Maker's Mark, Sally," I added cheekily.

At this, the shop owner bent over in a renewed fit of hilarity. He slapped the counter with an open palm. He

43

grabbed the bottle and put it on the counter in front of me.

"Anything else?"

"Yeah," I grabbed a pack of rolling papers and some tobacco and shoved it next to the bottle.

"Thirty-six twenty-four," he said scanning the items.

I pulled out two twenties and slapped them on the counter. He bagged the bottle and two cans in a brown paper bag before grabbing the cash.

"Keep it," I said. "What's your name?"

"Eddy," he replied with a wide smile.

"Leo," I stuck out my hand to shake his.

"I don't give a shit, you filthy street rat. Get the fuck out of my store!" He waved his hand toward the door without shaking mine. The ding-ding of the door sensor rang out as he roared with laughter in his now empty shop.

Fred was outside leaning against the side of the building, Donnie at his feet. The dog's eyes lit up when he saw me but the rope stopped him from doing little more than jump and pant in greeting.

"Took long enough," Fred muttered. "Let's get outta here."

At that, we headed back home. I cradled the brown bag in my left arm like a newborn child. I pulled out a can of chelada and handed it to Fred.

"What is this shit?" He complained as he cracked the can open. He tested a swig and shrugged acceptably.

"Don't worry about it, just drink," I told him as I pulled one out for myself. Over the years, I had developed the ability to hold and open a can with one hand. Not the most groundbreaking skill in the world but it still made me feel talented. We sipped the tomato juice-and-alcohol mixed drink as we made our way back to Fred's house. In these moments of silence, I wondered what the next few days had in store for me as Fred fixed my car.

Donnie led us all the way back to Fred's house. Fred looked up and down the street briefly, and I caught a hint of what looked like a moment of pained disappointment. It occurred to me that he was probably looking for Nicole's car. Apparently it was gone. I mildly wondered where it had taken her.

Fred threw the door open and unclipped Donnie. I followed him in, placed the bottle of mid-shelf whiskey on

45

the solid oak table, and took a seat the couch.

"I approve." Fred examined the bottle with the melted red wax top. He stood, strode to the kitchen, which separated the living room from the two back rooms that I assumed were bedrooms. He returned with two tall glasses. Not intended for taking shots, but who were we trying to impress? We were going to drink that whole bottle anyway.

We drank long into the night. I struggled to keep up with this bearded Latino's pace, but we had little problem going through what I bought at the store and even continued on through Fred's fridge.

I don't remember falling asleep but I woke up with my head pounding. I was covered with a blanket, and there was a glass of water and a Tylenol on the table in place of the bottle of whiskey and beer cans that were there the night before. I was grateful for the hangover cure, and I tossed back the pill, chasing it with the water. Sat back and waited for it to work. I closed my eyes. Hushed whispers, sounding somewhat angry, drifted out from the adjacent kitchen. I didn't want to eavesdrop but I opened a curious eye. I had a feeling the whispered conversation was about my intrusion in the house. A few minutes went by. The whispers were interrupted by Fred's voice.

"Alright, enough. I have to go to the shop." He strode

into the living room, and I sat up, pretending to have just woken up.

"Hey, Fred, thanks for everything again. I really appreciate the couch and hospitality." I lifted the glass of water, and motioned toward the blanket. "I'm going to head out soon."

He ignored the last part. "Yeah, no problem, man. Hopefully, we can figure your car out today." He grabbed his jacket and headed for the door. "By the way, you can thank Nicole for the blanket and water and Tylenol. She figured you might need it after last night. She's a sweetie, ain't she?" I couldn't tell if he was being sarcastic or what.

Fred Briggs walked out, closed the door behind him. Donnie trotted into the room and greeted me with a few licks to the face.

"Alright, man. Take it easy," I mumbled as I sat up, out of the reach of Donnie's tongue. I scratched behind his ears, and simultaneously felt the beginnings of a vicious hangover scratching the back of my skull. I gulped the remainder of water in my glass. As I stood to go refill my glass in the kitchen, I heard the faucet running and the easy clinking of dishes. I was a little hesitant to approach Nicole, so I pulled myself together in the most courteous mindset I had available.

I knocked on the doorjamb before entering the kitchen. "Good morning, Nicole!"

The kitchen was an off-yellow Post-It color and the countertops were covered in dark-brown tiles. The kitchen was the center of the house, leading to a bedroom to the right and, to the left, a short hallway, bedroom and the backyard. A small window allowed light in from the backyard.

"Good morning, Leo. How are you feeling?" Nicole greeted me with a warm smile, and her voice seemed sincere. There was a breath of a moment where she looked me up and down, but it was barely noticeable as she continued. "Need some more water?" She took the glass from my hands and filled it from the tap before I could answer.

"Thank you - so much," I said as she was filling the glass. Not used to someone looking after my well being. I took care of myself, worried about myself, dug myself out of hangovers and other troubles. When I did stop long enough to connect to someone, those someones didn't usually do me many favors. I felt friendly enough but I always thought it rare for someone to go out of their way to help a stranger.

"No problem. I just felt like I was a little short with you

last night." She turned from the sink, holding the glass in her right hand. She held it close to her, and I reached out to relieve her of my glass. Her eyes remained locked on mine. Her eyes were a brilliant blue-green, and her light brown hair hung over her forehead in straight, neatly maintained bangs. Her lips curled up slightly in a Mona Lisa smile. I felt unease but could not place the source. A painful awkward eternity.

"Appreciate the hospitality. I don't think I'll be here more than a day or two." I paused, slightly reeling. "I think I am going to lie down for a bit. Just got another wave of hangover."

She smiled and nodded and turned back to her dishes. I went back to the couch, head spinning from the strange situation and the hangover. Donnie was curled up on the couch so I took a seat next to him. I set the glass on the coffee table and stared at it.

What a strange human being, I thought. She was attractive, sure. She dressed nicely, and she was polite. But there was something in her that was off. She apparently worked hard to keep up this nice and polite facade, but I caught a glimpse into her true self in that silent moment standing at that kitchen sink. Fred Briggs seemed to be a considerate, generous man. And trusting. He trusted me to be alone with Nicole, and trusted Nicole to be alone with me. I didn't know what she was all about but I knew there was something I didn't like. Or maybe I was just hung over.

The running water in the sink stopped, and Nicole appeared, leaning casually on the doorframe.

"Hey, I'm going to take Donnie to the beach. You want to come? The best cure for a hangover is a dip in the ocean."

Of course, I paused. Caution. Then, I came to a few conclusions. First, I am fairly sure she wants me to come with her so I won't be in their home by myself. Second, I hadn't been to the beach in months, though I had driven by it many times. Third, she was right. The cold, salt water always cured hangovers. So, "Sure. Let's do it."

* * * * *

Donnie jumped in the back seat of Nicole's Jetta, tongue-lolling out, excited for the adventure. I slid in the passenger seat as Nicole was buckling in. She wore a huge hat and sunglasses. Off we went to a nearby dog-friendly beach.

"So what do you do, Nicole?" I hated small talk but I was good at it. I much preferred unusual topics that made all parties slightly uncomfortable. In most cases, it didn't matter if the talk was awkward since I would most likely be leaving shortly anyway. Still, I only engaged people in that way under the right circumstances. Nicole seemed pretty vanilla, so I offered a generic how-do-ya-do question. And her answer was possibly more boring than my question.

"I work as an assistant to an accountant down at the city hall," she said with some manufactured enthusiasm.

"Ah, ok. How do you like it? Good job?" Again, an easy vanilla conversation.

She followed up, "It's nice getting a steady paycheck, and the guy I work for is great. I am just putting in my time now so I can work on up that ladder. Accountants get paid!"

"Oh yeah, that sounds like a great gig!" Ugh.

Still, I don't hold that against people. At times, I wish I could be like the Nicoles of the world. I think about my priorities often. Personal achievement, experience, loyalty to friends and family, love, health, faith, morality, money. These all had their place. I was constantly weighing the benefits of chasing each of these. My mama said life was like having a roomful of floating balloons, slowly falling toward the ground. You run and bump one balloon into the air, preventing it from hitting the ground. If you had more balloons, you would have to put in more effort to keep them all in the air.

Imagine if you had just one balloon. Nicole's one balloon was money. Or so it seemed. Maybe I was being premature in judging her.

As we cruised down the road, the pain of last night crept in. With each bump in the road and each glimpse of reflected sunlight, the hangover panged around my head. On the verge of puking but I held it in with bland conversation.

"So how do you like living in San Labre?" I asked.

"It's great. You can't complain about it. Weather is always nice, the people are always friendly, there is a Target and Costco right in town. It's easy, very comfortable. Still, I would probably change a few things..."

"Yeah? Like what?" I felt we were on the brink of a real conversation. But she refused the uncomfort.

"Oh, never mind. Look! We're here!"

Her deflection annoyed me. I was instantly relieved by arrival of the ocean in our view. The yellow-brown of the sand stretched out to the deep blue expanse, meeting the horizon with a lighter blue of sky. The beach itself was not even that busy. People walked about the near empty beach, all smiling, laughing, talking. Outer clothing hung loosely, covering tiny clothing underneath.

Nicole pulled to the side of the road bordering the beach. Donnie whimpered in anticipation. I could relate. I popped the door open, while Nicole leashed Donnie before opening his door. We walked down the stairs leading to the sand. I kicked off my shoes, letting the granules warm me from the feet up.

Nicole unleashed Donnie, and he ran off down the beach. I ran after him, leaving Nicole in our wake. We ran parallel to the water for a few hundred yards until Donnie turned back toward me. I changed my path toward the water. The waves were gentle, too small for surfers, but perfect for swimming. With Donnie on my heels, I headed straight for the water. I threw off my shirt and stepped out of my jeans, leaving them clear of the waves. In my boxers, I stomped and frolicked into the water like a childish idiot.

The water was cold, but refreshing. My attention switched from dealing with the hangover to dealing with the cold, then switched again to a pure, joyful bliss. I swam out just far enough to avoid the breaks, then looked back at the beach. Donnie paced at the water's edge.

"Here, Donnie! Come!"

He whimpered, laid down then stood up and paced. He was scared to come in. For such a strong dog, I was surprised to see him so fearful. I liked him a bit more.

I splashed my fill and headed back to solid ground. As my body left the sea water, the warm sun went to work drying my skin. The pain of yesterday was now completely gone. I looked up to see Nicole holding my clothes. She approached me, handing me the bundle.

"Feel better?" She smiled as I struggled to pull my pants over wet legs.

"Yup, good to go."

She drew a tennis ball from her pocket and tossed it down the beach. Donnie chased after it.

* * * * *

"Want to grab some lunch?" Nicole asked as we jumped back in her car.

"Yeah, I could eat," I said.

"What are you in the mood for?"

"What's good around here?" I liked to try the locals' favorites in places I visited.

"Hm… well what kind of stuff do you like?"

Are you fucking kidding me? I thought. The conversation was stuck in a loop. I didn't know what was good around there, and I just wanted her to make a recommendation, a decision. We passed the pier, and I spotted a sign that read Splash Cafe.

"How about that place?"

"Clam chowder? Sure, if that's what you want." She pulled into a parking spot, and cracked the window for Donnie. We went in.

I just wanted a cup of chowder and some fries. I beckoned Nicole to order, so I could pay for her lunch, but she adamantly refused.

"No, no it's ok. I don't know if I'm going to get anything."

"What? Why not?"

"I'm allergic to clams." What the fuck?

"We can go somewhere else then, that's fine with me."

"No, no, it's ok. Go ahead and get your chowder."

Now we were holding up the line and causing a bit of a scene. I apologized to the cashier and stepped out of line.

"Why didn't you say something when I suggested this place?" I asked her, peeved.

"I didn't want to say anything. I wanted you to get what you wanted."

"Do you like hot dogs?" I asked her directly.

"Yeah, I could go for a hot dog."

"Cool, looks like there's stand over there." We walked down the boardwalk, where a hotdog vendor was selling out from his cart.

"Two hot dogs, please."

"NO, Leo! Let me pay for mine!"

"It's not a big deal, Nicole, I got it." I shoved some cash in the vendor's hands.

"OK, well do you have any veggie dogs?" Nicole asked the vendor.

A look of disgust at her before he answered, "No. Sorry, young lady."

"OK, I'll take a bag of chips and a Coke, then."

"No hot dog?" the vendor asked.

"No, thank you, I'm vegetarian."

What. The. Fuck. "I thought you said you wanted a hot dog?" I asked her, my own frustration oozing. I briefly wondered why I was getting impatient with this girl.

"I just didn't want to say anything."

* * * * *

We returned to Santa Labre. Me, quiet in contemplation and some annoyance at Nicole's indecision. Nicole was quiet as well, but blasted pop Top 40 hits to ease the silence. That dug into me a bit more; not a fan of that pop nonsense. When we stopped in front of the house, I opened the door, eager to get out. Donnie trotted to the front door. Nicole and I followed.

"I'm going to take a shower, get this beach off of me," she announced.

"OK, sure." I glanced at her.

"Can you let Donnie out into the back?"

"Sure."

Nicole left to the shower connected to the master bedroom, and I went to let Donnie out into the backyard. I stayed inside and sat down on the couch. I was going to write but instead fell asleep, half-sitting.

I woke to Nicole's foot toeing at my knee. "Hey Leo, wake up!"

I was surprised to see she was only wearing a towel, wet hair draped over slender shoulders. I rubbed my eyes to avoid the possibility of staring, and sat up.

"Leo, where's Donnie?"

"I let him out back, like you said."

"I didn't see him back there."

"Are you sure? Where'd he go?" I started to stand.

A Nicole hand met my shoulder and pushed me back to the couch. "Don't worry about it, Leo. He runs away all the time. Just relax."

Listen. I'm not an idiot. I understood what was happening at that moment. My time on the road taught me when hungry scavengers were on the prowl. My time on the road also hipped me to the risks of consorting with such scavengers. Particularly when the boyfriend of that scavenger is both providing housing to me and currently holds the keys to my only means of transportation.

So, I escaped. "I better go find Donnie." I slipped passed the booby trap and out the backdoor. Donnie was nowhere to be found. I swung around to the side of the house where I saw a gap underneath a chain link fence. The pup was out on the streets. I followed.

"Donnie!" I walked the streets. "DONNIE!" I called out. What the fuck was I doing? Why would this dog come to me, even if I found him? He didn't know me, I didn't know him. At least I was out of that situation with Nicole. Just then, I heard a rumbling coming down the street. Fred Briggs' Chevelle turned the corner and he pulled over to the side of the road. Donnie was grinning in the passenger seat.

"You lost, Leo?" Fred asked with a smile.

"Donnie ran away, and Nicole was ... busy."

"He runs away all the time. Thanks for trying. Jump in." Fred Briggs shooed Donnie to the backseat, so I could climb into the passenger seat. "Let's get some beer." Off we drove to the liquor store. And so it went.

can't trust polite.

About 1AM, Donnie perked up his ears. He sat up, faced the door, a low rumble rising from his throat. Seconds later, the door burst open. Nicole stumbled in. She was clearly at least as inebriated as we were. Her eyes widened with surprise as they moved from Fred to me to Donnie and back.

"I thought you weren't going to be here..." Nicole stammered and slurred. Another figure appeared. A twenty-something dude with a backwards Giants hat stood in the doorway, half in the house, half out. Shock, confusion, then fear flashed on his face before he stepped out of the house.

"Who...the fuck...was that?" Fred's frugal attempt to control his voice. He rose to his feet.

"I wish you didn't find out like this..." Nicole looked

can't trust polite.

down and away, avoiding his laser beam gaze. Hell burned in his eyes. God damn, I was uncomfortable.

"What am I finding out?" Fred was gesturing wildly, beer in hand.

"I...just didn't know how to tell you..." She avoided eye contact.

OK. I was sitting on the couch. Nicole was near the open door, and Fred was standing on the opposite side of the room. I stared down at my beer can, trying to be invisible. I wasn't.

"Who the fuck is that out there!"

A long pause. "Fred. I don't know what to say...I didn't want to hurt you."

"You...you think this is protecting me right now?" Fred's anger was boiling over.

Silence.

Fred breathed out steam but regained a smidgen of composure as he did so. "I think you should leave, Nicole."

"Fred. I didn't want to tell..."

"I KNOW. OUT."

She turned and passed through the doorway. I only saw her once after that. A few days later, she came back to the house with a Ford Expedition to take all of her stuff. She waved sheepishly in my direction but avoided eye contact. Fred never talked about Nicole again. Days went by, and I would occasionally bring her name up but Fred ignored me every time. Until one time.

"You ok, man? Want to talk about Nicole?" I offered to Fred as we walked toward downtown

He paused and turned to me. He grabbed me by my collar and shoved me into an alley with tall brick walls. "Don't say her name to me ever again." And, I didn't.

I thought about how that situation unrolled. Nicole seemed like a mostly amiable, if slightly unsettling, person. And, from all of Fred's accounts, she seemed like a gentle, polite, innocent girl. Likeable. She clearly worked hard to gain the approval of others, leading her to diffuse bad news, sometimes hiding it.

Fearful of honesty, polite to avoid conflict. Can't trust polite.

* * * * *

The storm passed through Fred Briggs' home, but the debris and rubble remained. Fred let me put my stuff in

Nicole's bedroom, which hadn't really been used recent-
ly anyway since Nicole had usually slept in Fred Briggs'
room.

"You sure this is cool?" I asked Fred as we rearranged
the few things in the room. There was a floor-folding fu-
ton, an empty dresser, and a desk against the window.
A few random boxes were stacked against a small closet.

"Don't worry about it, Leo. We will figure out your car
soon," Fred smiled through the pain. "Until then, Donnie
can keep you company. Just do me one favor. If you find
anything from that fucking slut, throw that shit in the trash."

"Consider it gone. Although, it looks like there isn't
much here."

Fred left me to settle into the room. The floor mattress
was twin-sized, and much more comfortable than my
typical sleeping surface comprised of a thin backpacking
pad and sleeping bag on top of gravel or grass. I took my
shoes and socks off and set them by the door. The room
was carpeted; it felt nice on my bare feet. I walked over
to the desk by the single window in the room. I sat down
in the swivel chair, and leaned forward to see the outside
world. It was beautiful out. In fact, I realized it had been
beautiful every day that I had been in Santa Labre. Perfect
weather. Damn perfect people too.

I unloaded my sleeping bag from my backpack and clothes from my duffel. I must admit, the washer and dryer was a welcome luxury and planned to do a load later. I pulled out my notebook, and placed it on the desk. I stared at my new digs, the carpet, the floor mattress, the small closet, the yellow-white-beige walls. My Vans Authentics by the door. They seemed out of place in this clean room. They were worn and ragged, with holes in the rubber sole bottoms and canvas sides. The once white material was now grey with dirt and age. I had hiking boots but preferred to wear the Vans. They had been places but now seeing them off of my feet and on the other side of the room, I decided it was time. I walked over, grabbed the shoes and threw them in the trash bin next to the desk. I took a seat, and opened my notebook.

I wrote.

> *My brother and I*
> *Travel wide*
> *Savior of souls.*
> *The world wears us down*
> *Together we die.*
> *Save our soles.*

I closed my notebook, pushed it into the corner of the desk, and reached in my backpack. I pulled out the yellow manila envelope that held the remains of my savings. It was heavy but getting lighter. A pit grew in my stomach as I wondered how much my car repairs would eat into that money. I stuffed the envelope deep in the backpack and into the back of my mind. Placed my backpack right next to the door. I didn't want to unload too much. Didn't plan on staying here for too long.

* * * * *

The young girl at Sonrisa called me back the shop to hear about my car. Again, I sat in the medical waiting room, this time talking to Fred's lead mechanic. There were a few other people in the waiting room this time, and they lay witness to the unfortunate prognosis. Miles through desert heat and dust plus idle days by the beachfront led to the deterioration of a once strong soul. The car was going to cost a fortune to get running again. It appeared that my stay in this town would have to be extended.

Then, from behind me, "That Jeep a '93?"

"'92." I turned to face the voice. He wore a stained t-shirt tucked into blue jeans, and was in his sixties. Boots stuck out from the bottoms of the pants. He seemed blue collar, except for his watch. It was a Rolex, and was quite possibly the most expensive thing in that entire auto shop.

"Shit, son. I used to have one of those. Gave it away to my son. But it's gone now."

"Yeah, too bad it's on its last legs. Not sure what I'm going to do with it."

"First off, son, that car is a 'he.' He has balls," the stranger gave a wry smile. "Second, how much do you want for him?"

"Excuse me?"

"You heard me."

I paused, speechless. Then threw out a number. "Fifteen hundred?"

"I'll tell you what. I'll give you a grand. And, I'll give you that Rebel over there." He threw a thumb over his right shoulder. A small motorcycle, a Honda Rebel, was strapped to a trailer behind a Ford truck. Again, I'm not one for handouts. But I was stuck, and this rich man's generosity was a welcome break.

"You sure about this?" As we lowered the bike off the trailer, I tried to grasp at why this man was helping me.

He pulled out a staggering stack of cash. He counted

out ten hundred dollar bills and shoved the stack into my hand. We traded keys.

"Young man!" The strange man called out to me.

I looked up at him as I strapped on the faceless motor-cycle helmet. It was loose. I would need to buy a new one.

"Let me know if you want him back one day. We can work out a deal," he said as he secured my-his Jeep on the trailer that once held his-my motorcycle.

"Thank you. I appreciate what you're doing."

"I don't know what you're talking about, I'm robbing you blind, chief!" He had a broad, straight smile on his face as he drove off down the street, towing my trusty sidekick behind his truck. I rarely felt sentimental but I felt a catch as I watched my Jeep disappear around a corner.

Farewell, old friend.

I rode back to Fred's place, testing the capabilities of the new bike. Feathered the throttle, revved the little 250cc motor, leaned into turns, straightened out. As I did, I thought about what I had to do in the coming days. As much as I liked my new mode of transportation, I would need something more to get back on the road. A 250cc was fun and acceptable for a small town, but not reliable for life on the road. I did some budgeting in my head as I rode around town. I wanted to give Fred some extra cash for letting me stay at his place, and hoped that he would continue to let me do so. I would need to save up for some new wheels, too. The chunk of cash the stranger gave me was a good cushion, but it was clear that I would need to get a job in this city. I throttled up.

what's up. I'm Fred Briggs.

From the head of Fred Briggs.

I like my life simple. I love my dog, Donnie. I love my car. I love whiskey. I loved my parents. Love my parents.

My dad opened up Sonrisa Auto in 1983, and built it from the ground up. Before that, he helped friends, neighbors, and family repair their cars. They would pay him what they could which sometimes meant he was paid via bartering. We always had plates of lasagna, golf clubs, other odds and ends from his customers. Can't pay bills in lasagna so it was rough. My dad, mom, my younger brother, and me huddled together to get through these rocky times. Eventually though, my dad slowly built a reputation for his upstanding service in the community. So, he made it official, and scratched together enough money to buy a dirty old garage. I watched him build that business with his bare hands into one of the largest auto shops in the county. Just when things seemed to be looking up, he had a heart attack. I was 23, my brother was 21. My mom took it the hardest. She passed six months after my dad.

Of course it was hard, but what good does it do to wallow over the past like that? Be a man, push down your emotions, walk tall, and pretend you know what you're doing.

Soon after my mom passed, my brother left town with some girl. I'm not sure exactly where they went but last I heard he was somewhere near Austin doing some shady jobs for some shady people. I didn't like that he left. For what? A change of scenery? But again, why fret over the past?

With everyone gone, the shop ownership fell into my young hands. Too young. But my dad cared for all of his employees, and they in turn supported me in a way that I could not possibly put in words. They did what they needed to do to keep the shop running, and it flourished. Beyond that, they mentored me, invited me to dinner during the holidays, made me little frozen meals. The employees of Sonrisa and their families took me in as one of their own, carrying on their long-standing relationship with my family.

Leo Mas seemed like a capable enough dude, but who would look out for him when he was in a bind? Could he turn to anyone? Would anyone listen when he did? Why was he out on the road taking unnecessary risks and never setting roots? I never asked him directly why he was on the road. I figured it would come up naturally. Or not. Maybe he didn't want to share.

There was something elegant in the simplicity of fixing cars. It was a puzzle that was solved by a part. Radiator busted? Replace part A10-356 and it will be good to go. Need a tool? The 3/8 sockethead is what you need. No experimentation necessary. Once you got in the flow of automechanics, it became a comfortable routine.

I woke up everyday, same time. Put on my blue workshirt with my nametag. Laced up my work boots. Drank one cup of coffee, ate a bowl of Honey Nut Cheerios. Watched SportCenter highlights. Opened up shop, worked all day, closed. Came home, ate dinner, drank beer or whiskey. Walked Donnie. Slept. Woke, repeat. Repeat. Repeat.

My routine was interrupted slightly by Leo's arrival. In general, I always felt that change is just an unnecessary risk. If things were going well, why change? Nicole left me. That was a negative change. Parents died. Negative.

Why would I choose to experiment and try the new Bud Light Lime when I know that I like Budweiser? I was still trying to gauge how Leo, the most recent change in my life, was going to affect me. Of course his Jeep troubles were none of my fault but I still felt some responsibility for at least giving him a place to figure his shit out. Anyway, this Japanese dude seemed alright. Maybe Leo would stay in Santa Labre, set some roots, become part of the community. Maybe he would set some roots and get into a routine.

I didn't really like many drugs. Sure, I enjoyed whiskey and the occasional spliff. Nothing crazy though. I did like cocaine, though. It didn't turn me into a different person or challenge my perception of the world. It just gave me a burst of euphoric energy all the way to my fingertips. I did try acid once. Well, not by choice. It was one of the moments that dissuaded me from trying new things.

It was a time of turmoil. I was approaching the age of manhood. Most of my friends and I lived a sheltered life, one that provided a nurturing hub for a specific type of growth. But as cliché as it might be, every baby bird must be pushed from the nest at one point. I was a straight-laced kid but there were a series of events that shocked me into the reality of the harsh real world.

I had only been to a few concerts in my life, and none of them like this. Well. This was a rave. This was my first time but three of my best friends were going to Awakening, a show that was fairly close to where we lived. I had only tried weed a couple times at that point. When Scott asked if I wanted to try a firecracker, a rudimentary edible, I reluctantly accepted. Ritz cracker, peanut butter, weed, Ritz cracker. Bake it in the oven, and you have the worst tasting sandwich you could possible imagine. He let me know that it takes about 30 to 45 minutes to kick in.

It was a long wait in line, so Scott and I both decided to eat our crackers in the parking lot. Scott stuffed his in his mouth, and headed for the line. I took a nibble, gagged at the taste, and tossed the rest of it in a bush. No fucking way I was going to push through that. I was a bit scared of the drug, too.

We stood in line for a while. I looked around, amused at the vast array of characters. Tall, lanky dudes in neon tank tops were joking with young girls with black make-up, dyed hair, and neon booty shorts. People in panda bear costumes. People with painted faces. It was bizarre how this was considered "cool." If these people were at the Renaissance fair, would they be held in high regard?

Directly in front of me, I watched a twenty-something

guy tilt his head toward the sky. I couldn't see what he was doing at first but then his neon top hat fell to the ground, and I saw him dripping something into his mouth with what looked like an eyedropper. He passed the dropper to his punky girlfriend wearing red and black lingerie. She dripped a couple drops onto her tongue.

After about an hour, I started to feel euphoria drifting into my consciousness. I looked back at Scott to see how he was doing and jumped as he threw a hand on my shoulder. I tried to catch him as he began to fall to the ground but his body was about as sturdy as an overcooked noodle. He slumped to the ground, and security was upon us in no time.

"What did he take?" They looked at Erick, Bryan, and me.

Of course I lied. "Nothing, I think he just has heat stroke."

They half-dragged him to a shady area, where he sat sipping water and smiling absent-mindedly. He eventually recovered and rejoined us as we entered the venue.

The place was incredible. I hadn't seen anything like this. Darkness was broken by the purple glow of black lights. Beams of red, green, blue, white lasers crossed through the air, landing on the crowd. The music. The bass was so intense that it rattled my organs against my rib cage. I didn't like techno or trance or drum-n-bass much but I was enveloped in the atmosphere. I could not help but move my body, jump, and thrash my arms.

Even so, I was still aware of my surroundings, and watched the other rave-goers. Asian guys wearing gloves with LED fingertips, waving and swinging them around to make vibrant streaks and patterns of light in the air. Ecstasy-enthralled girls hypnotized by the light shows around them. Groups of frat guys jumped together, bobbing so violently, I was sure their heads would pop off of their necks. Couples grinded against each other so passionately and rhythmically, there was bound to be thousands of pregnant girls by the end of the night. And everyone, everything was moving to the beat of the music. It was like *Fantasia* on drugs. Well, I guess it was just like *Fantasia*.

I waded through the crowds, feeling energized by every shoulder I bumped, every dancing girl. I became accustomed to the constant human contact. But amid the elated din, I felt something graze my arm.

I looked at my forearm then back behind me as I saw a young woman walking away with something clutched in her palm. She called back to me as she disappeared into the swaying droves.

"Welcome to ACID."

The booming bass stopped. The room emptied. I stood alone, sweating profusely, trying to process what had just happened. Was I being paranoid? She had smiled as if to comfort me. She had spoken as if I was arriving in a foreign land, naked to the experiences that this new world could offer. I took a deep breath and started to relax. She was just fucking with a young kid. There's no way she dosed me. Right?

The music and crowd returned, and I continued pushing through the hordes of dancers. The lights sliced through the crowd, revealing smiling faces and dilated pupils. Feet stomping. Hands flailing. Sweat flying. And strobes. Strobes. Strobes.

I found that each time I opened my eyes, I saw a new scene, new people around me. I lost a few chunks here and there but somehow it didn't concern me. I remember darting through a maze of humans, dodging while dancing, sometimes stopping to enjoy the atmosphere, sometimes charging through for the sport of it. The rave had become a video game, and I was Player 1.

Around 4AM, the concert was coming to a close. I somehow stumbled back into the huddle of my long lost friends whom I had not seen in about three hours. The ride home was filled with flashes of passing cars as my imagination saw us challenging hundreds of cars up the 15 North. Probably thanks to one DD friend, Player 1 made it home that night.

And Player 1 survived til the next morning, still in a slightly fragmented world. I woke at 8AM as I did every Sunday to play baseball in a city league. I was in an epic tug-of-war with Player 1 over my splintered reality. I pulled on my pants and grabbed my cleats and team shirt. By the time I got in the car, I was starting to win the battle, and it seemed Player 1 was packing it in. I drove the 35 minutes to the field, and I sighed in relief as I strode toward the dugout. Made it.

I gave an friendly up-nod to my teammates as I tossed my gear under the bench. Our team was mostly old farts so the younguns usually had to play the most time to give them a rest. As I was lacing up my shoes, my cousin tapped my head.

"You're up." He tossed me the ball, letting me know that I was going to be the starting pitcher. I groaned under my breath. But being the rookie on the team, I had no choice.

Grabbing my mitt and the ball, I headed for the mound. I kicked dirt and adjusted the surface with my cleat, half to fix it, half to kill some time. Finally, I lifted my head from my digging and made eye contact with the catcher to start warming up. Fastball. Fastball. Change-up. Slider. I continued for a while until my arm was loose. On the last pitch, I threw my specialty, the cut fastball. It sliced through the strike zone and thudded in the catcher's glove. He tossed it back to me.

Wait.

I felt the first drop of sweat escape my forehead and run down the side of my face. I looked at the ball. It was floating midair, halfway between the catcher's outstretched throwing hand and my outstretched glove. The murmuring crowd went completely silent. A slice of sunlight cut through the clouds and illuminated a child sitting in the stands some 75 feet away from me. Making direct eye contact with me, the child whispered without smiling. Her voice was clear.

"Welcome back."

My heart sank as I looked back at the ball in time to catch it. Well, Player 1. Let's see what you got.

* * * * *

78

Some folks say that hallucinogens help them reach some dramatic turning point in their lives or produce some introspective journey through space and time, and then coming out of it a "better person." Bullshit. I was plunged into a strange world of terror and unfamiliarity. Don't get me wrong. I loved my share of intoxicants. Whiskey was my go-to, but I would be fine with a beer or a bit of coke, too. I felt more in control, I knew where I was. Cocaine doesn't pick you up by your collar and toss you into a black sea of psychedelic waves and melting faces.

How could this state possibly bring out positivity? Why would I purposefully put my mind and body in a place where I know I am going to be uncomfortable? Why would you risk losing something good, just for a slight chance of getting better? I am fine how I am right now. I don't need to change. I am just fine running this auto shop. I am just fine walking my dog every day. I am just fine living in the same house. I am just fine living in the same city.

I am just fine.

enso.

I was grateful for Fred's unending hospitality, but still I was uncertain of what the future held. He never mentioned an end date but Nicole's departure likely left him in a place where he was open to some companionship and a drinking buddy. I could at least provide the latter. After one such inebriated therapy session, I had a dream during my drunken slumber. A dream or a flashback...

I am in my grandparents home, looking up at a strange painting on the wall.

"Grandpa, what's that black circle?"

I point at a canvas hanging above the fireplace. A single stroke, a seemingly perfect circle. The black contrasts the clean, white canvas.

"How old is that, Grandpa?

He stops from cooking his ramen, looking down at me with an odd, beaming pride.

"A young man grown painted that in June of 1949."

"What's it mean?" I really meant, *Why would you hang this thing on your wall?*"

He pours the ramen into two bowls, and pushes one over to me. Steam rises from the noodle soup. The brown broth swirls and I see hints of beef, cabbage, carrots, and other goodies surrounded by a flowing forest of thin noodles. As I let it cool I think about my grandpa as a young man in his hometown nestled in Maui. I imagine him coming home after working in the sugarcane fields, tired and cut from the sharp plants. I wonder how much strength he must have gained from the hot ramen that his mom had waiting for him after a hard day of labor. I envy it in some way.

"Ah..." a broad smile stretches across his face as he leans in and breathes in the aroma from the soup. He wouldn't smile at baseball games, at birthdays, for photographs. Which made this smile so much more meaningful. He takes another deep inhalation, as if it were the last breath, and his smile persists. He sits back in his recliner to let the soup cool.

I look at the canvas, trying to uncover its importance, its meaning. Then, I notice.

"It's a perfect circle."

He nods and turns slightly toward me. "Well, close." I look back at the canvas.

"So what's it mean?"

"That's an enso, Leo." He stirs his bowl of ramen with his chopsticks before leaning back to let it cool more. "It represents a path to enlightenment. The only way to get it right is through muscle memory. Practice. Practice. Here." He grabs a tattered sketchbook from the table next to him. He flips through to find a blank page and hands it to me. Reaching in his front pocket, he pulls out a ballpoint pen. "Go ahead, give it a try."

I swoop a lop-sided oval. Terrible.

He smiles, ruffles my hair, and turns to slurp some noodles. I flip to a new page. Take it seriously this time.

I place the tip of the pen so it just barely rests against the clean white page. Focus. Close my eyes. Envision a perfect circle in my mind.

> *I was told that Descartes thought that a perfect triangle was impossible to draw, but one could*

imagine what a perfect triangle would look like. Was it Descartes? Or was it Hume? Socrates? Either way, I could imagine the perfect circle. I knew the pattern my arm had to move in. I could prove that philosophic fuck wrong. I inhaled slowly like a sharpshooter. I opened my eyes and exhaled slow as I swished my hand in a quick, roundabout motion.

"Shit."

"Watch your mouth." Grandpa pauses from his soup and takes the pen from me. A nonchalant swoop from him, and he makes a near perfect hoop. I sit for a second and admire his enso.

"Keep trying, Leo. It's the only way."

* * * * *

I awoke from my dream. Still at Fred's. I grabbed my own notebook. Maybe this would be the time. I closed my eyes again, envisioning a perfect circle. A practice swoop in the air before my pen met paper. A single swoop.

Shit.

living poor.

"Leo!" Fred Briggs wanted something. "There's another one over here!"

Fuck. I already knew what was jabbing at him.

It was one of the very few heavy rains of the year. Rooftops and trees were beaten wet. Gutters filled and overflowed, spilling onto sidewalks and waterlogging yards. It was a much-needed gift in this devastating drought, but much like the poor man who wins the lottery, the land didn't have anywhere to put all the water. The land stashed its lottery winnings in every pocket, hole in the ground, and truck bed available, sloppily covering the town in puddles and runoff. The flood drove all to shelter, including rodents. So in they came, and soon we found our refuge shared.

Fred Briggs and I approached the pantry to hear

scratches, hear gnawing, hear squeaks of gluttonous excitement. Holes would magically appear at the bottoms of our Wheaties boxes, and the grains were strewn about the shelves. It was not long before we decided to invest in some defense. Mousetraps were our first line against the rodent horde.

The calamity had just begun. We set the traps at night with the plan of retrieving them in the morning with clean, dead mouse captives. Come to think of it, the corpse clean up did not cross our minds while we were setting the death traps. The aftermath proved to be more unsettling than we were prepared for.

I was first up on that March morning. I dragged my way to the kitchen to start some coffee. Sun was not yet up, and the kitchen was dark as I walked across the living room. I heard a familiar scratching and clawing but this was much louder than before. A squeak filled the quiet of the room as I flipped the light on.

To be honest, I was almost smiling up to this point. These rodents had been a major annoyance to us. I was a bit uplifted that we had found a solution to the infestation. But, as I turned on that light, my stomach clenched at what I saw. The mouse was fairly small, could have nestled in a child's dainty hand. Now shrieking uncontrollably, the mouse had flipped the trap over, and was pushing itself in circles on the kitchen floor in some bizarre, desperate death dance. The wood base of the trap covered most of its body with thin, circular trails of blood marking the floor as the mouse figure-eighted a grotesque scene. It appeared the cheese had been too much to resist. I flipped the trap over, revealing the furry victim's wounds. The spring-loaded bar pinned the mouse's arm to his neck, which in turn was pinned to the wood base. It looked like he was trying to push the bar off of his throat with his tiny arm. He let loose another shriek, this one with less energy backing it. He was on his way out.

Again, we hadn't planned for the cleanup. I threw open our only closet and grabbed the first object that could serve out an execution: Fred's hockey stick. I glanced around and grabbed a plate from the kitchen table. Using the hockey stick, I scooped up the mouse and carefully put him on the plate. We went outside to the street. The brisk morning air bit at my skin slightly but my face was already tingling in preparation for my task at hand. Placed the plate on the black asphalt. The mouse was barely twitching now. Dried blood caked the fur on the side of his neck and face. His eyes were still open and stared up at me. I lifted the hockey stick high. The plate shattered the morning still as I put the *living poor.*

mouse out of its misery.

This went on. Everyday we would wake to find more victims. Some days we would find one, other times two. Sometimes they would be dead already. Other times the mice would escape, leaving the trap empty. There would be a part of me that was relieved. Most days didn't bring fortune for the rodents. We used shovels to end the mice, and bought a dustpan to be used specifically for the scooping of mice. It became a grim chore, a melancholy routine of waking and executing. We did not think ourselves sentimental but doing this everyday began to dig at us. Dark business, this was.

* * * * *

After losing my car, days were spent searching for odd jobs. I had done the burger joint gig while I was passing through Texas and tried to avoid that route. The burger joint route, not the Texas route. Anyway I applied for positions as assistants, bartenders, busboys, data entry. I submitted myself for a paid study where I took some surveys, tried some new-to-market sports drinks, and got $100. It was frustrating getting rejected from job after job. I would need to sample many more Gatorade knockoffs before I could afford a new car.

Days were filled with applications, with interviews,

with kissing the asses of potential employers. Nights were filled with drinking and storytelling with Fred Briggs, with the occasional card and chess game. And walking Donnie.

In need of a break from my endless job hunt, Fred Briggs and I grabbed some fishing rods, a handful of hooks and weights, and Donnie, and headed over to the Avila Beach docks. We picked up some anchovies at the bait shop and settled in at the far end of the pier. Fred dropped in the lure, half hoping for a catch but mostly just sitting back, sipping coffee, Donnie laying at his side. I wandered along the pier, people-watching in the early morning. There were a few sport fishermen with kids warming their hands in their pockets, fishing lines taut in anticipation of a bite. Further down toward the dock, a man crouched by an enormous pile of fish. He worked next to the deck of a commercial fishing vessel, sorting, cleaning, and wrapping the carcasses. The rest of the crew was nowhere to be seen. I walked over.

"What'd you get?" I said as I approached.

"Cod, salmon mostly. Some other stuff." The man answered me but kept sorting without looking up.

"You look like you could use a hand."

He paused just long enough to give me a quick look up and down before continuing his work. "You know fish at all?"

"Sure, I know enough," I rolled up my sleeves and started sorting.

We worked in silence without resting for an hour and a half. Reeking of fish guts, wet with blood and seawater, we threw the last of fish into their assigned bins. Stretching my back, I sat back on a bench near our work station. The man cracked open two cans of Budweiser from his ice chest and handed me one.

"Cheers, brother." He tapped his can against mine, spilling a bit from both of our full cans. "Appreciate the hand. I would've been working on those fuckers for hours."

"No problem. I couldn't let you sweat that by yourself."

"Hey, man. I wasn't sweating." He took a gulp of beer before shooting out a hand. "I'm Matt."

"Leo," as I shook his filthy hand with mine.

"So, Leo, what are you doing at the docks this early?"

I told the most recent chapters of my story. My damaged car, the mysterious buyer, Fred Briggs and his generosity, my motorcycle, and my need for a job.

"Sounds like you're in a hurry to get out of here," Matt glanced at me. "But, we could use another deckhand. Our last guy left."

"Yeah? Sounds good to me."

"Well, you can talk the captain sure enough, but he trusts my opinion."

"What's the pay?"

"Well, you'll get all the cod you can eat," Matt bellowed with laughter. "I would guess a hundred or so for a day's work."

"Matt, if you can give me that, you can consider me your newest deck hand."

Donnie ran up and jumped on me. He licked the fish blood off my fingers. Fred followed, carrying the rod in one hand, and a couple rockfish in the other.

"Matt, this is Fred Briggs. Fred, Matt."

"Good looking rockies you got there, Fred." They shook hands.

"Thanks, man. Gonna go try to cook these guys up. Ready to get outta here, Leo?"

"Let's do it," I replied before turning to Matt. "When do I start?"

"Get here at sunrise on Monday. I'll introduce you to the Cap and crew. If they like you, you're in. Just don't bullshit them. You'll be fine."

Looks like I am going to be a fisherman.

too fucking quiet.

Over the next couple of weeks, the Captain only had me come in for a handful of mornings but the work itself was pretty easy to pick up. Grunt work for the most part. Cleaned equipment, washed the deck of the boat, prepped the gear for the next outing. They did pay me in cash though. Not the best gig I had had but not the worst.

An unforeseen benefit of this job was the trip out to Avila. The short ride on my motorcycle was a refreshing start to the day; the early morning crispness carried the sea spray. I had grown accustomed to the dry stillness of the desert but this new atmosphere was a pleasant change. I settled into this new rhythm. For now.

I came home, scratched Donnie on the head, let him smell the day's grime on my palms. He would stuff his snout into the grooves of my hands, looking up and understanding as I told him about my day at the docks.

too fucking quiet.

Fred Briggs' stereo was nice; it filled his small home with sound. Some days I would play Bob Marley and Toots and Sublime. Some days I would unwind with Jimi's or B.B.'s blues. The licks would roll all over the house and through me as if they too knew how my day went. Music was the calming static that held my brain together, allowing it to unwind from itself. It was as if my mind needed something to preoccupy itself to prevent it from digging too deep.

At the docks, I once overheard the Captain talking to a marine biologist-tourist. They were talking story about sea creatures and critters including the high intelligence level of the octopus. The scientist explained how octopuses held in tanks are one of the few animals that appear to die of boredom.

"Boredom?" The Captain scoffed. "What are you all about?"

"No, sir, I'm serious. Trainers and care takers at aquariums often have to give food in a puzzle form, or provide the octopus with some kind of toy to play with."

"Yeah? Sounds like a load to me," the Captain sneered but I could tell he was interested. At his heart, the Captain was as curious as any. But he was a man's man so he kept up appearances. "So what happens when these octopus die of boredom?"

"Well, they will often explore themselves into a situation where they can't get out. Or, more often, they will escape the tank and end up dying."

"That sounds more like suicide than dying of boredom, son," the Captain beamed as if uncovering a huge flaw in the scientist's theory.

"We prefer to say it dies of boredom," replied the scientist.

Mornings of stories and fish and grime, followed by afternoons were filled with Jimi's sweet riffs. This day, I came home, selected the Black Keys' *Brother*, and was greeted with a loud snap and a rush of electronic static. Nothing. Fuse blown, and the music that balanced my day was gone. I was too tired to run to the store to grab a new fuse so I slumped on the couch. I heard Donnie rummaging in the backyard but had no energy to join him. I sat in silence. I reached for my notebook then tossed it on the coffee table. The notebook and I stared at each other for minutes, anticipating. I broke. I picked it up and opened to a fresh page. I wrote.

> *It's too fucking quiet.*
> *Too quiet to think,*

too quiet to talk.

Too quiet to reach out.

Too quiet to listen.

The Still ping pongs around my head

dislodges long-passed thoughts

and memories forgotten.

They noisily claw and dash, adding to the para-
lyzed din.

This quiet is too loud.

I hope for a Peep,

a Tap,

an Explosion.

This complacent air is an assault on

my senses.

Tap a rhythm to combat that Still.

Shh.

Hum a hymn to break the calm.

Shh.

Fire a gun in the sky to rattle the cages.

Shh.

Even the Quieter is quiet.

Holster your gun, son. I give up.

Embrace the silence, add to the silence.

My own voice is forgotten by my own mind.

Another voice enters the Still:

"It's too fucking quiet!"

Shh. I say.

Angry or disheartened. She the Voice was one of those.

I turned to retract my statement, but it was too late.

Gone.

I sighed.

Shh.

Hi, I'm Kat Scindo

From the memories of Kat.

"It's just wires and batteries. It has no reason to hate you. It can't hate you. You are just being stubborn, Kat." The bartender strode over as I fiddled with my point-and-shoot camera. I was just getting into photography, a wiry twenty year-old sitting alone at the bar amid grown men.

"Fuck you, Roger. I'm not stubborn," I shot back.

Barkeep Roger smiled, pouring a beer for a customer. A hand reached from behind me and pinched my ear.

"Watch that mouth, young lady."

"Ow! Mom!" I spun around, greeted by a concrete gaze dissecting my awry attitude. I couldn't help but soften at this non-verbal assault, and I saw a glint of a smile behind that stone.

"Give Roger some respect. You're lucky he doesn't kick you to the streets."

"It's alright, Jacky," Roger chimed in. "My feelings ain't hurt. Anyway, I couldn't kick Kat out; who would jam on that piano on Saturday nights?"

"Talent is no excuse for disrespect." Mom went back to serving customers club sandwiches, chicken fingers, and Jack-and-Cokes.

My attention returned to the disassembled camera in front of me. I was sure I would be able to see the problem after it was taken apart. I thought I could figure it out. But I was in over my head.

I piled all the pieces of the camera onto a cloth napkin. Walked over to the trash bin at the end of the bar. Dropped the scrap in, napkin and all. Neither Roger nor my mom noticed the dump, and I slipped out of the bar, as I had a thousand times.

"I'll need to save up for a new camera," I thought to myself. Fresh air was needed.

The streets of Venice Beach. Not sweet. Not friendly. Not even that clean. But that beach town was my home. Some neighborhoods you tried to avoid, and some you couldn't.

Home, but I had an itch to get out.

My phone rang in my pocket. My heart sank and lifted simultaneously when I saw the caller ID. I braced myself.

"Hi, Papa."

A raspy voice, both familiar and unfamiliar, was on the other end.

"Kat, my baby. Kat." A deep breath. "How have you been? Still rockin' those keys?" He asked me this every time we spoke. It was the one consistency we had in our relationship.

"Yeah, still playing at the bar."

"Good, good, that's great, Kat." Another deep breath before continuing, "How's your mother doing?"

"Good, just working."

"That's good too, that's good too. Glad to hear you girls are busy."

I wanted to ask where he was. I wanted to ask when I could see him. I wanted to ask why he called.

When my dad called like this, I thought about my parents' life before me. They met in a methadone clinic in Santa Barbara, and promptly proceeded to spiral downward in a tornado of love and drugs. Somewhere in this storm, my mom got pregnant. Me. That's when my mom went clean. My pop couldn't cut his habit and tension began to build between them. Mom ended up moving south to Venice Beach and went to rehab, while he stayed in Santa Barbara. They were never married but I knew how much it tore at my mom. Once in a while, I would hear her talking and sobbing on the phone, late at night, begging my dad to get clean. He didn't.

I tried to avoid too many questions, and this phone call with Pa was no different. Roundabout responses never satisfied my want for an answer. I was beyond that.

"Is your mother close?"

"No, I already left the bar."

"Oh, ok. I'll call her later." He wouldn't. "Anyway, I have to run to a meeting. Nice to hear your voice, Kat!"

"Bye, Pa." Dial tone.

I tried to brush it off. I pulled out a cigarette that I lifted from Roger, lit it and put my lighter back in my trusty denim jacket. On my 16th birthday, my dad gave me this killer denim jacket. Brand new, crisp, pockets up the wazoo. This jacket I took everywhere. He also gave me a beautiful camera. That introduced me into photography.

That was also the one I had just trashed.

On my 18th birthday, my dad came down again, near broke. In the two years that I hadn't seen him, he seemed to have aged twenty. He was thin as a rail, and his once thick, Italian hair was thin and unkempt. His eyes had bags beneath them, but they were still comforting, filled with energy. I treated him to pancakes, and we walked the boardwalk. He stopped me in front of a tattoo shop.

"What do ya think, little girl?" He beamed at me.

"Yes!!" I hadn't given tattoos much thought, but I wanted to bask in any Dad-related experience. All the better if this experience stayed with me forever.

He was riddled with ink that attached to him through the years, but he found an empty spot on his back, on the right side. We both got sparrows in the traditional, Sailor-Jerry style. I got mine on my upper back, right side.

"I got your back," he said to me as we compared his ink to mine.

I hadn't seen him since. I knew he was still around, somewhere in California. He would call my cell from strange numbers at random times during the day or in the middle of the night. Sometimes he sounded calm, collected, happy. Other times he was frantic, almost panicked.

He always tried his best to present himself as happy as possible, even if just on the phone.

I was afraid I would eventually lose contact with my dad after I left Southern California. But through all my changes of address, he always kept my number. I later found out that he had it tattooed on his inner forearm. I always wanted to help him, to save him, but deep down I knew that that time had likely passed. He was who he was, and would always be.

I continued down Venice Blvd and took a last drag of smoke. Little did I know that less than two years later, I would be walking down that same street of that beach town, reeling from the passing of my mom. Alone and lost, I struggled to find my way. I took to the road with my music, photography, or whatever else I had to do to make money.

I stomped out the butt of Roger's cigarette and moved onward.

* * * * *

Fast-forward six years. I was walking down another boardwalk, this time in Avila Beach. I had a pocketful of cash. It was late afternoon but there was still plenty of light as I looked out toward the ocean. The sun was getting ready to lower itself to the horizon, and orange streaks were beginning to spread across the sky, illuminating low clouds. I snapped a photo. I had seen thousands of sunsets, yet stopping to appreciate one still left me with a calm. I continued on my walk.

On a bench sat a dude, about my age. He slouched over a notebook, writing furiously, ignoring passersby, oblivious to the oncoming sunset. As I approached him, I recognized his face. Leo, the traveler that I met at the bar a few weeks ago.

"Buenos tarde, hombre," I stood directly in front of him, casting a shadow on him and his notebook. He looked up and blinked a few times as he adjusted to the change of scenery. An awkward pause. *Shit, he doesn't remember me.* A broad smile swept across his face.

"Kat!" He hopped up from the bench and gave me an unexpected hug. He let go suddenly, and cleared his throat, realizing he overstepped the boundary. We really only met once in that bar a few weeks ago. But yes, he remembered me.

"What are you doing here?" He glanced at me, cocking his head. I was wearing a mid-length black cocktail dress with some fancy heels. I was also wearing my denim jacket. Tattered and worn, I never went anywhere without it.

"I had a gig over there at that new wine bar. Those hoity-toities paid me to play piano so I took their money."

"Clever. You live around here?"

"Nah, I live in Santa Labre."

"Me too. At least, for now. My car broke down so I'm staying with this dude that runs the auto shop. I got a pretty good job with this fishing crew here."

"Fishing? Is that why you smell like shit?" I smiled and tapped his notebook. "What are you writing?"

"Just some bullshit," he quickly changed the subject. "Where are you headed now?"

"Nowhere, home maybe."

"Fuck that. Know some place to get a drink?"

"Ye, andiamo."

"What?"

"Let's go. It's Italian, you unsophisticated fuck."

Over the next few weeks, I met Fred Briggs the mechanic and Donnie the Dog. I usually didn't like dealing with people, especially those who were consumed with their dull, monotonous suits and cubicles, talking about the weather and going to happy hour after an eight-hour workday. But these two dudes, Fred and Leo, were good people, even if the three of us kept each other at arm's distance. I still didn't even know exactly how Leo found himself in Santa Labre. I wanted to ask him about his past, but the past is the past, I suppose.

I also avoided conversations about history so mine wouldn't come up. Now passing through my mid-twenties, I felt like I was carrying way too much baggage for my age. Even so, I had no regrets, really. I enjoyed life, and I was determined to get the most out of it while I could.

I was never one to set roots. Jobs, relationships, homesteads, sunglasses - all came and went. I never held onto a pair of sunglasses for too long so I hated investing in a nice pair. I would get some cool shades and take them everywhere with me. They would help me hide from the world when I felt down, and gave me a confident energy when I felt good. But inevitably, I would fuck up. I would break them, I would lose them. Sometimes, I would get too self-aware and think that I was too dependent on them, hiding behind the dark lenses. Sometimes I would come across prettier ones, and I would be tempted to wear that pair for a while. So, I stopped getting too used

to any one pair of shades. I bought cheap ones at gas sta-
tions, expecting that I would fuck them up somehow. I
just came to accept the fact that I wasn't made to keep a
single pair of shades.

Spending my leisure time with Fred, Donnie, and Leo
wasn't so bad. I liked those folks. They seemed to understand me. But, once in awhile, I would notice Leo staring
off at the ocean in the distance, to the mountains in the
east. I wondered how many shades he went through in
his life.

relate.

As the owner of the shop, there were times when Fred Briggs had to put in long hours. He would sometimes leave before me, before sunrise, and sometimes return late into the night. Those days he would come home, eyes bloodshot, shirt smeared with black grease, reeking of the warm must of motor oil clung to him, and his work shirt would be smeared with black grease. He would shoot a whiskey and go straight to bed. If his eyes were open, they would be bloodshot. I am fairly sure they were bloodshot when they were closed, too. It was one of those weeks.

I had just come back from a walk with Donnie, and we were both sprawled on the couch, listening to Johnny Cash and rolling a couple cigarettes. Kat came in without knocking, and slumped down on the couch without a word. Neither Donnie nor I stopped what we were doing. The three of us just slumped in that room for a moment while *Folsom Prison Blues* crooned through the air. The room was still except for my fingers rolling the cigarette and Donnie's wagging tail.

"Have you eaten yet?" Kat asked me.

I leaned back and stuck the two finished cigarettes in my front pocket. "I could eat."

"Let's go somewhere. Let's get a steak. On me." Kat offered. She was very sporadic with her money. There were times when she would get a big check from some gig and buy meals and drinks for Fred and me. Other times, she seemed to be near broke, and survived off Top Ramen and oranges. This time she had money.

"Let's do it. I can go for a steak." I scratched Donnie behind his ear, grabbed a jacket, and headed out.

"You drive," Kat said, walking toward my bike.

"OK, but I only have one helmet." I grabbed my helmet, placed it on her head. I laughed as the helmet swung loosely around her head. She pulled it off, handed it back to me, and walked over to pop the trunk on her little red Honda. A staggering mass of junk hid the bottom of the trunk. She dug for a few moments before producing a beat up skate helmet. It was small, even for her, but she made do and buckled it.

relate.

"We're good!" She gave a foolish grin, revealing a full set of white teeth with a hair-thin gap between her front two.

I put on my own helmet and climbed onto my bike. Turned the ignition and started it as Kat hopped on the back. She put her arms around my chest as we zoomed off down the street toward downtown Santa Labre. She gripped me closer as we took the first turn, and I could almost feel her pulse quicken. I smiled inside my helmet, and took the next turn a little faster.

A red light stopped us, and Kat leaned forward and yelled over the rumbling of the motorcycle engine, "McLaren's!"

"Alright, easy. You don't have to scream." She had overcompensated and yelled straight into my ear. McLaren's was a fairly nice steakhouse downtown that turned into a bar in the late hours of the day. I was a bit hesitant because it was a bit more expensive than I wanted to spend. But I said nothing. We pulled up and parked.

It was a cozy place. We were seated next to the window where we could watch and make fun of passersby. Kat and I had been spending more time together, but we still never talked about our past. I was able to piece together a patchwork of the flavor of Kat's life through her stories, but I had to connect dots myself. She didn't talk about her family, her parents. I was equally vague. We grew to just enjoy our time together.

"Look at these fucking squares, nine o'clock," Kat shoved a none-too-casual thumb in the direction of a middle-aged couple. Matching baby blues made it easy to distinguish them as a pair (button down shirt for him, sundress for her). Pleated khaki's covered his legs, ending in dark dress shoes. She wore her hair in a ponytail.

"They seem alright to me. Those Dockers look a little uncomfortable, though." Square Man Blue adjusted his belt as he sat down. He looked like he wanted to scratch his balls but did not want to do so in public.

Kat snickered, "He makes me uncomfortable just looking at him." Square Man Blue pulled out his phone, and, from my angle, I saw that he was checking his Fantasy Football lineup. Square Lady Blue stared at him, attempting to gain his attention, but soon gave up, rolled her eyes, and began pawing at her own phone.

"I wonder why they're here," I said. "What's their story?"

Kat turned toward me and smiled. "They are actually on a first date. Maybe a Tinder date. I think they are swiping for their next date right now. Or maybe they are both texting their friends, complaining about their lame-ass date."

I contained my laugh, and gave it a shot. "That's a possibility. Or maybe this is their weekly dinner out on the town. Babysitter. Matching blouses. Same meal at McLaren's. How exciting."

Kat snorted, "Yeah, fuck that."

Just then, our food came.

"Fuck yeah, T-Bone!" Kat hooted loudly as the waiter brought her an enormous steak with potatoes, baked beans, and garlic bread. People turned, looking over their shoulders at the little tattooed girl with glasses hanging from her neck. I usually wasn't one for loud outbursts or cries for attention, but Kat's attitude was one of pure, child-like joy. She allowed herself to get swept up in a moment. That we shared.

That night Kat and I ate our steaks and talked nonsense. We talked about our misconstrued understanding of philosophers, and promptly dug into each other when the other ran into unknown territory. We talked about music, but found Kat's knowledge far outreached my own on that subject. We talked and enjoyed the moment.

"So, Leo. How exactly did you find yourself in Santa Labre?"

"Hm? I was just passing through and my old Jeep died out on the way out of town. The morning after I met you at that bar, actually."

"Yeah, yeah, I know that part, dummy. I meant where are you going?"

I paused a moment before answering. "Not really anywhere in particular. I did some exploring, did random jobs in Arizona and Utah and a few other places, but it's not like I have some kinda master plan. I headed out here mostly because I wanted to see the ocean."

"So now what? You saw the stupid ocean, you hippie. Why stay here?"

"Well, I don't exactly have a car right now. That little Honda bike can only take me so far."

"Hm. Yeah, sure." Kat gave me a bit of a sideways glance. The bill came. Kat grabbed it.

"How much is it?" I reached in my jacket pocket, fingering out a few twenties to cover our meal.

"Nah, don't worry about it, Leo." Kat put a hundred dollar bill on the tab and the waiter came by and swooped it up before I could stop him.

"What? Are you serious? I can't let you do that. Here, take this," I grabbed her hand and stuffed three twenties in it. She closed her fist, wound back, and threw them in my face, laughing.

"Nope! You get the next one."

"How dare you - I am offended," I said with a smile. I collected the cash and put it in my front pocket.

There was an easy comfort between us. Yet an unspoken, unseen glass wall separated us. I can only speak of this in retrospect, for neither her nor I appeared completely aware of it at the time. Well, at least I wasn't. It felt natural to drink and spend time with her, but we resisted each other in some way. We passed out on the couch together, and I would wake in the midst of a deadly hangover with Kat using my shoulder as a pillow. That hangover did not seem so bad. We would get close, drinking face-to-face, but always interrupted the moment by another shot of whiskey or a playful wrestle. If things got a little too close in our drunken antics, we would sometimes take a break for a day or two. After a time apart, we would always reconvene, and continue as normal. It was just too damn fun.

It was a delicate balance we had. Neither of us wanted to point it out for fear of destroying what we had. Still, there were times when I look at Kat, gesturing wildly with one hand, steadying a glass of whiskey with the other. Talking some bullshit about her stance on Descartes' proof of God. Tattooed wrists barely showing out of her denim torn jacket. Thick-rimmed glasses swinging from her neck. Deep, dark eyes flying around the room as she searched for proof of her theories. Her passionate eyes rarely made direct contact with mine. When our eyes met for a split second, she would break it every time. There was a part of me that did not like that quirk in a person's character. I always believed that eye contact was an important part of communication. Avoiding it seemed weak. Somehow it did not come from a place of weakness in Kat. Whatever it was, I didn't want to change it. She seemed fine as it was.

As Kat and I grew closer, it occurred to me that we could be using each other as a crutch. It quickly became apparent that Kat's thirst for addiction matched or exceeded my own. We rolled cigarettes and spliffs, poured whiskey until bottle's end. Painful hangovers did not slow us. In fact, there was something almost romantic about a hangover. Pain searing through our heads on the verge of puking, it became impossible to focus on anything but the hangover at hand. Life became simplified, even if it was filled with pain. We did our best to time our heavy drinking nights with off days for work, even though we weren't always successful. The guys at the docks never seemed to mind my hangovers as many of them were drunksick themselves. As for Kat, she always had a remarkable ability to pull herself together. Inside, I was sure she was a writhing, dizzying mess of sickness. With one glass of water to drink and another to splash on her face, she managed to carry herself as if in clear-headed sobriety. At the end of the day, she would collapse like a dying star, sleeping coma-like for hours. But, in public, hung-over Kat was true revelry.

* * * * *

Fred Briggs was not always busy. When we three were free together, we would spend late nights dancing and stomping to Nirvana or the Black Keys or some funk. Fred had a special love for funk. We sometimes smoked. We usually drank. But we always played music.

Fueled by Fred's unending hospitality, we spent hours and nights together at his place, but also frequented Kat's apartment a few blocks away. We moved back and forth, Donnie always close at our heels.

Sometimes it is some catastrophic event that brings

people together. Sometimes people use the company of others to distract themselves from their own thoughts. Sometimes people just find someone and hold on for a while. Reacting outwardly, instead of evaluating inwardly. Other times, it simply takes a shared interest to produce a friendship. I'm not sure why we ended up spending so much time together, but we three shared at least one interest.

We had our alcohol. We would work during the day, Fred Briggs at the auto shop, me at the docks, and Kat at some photography or music gig. Kat was apparently pretty successful because she seemed to be busy. After our separate workdays, we would collect at some table at some place and we would drink. I taught Kat to roll cigarettes, and she taught me to play the harmonica. Fred taught Kat how to open a beer with a lighter, and I taught Fred to box while drunk. Well, maybe we taught each other.

I sometimes got anxious about the road, and when I could or should get back on it. Sure, these were fine people, but I had met fine people before. I met people who seemed trustworthy and nice and friendly. I knew you can trust people, but you can't trust their insecurities. Sometimes these insecurities would reveal themselves at inconvenient times. Whether I liked it or not, I was stuck in this town for now. I couldn't make it far on that tiny motorbike, and I used most of the money I got from selling my car to pay Fred for letting me take Nicole's room after she moved out. So, I was broke and stuck. At least I had these folks for company.

We three and Donnie sat in Fred's living room one evening, decompressing. Kat lay on the loveseat, her Converse-clad feet propped up on the arm. Her head rested on a folded pillow, face aimed at the TV. Fred Briggs sat to my right, manning the remote, with Donnie in resting his head on his lap. I sat in front of the coffee table with my black notebook.

Fred Briggs surfed through the channels, illuminating our faces with flashes from the screen. Movies from the past, cartoon reruns. I saw a flash of CNN featuring some new conflict in the Middle East.

He stopped on one of those celebrity news shows. Kat kicked and stomped her feet on our couch defiantly, throwing a nonverbal tantrum for a channel change. Fred ignored her pleas completely, his eyes glued to the screen as pictures of the Kardashians and goofy graphics filled the screen. I looked at Fred in amusement. He was genuinely drawn to this, and I wondered why. It was senseless babbling about people whom we had never met, never would meet, and probably wouldn't even want to meet.

I heard the *vrmmmm, vrmmmmmmmm* of a vibrating phone. Kat lazily grabbed the buzzing device from the coffee table, glanced at the caller. Her eyes went wide, and she sat up straight, posture perfect and alert.

She jumped to her feet and flew out the door. "Hello? Hello...." Her voice faded as she took the call outside.

I turned my attention back to the buzz on the screen that was now holding Fred Briggs, transfixed. I guess everyone needs a distraction. The nature of existence is infinitely more complicated than non-existence, and everyone deals with it differently. How could you fault someone for seeking distraction? Good for Fred. I concluded that I was happy he could find solace, find haven from the drag of real life in such a simple form. An image of Justin Bieber's clothing choice popped up on the screen, and I tried to watch it, to let it absorb me. But I could not. Maybe someday I will be distracted a little easier.

Kat re-entered our atmosphere in a colder state. She sniffled for a second and stared at her phone.

"Who was that?" I asked.

relate.

"Don't worry about it," Kat sniffled again, then cleared her throat before regaining her composure to attack us. "You pansies finished watching your drama show? This whiskey isn't going to drink itself."

And so it went.

stumble.

Some people leave a profound mark on your being even though their time in your life may be short-lived.

One night, after a heavy night of drinking at the bars, Fred Briggs and I were strolling back to our home. Kat had a gig so it was just Fred and me. Our pace was slowed by frequent piss breaks and stumblings over feet. Fred was a few steps ahead of me, talking loudly, but was walking backward so we could talk face-to-face. We approached an intersection, when not unexpectedly, Fred collided with another body. The two guys tangled in a heap on the ground, both obviously weighed down by the lead blanket of alcohol. Although Fred's fuse was usually not short, he was also not one to back down from an altercation. I stood over them with hands in my pockets, anxious to witness the next scene in this episode. Alcohol prevailed, and the two of them burst into laughter and apologies. They struggled to stand, managing to help the other up. Friendly slaps on the back all around.

"You alright, man?" Fred Briggs offered. He was greeted by a wide grin. Maybe a few years older than us. His grin exuded a warm aura and he seemed genuinely happy. His smile, however, was not quite complete; his straight, white teeth were interrupted by a gap where an incisor once stood. A tongue poked out of the window.

"Shit, man...my tooth."

I laughed while Fred Briggs, ever hospitable, was concerned. "What're you talkin' 'bout, man?"

The guy dropped to his knees and began groping the sidewalk in search of his lost chomper. Fred followed suit, as did I. We must have looked ridiculous: three men on their hands and knees, hammered as nails on boards.

"Is this it?" Fred lifted an unmistakable white tooth up to the streetlight.

"BEEE-YAAAHH!!!" The toothless drunk danced around, waving his arms like a fucking madman. He took the tooth from Fred and tossed it into his front pocket. "You're the fucking man!!"

He doubled over, out of breath from his antics. He

stood suddenly, and rested a hand on each of us. "Where you guys coming from? You want to party?"

It was late and I was about to decline, but my reluctance was lesser than Fred's enthusiasm.

"Fuck. Yeah."

We proceeded to follow the guy around the corner behind the liquor store near the downtown center. He conjured up a small baggy from his pocket. The white powder and his ear-to-ear grin glowed as the shadows semi-hid us. He pulled out a house key, dipped the tip into the baggy, and took a snort.

"Oh, wah, ah-OOOOH!" This fiend clearly gave very few fucks about drawing attention to us. Or maybe the drugs were just that good. The fiend offered Fred Briggs, and, to my surprise, Fred accepted.

"What's your name, man?" Fred Briggs asked as he took the key and dipped it. He snorted it quickly, and whispered something under his breath before our new friend answered.

"Kristoff. Greg's my first name, but everyone calls me Kristoff."

"Pleasure to meet you, Kristoff. I'm Leo." I declined

the powder. Wasn't really my thing.

Turned out that Kristoff lived in the same general direction as us so we gained a stumble buddy on our journey back home. Fred and Kristoff took a couple more bumps as we entered a residential neighborhood and left the bar area. We laughed, pushed each other into empty street, pissed on street signs. We were having some good fun. And, as it often happens when three young men mix with alcohol and drugs, our mischief escalated.

Kristoff ran forward about 50 feet to release some of his pent-up chemical energy, while Fred and I trailed behind, guffawing at this crazy fuck. Kristoff, suddenly turned back toward us, yelled an incomprehensible outcry, and gave a handy roundhouse kick to the nearest parked car, knocking the side view mirror clean off. Fred and I stopped laughing and looked at each other. We looked into each other's dilated pupils for a second. We could run. Kristoff would make it home fine on his own, and this wasn't the most inconspicuous crime. We both burst into a renewed fit of laughter, doubling over. We couldn't run. Fred did have the presence of mind to tie his shoes tighter. "Just in case we have to leave in a hurry," he smiled.

It didn't end there. Kristoff proceeded to kick off every

single side view mirror on our side of the street. Some dangled, hanging on with exposed wires. Others flew off, sailing into the night, and into the night sky. In my inebriation, I somehow thought it a good idea to keep one mirror. I stuck it underneath my jacket.

Kristoff stopped at a house on a corner, some 18 roundhouse kicks later. "You guys want a beer?" Fuck it. We had come this far.

Kristoff was one of the most hospitable people I had met. His house was clean, but he still apologized for the mess as he obsessively stacked some magazines neat on his table. He cracked two long necks, and gave them to us. I rolled a spliff as Fred took another bump from Kristoff's now dwindling bag. Blasted ACDC out of his shitty speakers, and we all sang and drank.

As they finished the off the blow, I realized I still had the side view mirror that Kristoff had dislocated with his foot. I retreated to Kristoff's kitchen. After looking around for a place to stash it, my drunken mind found the freezer. It was mostly empty aside from some frozen pizzas. I left the broken mirror next to the pizzas, and smiled to myself as I thought what our host would think when discovering this in the morning. I returned to the living room. The three of us smoked the spliff, polished off our beers.

"I'm fucking beat." My eyes drooped.

"Let's get outta here, gypsy," Fred slurred. The three of us stood simultaneously. Kristoff grabbed each of our hands with each of his, and bowed his head in mock-prayer. He only held it for a few moments before bursting out in guffaws.

"Later on, you crazy pieces of poo!" We walked out the door and began the short walk home.

We had not made it a block, before a cop car pulled around the corner ahead of us.

My heart sped up a bit when the Santa Labre black and white pulled into view. Adrenaline shot through my veins and I felt a strange sense of excitement, a tinge of thrill. The car cruised down the street in our direction.

I could feel the air tighten around Fred Briggs and me. "Fuck, I'm high as David Bowie on a space shuttle. I gotta run," He murmured.

"What? No, be cool. He's just driving by. He doesn't know we did anything." I was wrong. As soon as the headlights reached and illuminated our forms, the engine roared and the car lunged forward. It pulled over to our side of the road. I could see two cops in the front seats, glaring with furrowed eyebrows at us.

"YOU! Put your hands behind your head and get on your knees!"

"NOOOPE!" Fred Briggs turned and was off. Good thing he tied his shoes tight. There was a split second where I could have decided to run and follow Fred. I could have kept up and had done that before. I could have easily done it. Jumped over a few fences and off into the woods surrounding the residential neighborhood. No chance they could have caught me. But I didn't run. Did I stay because I thought myself innocent? Did I stay to give fugitive Fred a chance to get away, sacrificing myself? Why the fuck would I do that? Or were my thoughts just slowed by the drugs and alcohol? I cannot claim that I made a logical decision based on a pragmatic cost-and-benefit analysis; this was solely a gut instinct. My gut said stay, and I did.

I stood straight, arms hung loosely by my side. The passenger door of the Crown Vic flew open, and a cop was upon me. He grabbed my wrist, wrenched my arm behind my back, and trip-threw me on the pavement. The impact knocked the wind out of me. My cheek rested on the cold concrete as he wrapped two, cold, hardened-steel *stumble.*

loops around my wrists. A few clicks and a snap. The cop pulled me up and sat me on the curb. Cuffed and blinded by bright halogen headlights. Fuck.

I lifted my head to adjust my eyes. As my pupils contracted, the world outside of the blinding white became increasingly clearer. The driver of the car was now standing, half in the car, half out. He held a radio to his mouth as his eyes remained glued to me. Another black and white turned the corner, slowed down to glare at me, then sped off in the direction that Fred Briggs had gone. No fucking chance that they were going to catch him. They were damn fools for wasting the gas. The cop that cuffed me approached.

"What're you doing out here, son?" Why did cops insist on talking down to people? I am not your son. You are not my father. I didn't even run from you. You drove up to me, slammed me on the pavement, and cuffed me before I said a single word.

"Just walking home, officer." My eyes were glued on the cop with the radio. No reason really, he was just looking at me so I looked back. I was slimy with feigned respect for these men. At this point, I knew that was my only shot at getting out of this.

"That all?"

127

I raised my eyes to the cop that was addressing me and nodded.

"You been drinking tonight?"

"A little bit."

"How much is 'a little bit?'"

"Just a couple beers." And three more. And six whiskeys. And a spliff.

"Where are you coming from, son?" Go fuck yourself. Stop calling me that.

"From downtown. I left my car down there because I was drinking." I lied to gain a few extra points. I think it helped.

"Why'd your friend run?"

"No idea, he wasn't my friend."

The cop raised his eyebrows and looked down at me. "Do you have ID?"

"Yeah, in my back right pocket. Can't really get it though."

"Just lean to your left." As I leaned, he tipped me just enough to slide my wallet out of my back pocket. He pulled out my driver's license and set the wallet on the hood of his car. He passed the card to his partner.

"Where are you headed tonight?"

"Going home."

"Where from?"

"From downtown. That guy and I were walking in the same direction so we ended up walking together."

"Is that right? What's his name?" The cop was a statue of suspicion staring down at a lump of a human on the curb.

"Manny, I think." My body may have been slumped but my mind was racing 1000 miles per hour. A flash of my countless nights sitting at a poker table came to me. Focus, I reminded myself.

The cop pulled out a notepad and flipped it open. "Is that short for Manuel? What's his last name?"

"No idea, sorry. I didn't know him."

The cop put away his notebook without writing anything down. Just then, I heard over the cop's radio sound. "Perp got away. Will continue search. Over."

Inside, my mind was shouting and celebrating for Fred

Briggs' escape. Outside, poker.

The two cops talked for a few minutes, and another cop car pulled over. A woman officer, clad with a bullet-proof vest, exited, and walked over to her fellow officers. She stood straight, rested her thumbs in the armholes of the vest, legs slightly wider than shoulder distance apart. A stern look spread across her face. I stared at her strange body posture, poised like a cobra preparing for a strike. I snapped out of my thoughts as the other male officer approached me.

"So what were you doing?"

"I was just walking ho..."

"He already told me that, don't be smart." He threw a thumb over at this partner who was leaning against the car. Were these guys serious? Were they trying to get me to say something in anger? That's what they were going to try and pull? I was insulted by their god damn routine. I remained respectful. Poker.

He continued his interrogation, and took a step toward me. "You know what I'm talking about."

I was so deep in my act that I had forgotten about the side view mirrors that the Kicking Kristoff had removed. I was just focusing on appearing sober. I looked at him with an authentically quizzical look, remembering what he was talking about while maintaining the look. He took another step toward me.

He not-so-secretly rested his hand on his holstered gun clipped to his Batman belt. "Don't play stupid with me. We have witnesses that described a man who was walking down the street and knocking side view mirrors off of cars on Chorro. The description fits you. What do you have to say?"

I saw a glimmer of hope. I was cuffed, surrounded by cops, with other cops chasing my friend through the city, and I was drunk and high. This is when you must ready yourself for an opportunity. The cop lied. I was not knocking off side view mirrors. I was at least 200 feet from Kristoff as he was doing it, and his lanky form looked nothing like me. The cop lied to force a confession. I grabbed this advantage, however slight, and chambered it as ammunition for myself. I remained stone faced.

"A description? I don't think, sir." I oozed sincerity, "That wasn't me. How far up on Chorro?"

"A couple blocks away," he growled.

"No, sorry, sir. It definitely wasn't that guy I was walking with either. I was walking with him since pretty much downtown."

"So you're telling me you don't know anything about the side view mirrors on Chorro? You didn't see anything?"

I shrugged and looked up at him innocently.

The cop scoffed and looked back at the other two cops. The woman remained in her power-stance, and the other cop's only reaction was a slight eyebrow twitch. Might as well been a shoulder shrug. I was starting to see daylight.

The interrogator turned back to me. He took the final two steps to me, and knelt so he was face-to-face. I'm sure he wished it was daytime. If it was daytime, he could have over-dramatically taken off his sunglasses to look me straight in the face, like in a movie. Still, I wondered if he could smell the spliff I had smoked only minutes earlier.

However, he lowered his growl to a low whisper, and, for the first time, a chill went down my back. "Do you think I believe you for a second?" Suddenly, I was aware of my vulnerability. No one was around. My hands were cuffed. I had no defense.

The chill shook me from my focus for a second, and my next words were instinctual. "I...I don't know what to say. It wasn't me." My slight stutter came off as genuine fear, and actually may have helped me. I saw a twitch on the officer's face, and he stood up and took a step back, as if realizing how his intimidation was working. A momentary glint of his humanity brought my focus back.

The Bad Cop strolled over to his fellow cops and they talked. Once in a while, they would glance over to me then continue in hushed tones. My focus wavered once again, and I felt my vision blur for a second. Tightness on the cuffs brought me back to reality. I just have to hold on to my sobriety. That's it.

Finally, the original cop strolled over to me. "Stand up, son."

I flopped on my side, and tried to stand. It was hard to stand while handcuffed when you're sitting on slow curb. He put his hand under my shoulder and lifted me up. He faced me toward the other cops, and moved behind me as he unlocked the cuffs. The other two cops scowled as they got back in their respective cars.

"You're free to go." He handed me my wallet and ID. "Watch yourself walking around at this time of night."

"Thanks, officer." I turned, and deliberately walked at a normal pace. My heart was racing, and I wanted to scream as loud as I could. Donnie greeted me at the door when I eventually made it home. He sat at my feet as if to comfort me as I sat in the darkened living room. I lit the cigarette I had rolled earlier and lay back on the couch, still feeling the indentations on my wrists from the cuffs. Exhaled a smoky sigh of utter relief.

Hearing the front door and smelling the tobacco, Fred came out of his bedroom, rubbing his eyes. Apparently, he thought it was wise to pretend he was fast asleep. He had taken off his pants and put on a loose tank top, just in case I brought cops with me. Not a bad move on his part, although he still had his shoes on, muddy from running through puddles and yards to safety. I smiled, and Fred saw it through the dark. He stood there for a second in his boxers, staring at me. We both burst into laughter.

I had his back, apparently. I didn't plan on putting myself in that position that night but somehow I couldn't betray him like that. So, trust grew between us.

life of a raindrop.

I wrote.

We gather en masse
far above the Earth surface
seeking protection.
Gravity pulls us
one by one.
We all fall
my brothers, sisters
streak through the sky to their end.
Cannot resist, no.
Scared, I wait. My time will come.
Last to go.
I live long enough to see them all die.
My scream leaves a trail through the sky.
The ground approaches,
I shed tears.

Like me, they fall down.
Splat.

miyamoto.

And again, I wrote.

Flames lick steel edges
I hold breath
Cold blade turns orange glow
Folding for strength.
Fold. Fold a thousand times
I force eyes to blink.
Concentration stands over body functions.
Precise focus
Precise craft
No worry of life, of bills, of sickness
This moment, this craft stands alone
Blocking all else from mine's eye.
Someday, we will defend against foe
and friend turned foe.
Someday, we will strike fear in all

and turn foe to friend.
Someday, we still stand, then fall.
We must fall.

build.

Morning came a bit earlier. Donnie put his heavy paws on my chest, lowered his square head, and lolled his tongue out, dripping gobs of drool on my forehead.

"Goddamn it..." I scratched him behind his ears then bulled his head toward my chest in a Muay Thai clinch, so his drool stopped water falling on my fucking face. "Alright, buddy. Let's go pee."

I dragged through the living room with Donnie jumping excitedly ahead. Fred Briggs was sprawled on the couch, long neck bottle of 805 still in his hand. I plucked it from his fingers and placed it on the table. Donnie licked his now empty fingers, and Fred Briggs groaned and slumped to a more comfortable nook of the couch. No sign of Kat.

I gripped the brass doorknob leading to the backyard,

turned it, and pushed. Donnie rushed outside, and the brisk morning air rushed passed me. The cold greeted the two of us like a quick rap on the ball sack.

Shit. Should have thrown on a jacket. I crossed my arms to hold my heat in. I watched Donnie sniff around for a suitable spot, and after careful deliberation, began relieving himself. He had such a look of satisfaction on his face, I decided to join him. I found my own spot that suited my needs. After careful deliberation, I chose a spot in the corner of the yard to relieve myself.

"Good morning!" A voice rang out from the other side of the fence, startling me. It cut my stream short. "Is that you, Freddy?"

I tiptoed to see over fence. "No, this is actually Leo. I am staying with Fred for a while."

"Oh, I'm sorry about that!" A wrinkled hand with turquoise fingernails reached over the fence. I clasped the hand but could only see the brown-red curly mane of a woman. "Pleasant to meet you, Leo. I'm Dorothy."

As I unclasped her hand, I didn't know how to tell her that just seconds before I shook her hand, my hand was helping aim at a spot on the wall. So I didn't. Some things are better left unsaid.

build.

"Nice to meet you too, Dorothy."

"So how long have you been staying with Freddy?"

"Only a few weeks."

"Such a good boy, that Freddy."

"Yeah, he's a good dude."

"So what are you doing up so early, Leo?"

"I am just taking Donnie out. And you?"

"Oh, I was just taking a look at this dreadful fence here." She rapped on the fence with her knuckles. "It has been years since someone's tended to it."

Since I couldn't see her face, my attention had drifted to the rough wooden planks, and had already noticed their worn and broken shape as she mentioned it.

"I will have to get an estimator out here to see how much it will be to fix this damn thing."

"You know, I can probably take care of this fence for you." I ran my fingers against the boards. I wasn't the most experienced craftsman, but I had enough comfort with tools that I could mend a simple fence without much fuss. "I'll ask Fred if he has tools that I can borrow."

141

"Oh, that would be lovely, Leo!" I saw two turquoise-clawed hands rise above the fence and shake, jazz hand-like. "Of course, I would pay you for your work. I'll even make you a fine meal."

"Thanks, Dorothy, but a free meal is fine with me."

I heard the backdoor to Fred's house creak open, and out walked Fred Briggs, awoken from his hung-over slumber. Wrapped in a blanked, bare feet gripped the deck as he swayed slightly with the heavy of last night. He looked like a burn victim, all bundled up like that.

He spoke up from the desk. "Hello, Dorothy, good morning."

"Oh! Hello, Freddy! I was just talking to your friend, Leo, here. He volunteered to help mend this pesky fence, if you will let him borrow your tools."

"How nice of Leo," Fred looked at me and rolled his eyes, but smiled. "You know, I've been meaning to work on that fence. I'll help too."

"How lucky I am to have two young men to help me! What would you like for supper? Do you like Swedish meatballs? I'll make Swedish meatballs."

"Thank you, Dorothy, that sounds great." I waved to

the poof of hair over the fence before moving over to Fred Briggs and Donnie, who was now sitting next to Fred's feet, looking up at the hung over mess.

"So," Fred crouched down and scratched Donnie behind his ear. "What do you know about fences, Leo?"

* * * * *

The sun angled higher as we prepped for the task at hand.

Tools

Fred has a couple hand drills, a wired one and a battery-powered one. He had a nail gun. He had a skill saw. He had a few hammers of varying sizes. He had one sledge hammer, too. Seemed like all we needed.

Design

While Fred Briggs took inventory of the tools we had available, I sketched out a rough plan of the fence with dimensions. I was no fence designer. But I had a decent eye for spacial design and support structures. Anyway, we showed the design to Dorothy.

"Well, boys, I love it. One suggestion, though. How much extra will it cost me to put a gate in that fence?"

"Well, ma'am," Fred chimed in. "That will cost you handsomely. One dozen more Swedish meatballs. Each." Fred laughed.

"Six." Dorothy mock-countered the offer, and Fred burst into a new fit of hilarity.

"Eight!" I said, slamming the table with my fist and a grin.

"Deal!" She stuck out a hand and I clasped it in concord. I was shocked at the strength of this seventy-something woman. Her turquoise-nailed fingers vise-like around my hand, and she cranked down with the strength of an Alaskan lumberman.

"Deal." For some reason, I choked up a little right then, clasping that little big woman's hand.

Materials

We made a list.

We borrowed Dorothy's truck.

We made two trips to bring the wood back to her house.

That's pretty much it.

* * * * *

build.

"Alright, Leo." Fred and I examined our supplies and tools strewn on the grass in Dorothy's backyard. Oh yeah, and a six pack of DBA's. "Alright, man. Let's do this right."

There's something to be said about physical labor. The grinding, the frustration, the physical exertion. It was something we miss out in today's world. And that satisfaction of completing a job, of seeing the fruits of your labor at the end of the day. The finality of seeing a project through. Seeing your vision manifest itself in a physical representation.

We started. We used the existing ground posts as our base, just replacing the fence planks. Measure, cut. Measure, cut. Splinters. Blood. Sweat.

At some point, Dorothy came out with a bucket full of ice for our beer. Neither Fred Briggs nor I knew until we took a break, but goddamn did those ice cold brews quench our Sahara throats. We replenished the fluid that we were losing with that amber-brown, carbonation. It occurred to me that we were sweating out the booze, and that I still felt focused. Looked Fred up and down. He seemed to be fully functional, sharp even, as we continued replacing the fencing. Splinters. Blood. Sweat. Gulps of beer.

"So," Fred Briggs took a seat on the ground, pulled a glove off with his teeth, wiped his brow with the exposed hand. "You and Kat have a thing, or what?"

"What?" He caught me off guard.

"Seems like you have a thing. You fucked her or what?"

I took my glove off and stuffed it in his face as I took a seat next to him. He flipped me off as I responded. "No, man. She's cool and all, but I don't know. She's not into it. "

"Yeah? You sure?"

"Yeah man, I'm pretty sure."

"What, she turn you down or something?"

"What the fuck does it matter to you, man? It's her business and it's my business." Clink. Shield up.

"Easy, Leo. Just wondering. Seems like you two get along, that's all."

I felt a tinge of guilt in my gut for snapping at Fred. It was just my reflex, didn't mean to take anything out on him. I'm not even sure why it hit a spot, but it did. I wanted to apologize but didn't. Luckily, he didn't think about it as much as I did.

build.

"Yo, gypsy. You taking a break, or what? Hand me that hammer or get moving."

Hours went by as minutes as the wave of our concentration pushed us forward in time. After the short mention of Kat, our talk was only productive. Only fence-related. No chit-chat. Dorothy even offered sandwiches, but we denied. She did replenish our bucket with more beers and more ice. That was appreciated.

Before we knew it, the sun that had been angling up had started its descent down on opposite side. We noticed that the air was cooling as we secured the final plank.

"Shit." Fred Briggs slumped down on the lawn, looking at the fence. I had just realized how sore I was, and I flopped down next to him. "We forgot about the paint." Fred said with genuine disappointment.

"Fuck." I felt it, too. It was too late in the day to go back to the store and grab paint. We shouldn't have rushed through the shopping.

Dorothy came striding out with hands raised toward the sky. She had changed outfits to a bright, floral dress of orange and red.

"Boys! Oh my goodness! It's magnificent." She walked over to us. She bent down and kissed Fred on the cheek, then repeated the act for me.

"What's wrong?" She asked, noticing our sullen expressions.

"We forgot about the paint."

She chuckled and patted me on the back. "Come on, boys. I have to pay up."

We stood and followed Dorothy into her home.

"Couple of perfectionists, you two are," she poked at us. We walked over to pull out chairs at her kitchen table.

* * * * *

"Hey, hey, hey! Go wash your hands!" She pointed down the hallway of her peach-themed home.

We walked down that hallway, and I went in the restroom first. Flipped the brass faucet on, first cold, then warm. Soaped my hands and scrubbed. Looked in the mirror. Sawdust in my hair. Lips slightly chapped. Forehead a little sunburnt. Dirt on my shirt. But I liked it. Washed my face in the running water, dried it on a towel. Fred followed me after.

When we sat at Dorothy's table, I felt a grumble deep within the pit of me that I had been subconsciously ignoring for hours. I am fucking famished. Lucky for us, Dorothy had prepared to feed a Hun horde after crossing the Asiatic steppes. She lifted the lid of an enormous ceramic Dutch pot, and the air immediately became saturated with the thick, savory aroma of the mushroom cream sauce. The meatballs lounged in the white-brown jacuzzi, staring up Fred Briggs and me. I breathed in, entranced. Dorothy ladled a bed of mashed potatoes and peas on each of our plates.

"Dig in!" She broke our trance and we descended upon the victim.

A blur of creamy sauce and hearty meatballs and wine and mashed potatoes and more wine. We feasted with abandon until our stomachs were full and our plates were clean.

Fred leaned back in his chair, balancing on its back two legs. "Oh, man. That hit the spot."

Dorothy reached out and slapped Fred's knee. "Don't lean back in your chair, Freddy!" She scolded, but smiled. "I'm glad you enjoyed it."

Fred leaned forward and got a little more serious. "Listen, Dorothy. We feel bad about the paint. We owe you a paint job."

"It's fine for now," Dorothy poured our glasses with more wine before polishing off the rest of the bottle in her own. "Someday you can give me a nice coat of white paint, but you have done plenty for today. Besides, the plain wood gives it some character."

We sat together and digested and finished our wine, trading stories. Finally, we stood up to help Dorothy wash the dishes, despite her protests to leave them be. While we dried the dishes, Dorothy packed some leftovers into large plastic containers.

"Here you go, boys," Dorothy handed me the stack of containers. She leaned in, held my face, and kissed me on the cheek before walking over to Fred Briggs and repeating the same act.

"Pleasure doing business with you, Dorothy," I said. She smiled as we walked down her driveway and back to our house.

* * * * *

Fred Briggs flopped on the couch, and Donnie jumped up, pouncing right on Fred's full belly.

"Don't, Don! I'm gonna yack!" But he didn't resist much.

build.

I put the bundle Dorothy gave us on the table, untied the cloth, revealing the contents. I laid each of the containers on the table. I noticed the weight of one container was a little off, especially since it was supposed to contain food. I opened it.

"Hey, Fred."

"Yo." He called from the other room.

"Take a look at this."

"Ugh, what?" He walked over to the kitchen with Donnie on his heels.

I tipped the container, spilling its contents.

Five thick rolls of twenty-dollar bills rolled out, each at least 50 strong.

* * * * *

Sore. Splinters embedded deep in palm. Satisfied. Satisfied by more than just the staggering meal and the monetary reward. Even though we did not finish the project, it felt good to work toward an end. It wasn't the reward. Yes, we initially agreed to take on the task as a favor to Dorothy. But what I felt now was not the gratification of helping a friend in need. No.

Physical toiling. Working with hands and thinking only in the moment to accomplish a set goal. Hard work. Real hard work. It was something I sometimes missed.

I walked over to the little desk below a window that faced outside my room. Although night had now fallen, I could see the fence we built, standing proud in the darkness. My notebook laid on my desk. I looked at it and thought back about what I learned today.

That day, I reached for my little ink bottle and the paint brush in my leather pen case.

Opened to a new page.

Ran my fingers across the crisp white expanse.

Tipped the brush in the ink.

Soaked in the black.

Closed my eyes as excess black dripped back into the bottle.

Thought about my hard work today.

Felt the blisters forming on my hand.

Felt the shirt that lay damp with sweat on my back earlier in the day but was now draped over my shoulders, dry.

build.

Thought of Grandpa. His enso.

Thought about what he would think of my present situation here in Santa Labre.

Intake. A deep, steady breath.

Envisioned a perfect circle.

Tip to white paper.

I was more ready now than I had ever been.

Fuck.

appreciate.

Days. Weeks. I would race the Sun to work every day. He motivated me to get going when I felt I couldn't go on. It became a game. I almost always beat him but he would eventually wake up and spread his warmth upon me. I often amused myself, thinking, "I know I might not rise for work if the sun did not rise. Would the sun laze in bed if I chose to do the same? Who was driving whom?" What an idiot I am.

I had fallen into a comfortable routine. Taking the gig at the docks as a fisherman's apprentice, I learned to clean ling cod, salmon, halibut. Sliced their bellies open, pulling their guts out. Throwing the corpses on ice. The guys would even bring back loads of crabs, writhing and clawing in the bins.

Even though it wasn't the most pleasant job it allowed me to zone in and focus on a simple task. Some called it a zen state. They can call it what the fuck they want. All I know is that I would concentrate on my hands making cuts through that silvery skin, over and over again.

The fishing boat, dubbed *Rascal*, would come in, and I would help unload their catch, throwing the fish into wooden crates. While docked, I would joke with the grizzled fishermen, and we would share cigarettes and stories. They lived a simple, yet demanding life. The amount of fish they caught didn't affect me too much in my pocket since they paid me by the hour. These hardened men, on the other hand, lived on a gambling edge, hoping their nets would bring in enough flopping fellows to feed their families for the next week. They didn't talk politics or religion. In fact, they spoke reverently only about the ocean. They were aware of the mercy and generosity of the sea, and their livelihood could end with a simple change of current or weather. Yet, they seemed happy. In fact, these were some of the generous, heartiest human beings I had even been exposed to. They were content with what was in hand because empty-handedness could be around the corner.

After a few weeks, the sea dogs finally took me with them on their vessel. My boss, Rodger, called me over.

"Mas, grab your jacket and a rod, you Japanese pussy."

His vulgarity invariably came with a warm, affectionate tone. I tried to conceal the surge of excitement upheaving in my stomach.

"Sure thing, Father Time. I'll hurry so we can get you back to the retirement home."

Rodger smiling wryly and clearly tickled that I had picked up their humor, shot back, "Just hurry up, rook."

Cast off, we headed north on *Rascal*. Everyone on the boat was older than me, and the closest was an early-30s man named Tom Carter, Jr. He was not quite as the other men, bristles only beginning on his sun beaten face. He came over, and slapped me on the shoulder. If a stranger had came up and hit me that hard, I might have turned around with clenched fists. Instead, I turned around to see a welcoming grin sprawled across a friendly face.

"The fish know when we are sober," Carter shoved a Bud Light in my hand. "We don't stand a chance if me and you are sober."

"Well, I'm not going to be a jinx on my first trip out." We snapped our cans open, tipped them back, and took a long gulp. I liked these guys.

"Where we headed?" I asked Carter.

"San Francisco, my friend." He glowed. He raised his can, and headed back to his duties. I took a quick gulp from my can before fitting a piece of anchovy on end of my rod. I cast out, set my rod down, and watched the weight, hook, and bait sail into the fog behind *Rascal*. I turned to join the veterans prepare bait, throw out crab cages, and store the catch that they were already pulling in. At one point, Carter filleted a salmon and handed me a thin slice of that sweet, raw fish. It almost melted in my mouth. This was not a bad place to be.

Unfortunately, my happy, beer-induced demeanor did not attract any fish to my personal hook. Three and a half hours bobbing up and down on the boat brought no suitors. I did not claim to understand why we took this trip up to the Bay, something about delivering fish, and hitting some new areas. Didn't matter too much to me. I liked being a part of the crew, I liked adventuring on the sea, and I liked catching fish. Well, I didn't do much catching.

Our stop in this Bay Area port had been fruitful. I heard the guys on the other side of boat talking and laughing; they were happy with their catch so far. I looked down at a bucket near me. A dozen large rock crabs were struggling over each other. Each panicked crab looked out for himself, pulling down the crab on top of him, only to get pulled down by the crab below him. Writhing, clawing in a seemingly everlasting fight.

I stared at the crustacean struggle for a long moment before turning my gaze to the shore. A man in dark, ragged clothes sat hunched on a bench next to the shoreline, the city skyscrapers rising up menacingly behind him. I watched the man, as the buildings seemed to rise up and stomp on him. I felt as though these structures were poised, waiting for him to stand up, only to be kicked back down to the dirt.

The man placed his hand on his knee, supporting himself as he slowly stood at the foot of giants, among the hustle and bustle on the street. His back was arched with the weight of years. Reaching behind him, he brandished what looked like some kind of stringed instrument. Fingers on the left made a pattern, fingers on the right plucked. I could hear the guitar weeping sweet notes. As his baby cried, he seemed to cradle her and comfort her.

From afar, I watched the scene unfold. The rush of the crowd began to slow. People turned their heads if only for a moment to witness the owner of the pained notes. Encouraged by his caring grasp, his baby began to cheer up. Mournful blues licks grew into a raucous, but melodic *appreciate.*

din. Faster and faster, the man began to move his body, stomping his feet. A suit-clad passerby released a yell that felt like it had been canned, masked for decades. The new-born man began dancing and stomping to the jovial rhythm. A woman, dressed in a navy blue suit, joined him, and they danced next to the musician, surrounded by the crowd of dark suits and red ties.

Moments passed in free joviality. Another suited man rushing out of a nearby building caught my eye. Pushing his way through the crowd, he appeared to confront the musician. The man wrestled the crooning baby from the musician's hands. Raising the guitar above his head, the man struck it on the sidewalk once, twice. Suited Man directed some inaudible command toward the musician, as he pointed down the street with an outstretched arm. I saw him towering over the homeless man, pointing away down the street.

The crowd dispersed. The once merry dancing couple dusted themselves off, embarrassed at their rash behavior, and walked quickly away in different directions. The man stood with his head down, staring at his mangled instrument in his hands. He turned and slowly plodded down the street. The buildings still stood tall, and the hustle and bustle of people near the shoreline returned as if the scene never happened. A single tear escaped the corner of my eye, and landed in the still-struggling bucket of crabs.

* * * * *

Rascal was going to be docked in the bay for the day so I decided to go ashore to explore the city. I mostly stuck around the Fisherman's Wharf area. It was crowded with tourists, even for a Wednesday. I strolled through the streets, weaving between skyscrapers fitted into the grids of the city. I finally came across a bar with no name on the outside but with large windows facing street side. I opened the door and went in.

An old chandelier hung from the ceiling of the bar, casting dim light on the wooden booths, wooden tables, wooden bar stools, wooden bar. I ordered a pale ale and took a seat at the bar adjacent to the window facing the street.

A group of people was gathered around the entrance to a building across the street. I heard faint chanting, and some of the people were holding signs and pointing up, scolding the building itself. I couldn't really tell the cause of their agitation but it was enough movement to keep my attention in their direction. A man with a beard and a tweed jacket broke off from the pack of dissent, and walked across the street directly toward the bar where I was sitting. He walked purposefully but stared at the ground as he walked. He was not carrying a sign. Before he reached the entrance to the bar, I turned away and looked deep into my ale, feigning concentration in my drink. He took the seat two over from me at the bar.

"Boilermaker." His drink order was one of a tired man, inside and out. Charles Bukowski's drink of choice.

"Cheers." He lifted his glass and tilted it slightly in my direction. I was slightly taken as I thought I was being sly in my eaves-looking.

"Cheers." I lifted my bottle before tossing a swig back. Now that my charade was up, I might as well engage with this stranger. "What's all the hubbub over there?" I tossed a thumb over my right shoulder toward the crowd.

Without smiling, he stared at his half-empty glass. "We are protesting the mass production of cheap technology using unethical business practices overseas. That building over there houses the headquarters for a company that hires underpaid, untrained and unprotected workers in Vietnam and India."

I braced myself inwardly, preparing for an onslaught of idealistic bullshit. It's not that I didn't care or believe him. I just didn't really want to deal with a heavy conversation. Luckily, I wouldn't have to.

"But I don't really want to talk about it." He sighed and scratched the back of his head, still staring into his glass.

This man was clearly deep in the quicksand of thought but apparently did not want to pull anyone else into his conundrum. Why would a man who is spending his time protesting outside of a building be hesitant to state his position?

"You alright, man?"

He turned to me for the first time. The bags under his eyes looked as if two tiny children were hanging from his bottom eyelids. A beautiful gold watch peaked out from his tweed jacket. He was probably about sixty years old.

"Tell me, young man. Have you ever fought for something you believed in?" he asked but continued without waiting for a pause. "It is exhausting as hell."

I wasn't sure what to say but I was intrigued. "How so?"

"I teach theoretical physics at UC Berkeley. That's easy. It's this stuff that is taxing on an old man like me."

appreciate.

He turned back away from me, fixating on his glass. "My whole life I have fought for causes like this. And you know what I've learned? It doesn't help a damned thing."

"So why do it?" He hadn't said anything profound but even before he mentioned his profession, I could tell that this man exuded an aura of calm intellect that few had access to.

He sighed. "Because I know there's no choice." He must have noticed the sense of puzzled silence in the air. He proceeded to explain.

"Allow me to present a scenario. Imagine that outside of this bar and around the corner, there are two men fighting in the alley, armed with knives. It is unclear who is in the wrong but the resolution to this fight will likely end in bloodshed. It is just past noon right now so there will surely be people passing by this alley. Among these passersby, you will find each will have a distinct human reaction. Ideally, you would want someone to intervene, preferably a police officer. But the police are spread thin with other crimes and likely will not arrive until it is too late. Next, there will be some people, we will call them Group A, who are either too busy or too oblivious to notice the conflict. These people cannot be blamed, for they do not see the problem. Then there will be people, Group

B, who see the conflict but perhaps are elderly or too weak to intervene between two armed men. These folks cannot be blamed either, since their involvement in the issue would likely worsen the situation. There are other strong, intelligent people, Group C, who are able to help, and have the means to intervene with limited inconvenience to them. However, out of fear, they choose to ignore the problem and go about their lives. These people are despicable; this group of people have a responsibility to try and help resolve the issue, even if the solution is not immediately obvious. They are more responsible to help than Group A or B because they recognize the problem and are able to help. Because of this, those in Group C who do not do something, are just as much at fault as those two men fighting. I don't want to have that burden on me. So, I do what I can even if I am certain my efforts are futile. I fear the alternative."

"Can I add to your scenario?" I posed.

A glint of excitement glimmered in this man's eye, and I saw the professor side of him. The side that was excited to teach, to see others learn, to inspire. "By all means, go ahead."

"There is another group. Group X is a group that knows there is a conflict but is unable to distinguish who is at fault. X can be considered a blind man with a gun. He can hear the struggle in the alley happening. He knows someone is going to get hurt, and someone is probably in the wrong. But he can do nothing. He must trust passersby to convey the situation to him and then he must accurately aim his help in the correct direction. How can he? Can he trust the image that he is told? Can he trust his senses? Does he do nothing?"

A weak, knowing smile paired with the professor's sad, bagged eyes. He threw back his drink, and put a caring hand on my shoulder. He covered his eyes with one hand and held the other hand out in front of him, as if he was blind. He peeked out at me from under his hand and gave a hollow laugh. The man left the bar and I saw him join the protest at the foot of the corporate building.

I followed suit and left the bar and slowly meandered back to the boat. As I turned the corner, a man with tattered clothes crossed my path. He was carrying a broken guitar. He gave me a solemn nod as I passed. I stopped for a second, shot my hand in my pocket, and grabbed a few bills and change that I had. I turned around to catch the man who had continued on along the sidewalk. I tapped his shoulder and pushed money into his front pocket. I extended my hand, and he looked up at me, puzzled.

He finally grasped my hand. "Thank you, son," he said without smiling. I nodded, turned back toward the boat.

Back on the sea, homeward bound. I could not get those two men out of my mind. One fought for causes in futility. The other fought for happiness, seemingly in futility. What could I do to help? Probably nothing, but I should still try. Right?

life of Donnie.

From the doldrums of Donnie the Dog.

I remember surviving.

As a pup, I had only my brothers and sisters. We looked out for each other as best we could. Our mom was accompanied by a vagrant human, some man who dwelt days on the streets of Fresno and some nights in the alleys of Bakersfield. Unable to care for our mom plus the four of us, the man left us to fend for ourselves.

Early on, one brother was picked up off the streets, and taken away in a mini van. We never saw him again. We were just puppies, and the world had yet to sully our innocence. The humans that picked up our brother seemed to be a family. Though we didn't completely understand it, we hoped they brought him in as their own. Not all humans were kind though, and it did not take long for us to realize this.

We remaining three roamed. Constantly searching for food and a warm place to sleep. Life was hard, looking back, but it was all we knew. We were happy to have each other. Every morsel of food was a gleam of happiness, and we savored it.

One day, we were digging through the trash behind a shopping center. Fast food restaurants were flanked by a grocery store and they all stood neatly in a rectangle formation. Behind these stores was a buffet feast of discarded hamburgers, meat and potato scraps, and other delicious throw-outs. So we returned. And returned again. It became our home base. Until one day a door opened, revealing a human in a shroud of light. We were blinded as we looked up from our excavation site.

"Hey! You mutts! Git! Git! GIT!" The man charged us, and we froze in terror. He swung back a left boot and hit my brother square in his ribs, sending him sailing into the night sky. He landed like a sack of potatoes next to a sack of potatoes. The assaulter tossed a bag of trash at my sister and me, and the three of us ran down the alley away from the monster.

Our young days, lean. Some called us scoundrels. Other, ruffians. As we grew, we were able to chase off cats and other dogs, earning bigger meals. Man always had the upper hand, though. Once, three men in a white truck ambushed us and grabbed my brother, tossing him in the back of their truck. They turned to grab my sister and me but we were fast, young, and strong. My sister and I grew up quickly. We watched the lights of the truck disappear around a corner. We never saw our brother again.

Smarter, stronger, bolder. Bigger. And with that size came two disadvantages: an increase in appetite and an inability to hide. So we were driven to the outskirts of town.

A train yard became our home. We found a corner where humans rarely passed. Dark, secluded, protected. The seclusion from the humans also meant that food trash was sparse. Forced to roam further, we turned to hunting birds and rats and lizards for food. I always feared starvation, and it drove me forward. My sister, on the other hand, immediately activated deep-rooted canine instincts. She thrived as a hunter. She smiled after landing a kill, and she ran with the speed of a seasoned predator. But we were not alone in the hunt.

Dusk. We had been hunting in a new area, near an open field that led to a forested area. We had not yet ventured that far but we both knew that the field and forest would need to be explored at some point. We heard a yelp, followed by a light bark. My sister's ears perked. Nose lifted off the ground, pulling in air. I did the same. We caught the scent that seemed familiar and foreign at the same time.

We saw our first coyote. He popped his head out from the brush, eyes reflecting in the darkness. He was smaller than us, a little more than half the size of my sister. He kept his distance but did not seem fearful. Curious. We just traded stares for a few brief moments before he yelped playfully and disappeared into the brush. As we returned home, I thought I heard a chorus of howls in the distance, but a train passed, masking all ambient sounds. The howls were almost eerie. Almost laughing. My sister did not seem to notice, so I put them out of my mind.

The next day, we were hunting pigeons near our train yard when we were greeted by two coyotes. They were less shy than the one we saw yesterday, and they cautiously approached us. My sister trotted toward them, her size giving her confidence. I followed. As they got closer, I caught the scent of rotting flesh in their teeth and breath. No doubt, they were killers. But, then again, so were we. I hardly even noticed when my sister's teeth were stained scarlet with a fresh kill. To survive.

The coyotes moved toward us, lowering their heads in respect. They allowed my sister and I to inspect them, and we ceremoniously smelled the base of their tails, and they ours. It appeared we had gained allies in this harsh world.

That evening, we hunted together, chasing night birds and rodents, and prancing through fields, almost joyously. My sister and I watched the coyotes' technique and realized how rudimentary ours were. We soaked in the lesson, especially my sister. The hunter in her drew her closer to the coyotes' strategies and I watched as she practiced the turns and twists and bursts of speed.

Our coyotes departed near sunrise, and I followed my sister back to our corner of the train yard. As the morning sun started to stain the sky, I again heard wild cries and howling from the field. Much closer than previously, and much louder. My sister and I lifted our snouts skyward and let loose our own howls. I noted that there were many more than just two coyote voices, and wondered why the others did not reveal themselves.

The sun beat down on us during the day so we typically didn't start our hunting day until the cooler evening hours. A few hours earlier than normal, we heard a single yelp. My sister perked up, tail wagging. It appeared our new friends wanted to show us some new hunting tricks. I was too tired from the previous night, and the heat made me lazy. I stayed behind as my sister trotted out into the blistering sun to hunt with our new partners in crime.

Not an hour went by when I heard the band of coyotes' yelps, more energetic than ever. I got up and trotted outside. The sun was starting to reach the horizon, and the air was beginning to cool. The dirt was still hot. I heard the coyotes, this time slightly further away, but the yelps were followed by a singular, deep howl that made my blood curdle. My sister had cried out in distress, somewhere in the direction of the forest, and I sprinted in that direction. Low to the ground, I didn't even feel my muscles undulating under my thickened skin, and the pads of my feet pushing me ever forward through the tall grass. My focus, resolute.

I burst through the yellowed brush to come upon a horrifying scene. In a circle, snarling and yelping and snapping like possessed demons were fifteen coyotes. They glared at me, opening their circle as I approached. Clenched and displaying my teeth, and I advanced. At the center of the circle was my sister. Blood matted her fur, and she was missing an ear. The scarlet life fluid

172

cascaded down the side of her head, dripping off her jaw as she glared in fighting stance, trying to ward off the traitors. They had taught us how to hunt but they didn't tell us that they preferred one big meal to a handful of small ones. I broke through their circle, intimidating them with my size. They stayed just out of reach of my powerful jaws. Retreating slightly, I saw them lurking just within the trees. They were blocking our retreat, forcing us into the open field, where we would be vulnerable. As I reached my sister, I saw her back leg was broken and bloody. I licked at it, trying to offer comfort. She whined in agony, and that riled the coyotes to a new height of aggression. They closed a tighter circle around us. The setting sun reflected in the blacks of their eyes as they drooled over their forthcoming kill.

Two coyotes charged me from the left. I turned my attention to them, and I lunged, trying to grab at their flesh in my sharpened teeth. They dodged, I lunged again. Another two coyotes sneaked behind me and snapped at my hindquarters, drawing blood. I turned to face them. A larger coyote stepped forward to challenge me, underestimating my speed. I clamped my jaws around his throat. I felt my teeth pierce through his wry fur and desert skin, and I tasted the warm blood ooze, then spurt from an artery. Some blood dripped to the dirt, and some spilled down my throat. I released as I felt my enemy's pulse slow. I turned to the others, teeth baring. I turned back to my sister to see her locking teeth with a smaller coyote. She turned as quickly as she was able to face another attacker, using her size to bull away other coyotes. But she was marred by her injuries. That's when the coyotes closed the empty space between her and me. They stood glaring in my direction, and my sister turned as she too noticed the gap pinch. Amidst the fighting, I saw a look in my sister's eye. Fear, sorrow.

From behind, a coyote jumped on her back. She tossed it in the air, but it was replaced by two more. She bellowed in terror and my heart broke as I watched five coyotes descend on her weakened body and sink their teeth into her flesh. I watched my sister get torn apart.

I tried to move in toward her but a wall of jaws, teeth, and ferocious eyes blocked me. Her gurgled howl was silenced sharply as a coyote pinched her throat closed with one last killing bite.

Agony. Distraught. I launched myself on the band of coyotes. My frenzied attack shocked the coyotes. I sunk my teeth into anything I could grab. My jaws broke bones, and tore fur skin. I hardly felt the sharp teeth tearing at my own, but they did not relent. Blood from dog and coyote alike stained the ground red in that dusk. As unconsciousness started to envelope me, I heard a single thunderous crack, and for a moment, everything was still. A coyote fell, dead. I remember the band fleeing, scattering in the forest. A part of me smiled as I saw most of them limping after their encounter with my vicious attack. I slipped into blackness as a human descended on me. I was terrified but unable to move. Blackness.

That man who saved me nursed me back to health, fed me, over the following weeks. Eventually, I was given to his nephew, Fred Briggs. I owe my life to that man and his family, and I will die to repay them.

Marco Scindo.

Fog retreated from Port San Luis as we entered. I was weary from the journey, ready for a beer and a bed. Unloaded the boat. Waved to my scally-wagic co-workers. Jumped in the car. Home. Shower.

I was rolling a cigarette when a pair of Converse All Stars tramped into Fred Briggs' house. I licked the paper, sealing the tobacco in the crisp, pale paper. I lifted my gaze and greeted Kat as she entered the room.

"Where you been?" She continued without waiting for the response. "Wanna head south tonight?"

I paused for a second. My tired legs felt weak. Eyes took an extra long blink, lids struggling to stay open. Then, the thought that drove so many of my decisions entered my brain: "Fuck it." I stuck the rolled cigarette behind my ear as I stood.

I followed Kat outside, where her car was still running on the street. I slumped in the passenger seat, and we rumbled down the street. Kat reached over me to her glove compartment and grabbed two bottles of hard cider. She threw one in my lap, coming dangerously close to my jewels. We twisted the tops off, clinked necks together. Kat was smiling, feeling accomplished at finding an accomplice. I took a pull from the fizzy alcohol drink. Looked down. I forgot my shoes.

"So, do we have a destination?"

"Santa Barbara."

"Ah. What's happening there?"

The car slowed to a stop before I got an answer. Kat jumped out and threw the keys at me in one fluid moment.

"God damn it..." I muttered. The keys hit me right in the face.

"You drive!" Kat called back as she bounded up the steps of a broken porch attached to a broken house sitting in a broken neighborhood. I slid over to the driver's seat. Was a fucking garden gnome driving this thing? I thought as bumped my knees against the steering wheel. I adjusted the seat and mirrors.

Looking to my right out the passenger window, I saw a rail-thin man wearing a purple spotted shirt, smiling and waving violently at me from just outside of the car. Kat emerged from behind him, and sheepishly climbed in the back seat.

"Marco, Kat's old man." Marco climbed in the car as he talked.

"Leo, nice to meet you." I realized I had not known a single thing about Kat's dad. I knew Kat had lived a colored past but her parents were never part of the conversation.

Marco was high. Not sure exactly what chemicals were running his brain but it was clear that his red blood cells carried some extra stimulants as they circulated through his body. Smelled a little funky. Not body odor. Or at least not just body odor. More of a burnt chemical smell, probably the clinging remains of crack smoke or crystal meth or something like that. Didn't make a huge difference. The point is, that man talked. And talked. I pulled onto the road, and south we headed.

That wonderful chemical cocktail fueled Marco to bombard me with an onslaught of conversation. Weather. Some reality TV shows. The Lakers. The price of gas. Astute and aggressive judgments of fellow highway-goers.

I slipped in a chuckle or a few words of agreement but it seemed Marco's lively discourse could be stopped by nothing. I didn't particularly enjoy small talk, but it was tolerable especially when that chatter came from such an extravagant, fiery, purple-shirted character. However, the tide of small talk slowly left the car, revealing some sincere moments featuring my main man, Marco.

He talked about Kat.

"I had...problems when Kat was young." Drugs? I thought.

"I was a fuck-up. No way I could take care of her. There were times when I felt so bad that I had to find...distractions to get myself through it." Drugs.

"I had some run-ins with the law," and in the same breath he screamed and punched the roof of the car three times, "FUCK THE COPS!"

"Ugh," he rubbed his knuckles after hitting the dome light. "Anyway, I was sentenced to 24 months in county on some bullshit possession charge. So, I had to give her up. There was no other way."

I glanced in the review mirror to the back seat. Kat's head was slumped down in the most uncomfortable position, sleeping. Did Kat know this conversation would happen? Did she want it? We passed by the beautiful coastline, seagulls calling out to us as we cruised down the 101 South.

"I love her. She takes care of me!" Marco cackled at this, slapping his door with fingers curled in a loose fist.

"Can I ask you something?" I finally got a full sentence in.

"Shoot for it, young man."

"What's the craziest night that you've had?"

"Well, this one time I needed my ix. The only guy around with stuff was this crazy vato down in Santa Maria. It was probably 3 in the morning, and I was fuuuuhhcked UP on vodka and blow. My girlfriend at the time was faded as fucking fog on a fireman's beer." What the fuck does that even mean? "One of us had to drive, know what I mean?" He nudged me on the arm.

"We drove all the way to Santa Maria in his broken ass Celica, got there, and realized that our lights were out the entire fucking time!" Howls of laughter filled the car. A glance back confirmed that Kat was still asleep.

"I fucking hated that vato. Every time, he would fuck with me, holding a pistol to my head, threatening me.

One time he hit me with the pistol butt and I hit him back with an uppercut. Then, his buddies grabbed me and beat the shit out of me with a baseball bat. No. Wasn't a fan of that. And I didn't like driving that far."

"But that night...sheeeeiiit..." His eyes closed. Lifted his chin, turning face upwards. His fist clenched again, knocking his knuckles against the door.

"Those were the days." Opened his eyes, head still back. For the first time, he turned to face me. Eyes full of memory. Dark bags of skin surrounded bloodshot eyes. Wrinkles ran down his face in a landscape of tributaries and streams down to his jawline. A mix of salt and pepper scuff grew from his cheeks, unkempt and running freely. He had a black eye. Based on the color and swelling, it was probably two days old.

It then dawned on me the reason for this spontaneous trip. In one way or another, I was taking an addict to his hell.

We arrived in Santa Barbara, and Marco had me driving in circles until we pulled up to a run-down yellow motel. He sat up and rocked back and forth in his seat to gain momentum as I slowed to a stop. He hurled himself from the car with renewed energy. He stepped briskly around the car to my side. I rolled down my window.

He pushed some cash at me. I protested. He shoved it in my front shirt pocket and kissed me on the forehead. I looked up, and his eyes seemed bright. For a second, I glimpsed young Marco, brash and adventurous. Bag-toting eyes were just masks for his spirited inner self. Deep inside, though, there was a hole, a sad, an unfulfilled vacuum. I could only guess where that vacuum started, but it was clear that he was fixing it with momentary band aids, fleeting blissful patches of needles and pipes.

"Thank you, Leo." He was calm as she said it. Kat had woken up in the back seat, and gotten out of the car to see her dad off. She gave him a one-armed hug, and he left her with a forehead kiss, just like mine. Kat hopped into the front seat, but didn't look at me.

"Andiamo."

I used the cash that Marco gave me to fill Kat's car with gas, plus two Pabst tall cans and an Arizona Iced Tea for Kat. Tossed the treasures in the back seat, leaned against the Honda as the pump pumped. I was trying to digest Marco, and Marco and Kat. I felt a wave of sadness, and wanted to reach out and hold Kat. But I didn't.

We hopped on the 101 North, in silence, until Kat sighed.

"That's Marco." She reach back and grabbed the tall cans. She cracked my beer, then hers.

"He seems like a cool dude." The words I offered were hollow and were met with a Kat scoff. She proceeded to turn up the volume on the radio. *Under the Bride* played as we continued up the coast.

Sun was nearly set. We pulled over to rest, allowing Kat to snag a photo of the coastline. Sun sloppily spilled reds and oranges and purples all over the blue table trimmed with white crests and falls. The two of us sat on top of her little red Honda, sipping the dregs of our cans.

"I know you weren't asleep." I took a gulp of the shitty beer, and stole a glance at my road trip buddy.

Her eyes were glued to the horizon. They were glistening. Her face remained stoic, lips pressed together, hermetically sealed. If she allowed even a sliver of her breath escape her mouth, a flood would let loose, drowning her, me, innocent passersby in a swirling turmoil of memories and anger. The floodgate remained, but a single tear escaped.

A sniff, and a bottoms-up chug. Kat thought she was being slick. As she wiped her mouth to clear some beer from her mouth, she wiped away the runaway tear from her cheek. That moment of vulnerability was gone.

She hopped off the car, both feet landing firmly on the ground. Placed the can, top-up, on the ground, and stomped it flat with one Converse. Picked up the disk of crushed aluminum that once contained piss-water-alcohol. She tossed the can up in the air, and punted it toward the horizon toward the near-set sun. It landed short.

"GET THE FUCK OUTTA HERE!!!" Kat screamed wildly after the can. She laughed at her own antics before turning to me. "Andiamo, Leo."

By the time we got back to Santa Labre, the sun had long since left, and stars speckled the ceiling. I pulled up to Fred Briggs' place, got out. Kat walked around the front of her car, intercepting me before I started up to the front door. She put reached up and put her tiny hands on my shoulders.

"Leo. Thanks, man." She buried her face in my chest and wrapped her arms around me in a warm embrace, and I held her. We stood there for 150 years. Kat then pulled her head back, and headbutted me in the sternum. She then took a stiff arm to me, and pushed me away like a running back clearing space.

"You got it." I ruffled her hair as I walked off.

"Chinga te, piece of shit!" she feigned anger as she hopped in her Honda and zoomed off.

I remembered the cigarette I rolled hours ago. Stuck it in the corner of my mouth, lit it with my Bic. I watched Kat's red lights disappear around a corner.

185

Death's relapse.

One late night in Santa Labre, my mind wandered. I wrote.

Still in my work clothes, I sat alone at the far end of the bar. Most would be put off by this dimly lit and dreary establishment. The staff was horrendously inimical, spurred by spite for the hot-headed owner. The drinks were expensive. Even the room itself was always kept at a temperature that most would find uncomfortable. I didn't. I stared down at the glass of single malt scotch, grateful for the liquid bliss that it provided. Lifting the glass to my lips, I angled it so the scotch slowly rolled out of the glass and into my mouth. I felt it tumble down my throat, the warmth spreading throughout my body, alleviating my brain that had been strained from a particularly hard workday. I wasn't happy with my job but it was a job. Most would not have found joy in my line of work. I was eager and ambitious when I had started but it had worn down on my bones more than I could have even fathomed.

Soon, I saw the bottom of the glass. I ordered another. Then another. After eight scotches, I glanced at my pocket watch and decided to head back to my apartment. I took care of my tab, and ambled out of the bar.

As the fresh air hit me, I suddenly realized the effect of the alcohol. The unstable sidewalk seemed to tip and rotate, and each of my steps became a test of my focus. The relentless force that is gravity eventually prevailed, and the concrete beckoned me close. Abiding the concrete's call, I fell to the ground near the gutter, where I lay for a few seconds, eyes closed. I finally gathered enough strength to push myself up into a crouching position.

What am I doing? I know I don't enjoy my work, and I know many people don't respect what I do. Many even fear me. Now on all fours but still facing down, I opened my eyes to find a puddle

187

reflection staring back at me. I pulled back my hood, revealing my head. Though it was dark, I could just barely make out the outline of my white, hairless skull. My bony jawline met my equally bony cheekbones. I stared deep into my own dark eyes and saw weariness and sorrow.

Ashamed at what I had become, I looked away. Using my staff as support, I was able to bring myself to a standing position. As soon as I stood, I felt the insecure ground tugging at me, clearly wanting me as close as possible.

My stomach dropped a bit as I remembered I had to go to work the next morning. Disregarding my reluctance, the never-ending workload continued. Was it strange that I wanted to join those that I served? True, they could no longer think, see, taste, or feel. True, their families were filled with sorrow for their passing. The departed themselves, however, were relieved of the exhaustion of life. For this, I was envious. I knew this departure was not in my future; it was impossible. For I am Death. Who would bring me Death if I were the one dying?

the Major.

"We gotta go, gypsies!" joshed Fred Briggs.

The sun was about an hour from poking over the hills to release daylight on our town. We almost made it through the whole night so we clearly weren't going to stop now. Just like so many other drunken nights, we had concocted a plan.

There was a water tower at the foot of Madonna Mountain, and we felt it needed our touch. We gathered all the spray paint cans we had in our house, and shoved them into a pack. A blue. A couple blacks. White. A quarter of a red. Yellow. And a Montana Purple. That purple was my favorite. Fucking vibrant. So, we each rolled a cigarette and a joint, ushered Donnie out the door with us, and headed out.

Kat was most in touch with her inner sober driver so

we jumped in her little red Honda. She opened the window so Donnie could stick is head out, tongue lapping in the wind. We drove about six blocks in the early morning fog to the trailhead.

We simultaneously hopped out and slammed the doors behind us. Donnie trotted next to me as we walked toward the dirt trail. Fred Briggs sparked his joint first as we walked the short walk to the fence surrounding the water tower. We tossed the bag of paint over. The fence was topped with nasty barbs but Fred Briggs and I jumped up and climbed. Fred Briggs ripped his shirt a bit, but other than that, we were unscathed. Little Kat was able to just slip underneath the gate. She brushed herself off, and glanced at us, beaming in anticipation of our shenanigans. Equally eager to be included, Donnie squeezed under the gate after Kat. Kat and I both sparked our joints of inspiration as Fred Briggs began coating a small area of the water tower.

Streaked it with blue waves. Painted glowing all-seeing eyes. Dotted and slashed the side with patterns. After we were satisfied with the sides, we all met up at the ladder to the top of the tower. Donnie watched us from the ground as we started our work on top. Kat went first, I followed, and Fred went last. Paint fumes filled the air, and our index fingers looked as if we had fingered some smurfs. Satisfied with our work, we sat on top of the water tower, dangling our legs over the edge.

"Not too bad, kids." Kat took a drag from her cigarette in celebration of our work. "Not bad at all, for a couple of dopes."

"This is my masterpiece," I said as I stretched out. My hangover was passing.

"I wish we had more of that purple," Fred Briggs stood and tried to get some perspective on our work.

Kat pulled his pant leg, beckoning him to take a seat. He obliged. "Don't worry about it," she said, as she leaned up on an elbow. "You can't control how the art comes out, really. You just have to be there to accept it when it shows itself. Like the ancient Greeks used to believe, ya know? It was the Muses that delivered inspiration to a waiting and wanting artist. Artists do not produce anything on their own."

"Wow, look at the philosopher!" Fred Briggs laughed.

Kat hid behind another cloud of smoke. "Shut the fuck up and just enjoy the view!" She turned away, blushing.

The sun was just rising, trying to catch us in the act but

he was too late. We watched the light of morning inch across the fields, shedding day on the fields sprawled beneath us. I felt a smile creeping over my face. I looked at Kat, and she had a similar stupid grin on her face.

We climbed down, Fred Briggs and I hopped the fence. Kat stayed on the other side a few extra moments to snap a couple pictures then followed him down the trail. We jumped back into Kat's car and we were off.

"Let's get some fucking burritos." I was glad Kat brought up food. I could go for some G-Brothers breakfast. We drove around a few blocks, enjoying the empty streets as we smoked our cigarettes. We were in a comfortable bliss. Yes, allowing creative juice to flow onto a canvas of any kind was a beautiful, satisfying practice that ultimately rewards you by improving your state of being. But, god damn, the thrill of doing it in such a public, yet forbidden place. I turned up Kat's blown-out speakers, and out came a Sublime's *Santeria.* We sang obnoxiously loud. We were happy.

As we pulled around the corner of Broad and Murray, we saw a man sprawled on the ground next to a toppled-over blue trash bin. Kat slowed, as we all looked at each other for a second, me in the passenger, Fred and Donnie in the back. Kat put the car in park but left the car running in the middle of the street. Donnie watched us as we three jumped out and ran over to the fallen man.

He was old. Very old. I guessed he was pushing 90. His chest rose and fell, labored but moving. His skin was darkened and wrinkled. A white tank top clung to his shriveled body. His eyes were open, staring straight up at the sky. And he spoke constantly, gasping a single word over and over.

"Yes. Yes. Yes. Yes, yes. Yes..."

We didn't touch him at first for fear of potential back or neck injuries. Kat offered quietly, "Sir, can you hear me? Are you ok?"

"Yes. Yes. Yes." His feeble arms attempted to wave us off.

"See, he's fine, guys. Let's get out of here," Fred chimed in to both of us. His apprehension was showing itself.

"Fred, call 911," I told him. He pulled out his phone, turned his back on the scene, walked a few steps away.

The man was starting to move more, and I knelt down and put a gentle hand on his shoulder. "Easy. The ambulance will be here soon."

He stopped his *yes* chant for a moment, and looked at

me in the eyes. He said nothing, but his eyes said, "Get away from me, kid." I stayed my hand but he kept moving, eventually rolling onto his side. As he turned, I saw long, bloody gashes staining his white tee. He was not bleeding profusely, but the apparent fall had scraped him. His thin seasoned skin sloughed off with the slightest abrasion. On his exposed arm, I saw a faded tattoo of the Marine emblem.

Movement, even slight, tired him and he rolled back on his back. He resumed his *yes* chant, and we stayed with him until the ambulance came.

"Where are you taking him?" I asked one of the EMTs as he closed the back door of the ambulance. The fallen man had ceased his *yes* chant, and was now lying on the stretcher behind those closed doors.

"We're taking him to Sierra Vista. You family?"

"No."

"Well, you might be able to visit him. Just come by the emergency room."

"Thanks, man."

We three watched the ambulance disappear around a corner, sirens blaring.

"So, now what?" Kat said absently.

"We go to the fucking hospital!" Fred turned and walked directly to the driver's seat of Kat's car. Kat and I followed. Donnie was still in the back seat, and we all had a new plan for the day.

The sun was fully exposed in Santa Labre, and presented a beautiful day to the city and most of its inhabitants.

being found.

The last gasps of the Major, the found man.

The sun beat me down, pinning me to the scorching pavement. I could almost hear my drill sergeant hounding our squad, pushing us, berating us verbally, physically. When I first enlisted to fight, I was a 20-nothing-year-old with naught but a strong back and weak mind to my name.

The Marines built me in ways that I couldn't imagine. Just when my body was on the verge of breaking down and collapsing, my mind would dig deeper. When my mind would start to break down, and something else kicked in. My will had become the Marianas Trench, but that fight within me would be sitting at the bottom with a shovel, saying "There's gotta be more down here!" My time in the military had allowed me to harness this energy that may have been within me my entire life.

Now, nearly 70 years elder, I lay on the pavement. No visible enemies to fight. No bullets to dodge. No friends to carry. Just me, alone. My pride had kept me from ceding to my age. Now I lay, a fallen man, body failing, with no help. Closing my eyelids, I looked within, beckoning my inner, shovel-wielding will, asking, "Is there any left?" A soft, strong wind rumbled in my gut, jostling its way up my chest and throat and escaped my lips. "Yes."

* * * * *

Faint sounds drifted into my head through the darkness. I heard the beep, beep of medical machines first. Then muffled murmurs. Voices, that's what they were. I struggled to open my eyes. Blurs and smudges. Then some colors, then some figures. Slowly, a doctor in a white coat revealed himself.

The figure in white told me I was in the hospital and I had fallen. I knew very well what had happened. I wanted to tell him, wanted to point out his dumb shit statement, but I realized I couldn't. I couldn't speak. I could barely move. My toes wiggled, thousands of miles away at the end of the bed. I could move my arms, though. Not the whole arm, but I could move my forearm. So, carefully, slowly, I lifted my left arm up. I extended my fingers toward the doctor, and I saw his eyes light up, happy to

197

see that I was responsive. Then, I turned my wrist, and closed all my fingers in a fist. Well, all my fingers but one. The bird flew right in the face of the doctor, and he turned and left the room. I couldn't smile or laugh, but I imploded with hilarity as I lowered my arm back to the bed.

Three kids walked in. Who the fuck were these children? They were dressed like slobs, but the smell of alcohol and tobacco coming from them was somehow comforting. Still, I preferred my solitude.

"You alright, sir?" The girl leaned over and put a hand on my arm to try and comfort me. I closed my eyes.

"Do you remember us?" One of the boys said. "Can we get anything for you?"

I said nothing, eyes still closed. Please go back to your toys, children.

A nurse came in and shooed the kids out of the room. I could hear the three of them talking to the nurse in hushed tones outside of the room. I was just glad they were gone. I tried to ignore them but I heard them talking about me, so I listened to the voices as I stared at the ceiling.

"Who are you, are you family?" The nurse questioned.

being found.

"No, just friends." The girl did all of the talking.

"Well, can you get in contact with his family?" The nurse asked them.

Silence.

The nurse was first to talk. "Well, we got his name from his wallet. We've tried to reach his family, but haven't had any luck. It seems like his closest relative, his nephew, lives across the country and we don't have any contact information."

More silence.

Then, the girl again. "So, how is he?"

"Well, I can't really tell you that..."

A male voice interrupted her. "Just fucking tell us, lady!"

"Watch your language, young man! There are other patients here!" The nurse turned her tone sympathetic. "It's not looking good."

A long pause, followed by footsteps nearing my room. The three of them re-entered the room. This time the girl sat on the side of the bed. Get the fuck off my bed, stupid little girl.

She started talking to me. I looked around, trying to find escape. I saw some of my belongings on a bedside table. My brown jacket, my brown leather belt, my brown leather wallet, and my little, brown leather-bound note-book. No escape, and this girl would not shut up. I did the only thing I could. I lifted my arm once again, and gave the one finger salute to the girl. Since she was sitting on the bed, I was able to put the middle finger inches away from her face.

More stupid, sympathetic words came out of her mouth as she held me hostage. The silent kid with a me-chanic shirt and beard now stepped forward and put a hand on her shoulder. She looked up at him. He gave her a look and a nod, and she stood up from the bed. The three of them started for the door.

I suddenly felt a pang of disappointment in myself. I spent my whole life pushing people away. Went to the war to escape dealing with friends and family drama. Left my wife for no good reason. These three were just nice young people reaching out to an old man as he drift-ed off. I raised my arm. It was much more difficult this time, and I felt myself getting tired. I rapped my knuckles against the bedside railing as hard as I could. Wasn't that hard, but was hard enough to grab the attention of the silent boy. The other two were already making their way down the hallway, but he turned and stood in the doorway, looking at me. He had a full beard, but kind eyes. He said nothing.

I pointed to the table, toward my notebook. He walked over and picked it up. He looked at it for a second, and I motioned for him to take it. He stuffed it in his jacket pocket.

He stood there. I lay there. We said nothing. We just stared at each other in a standoff. Finally, I lifted my arm a final time, using the last of my strength. I turned my wrist, made a fist, but left that one finger up. A smile appeared beneath his beard. He lifted his own middle finger, aiming it right at me and walked out of the room.

I closed my eyes. That exchange with the bearded boy, though brief, felt like nothing I had felt in a long time. I felt like a great weight was lifted off my chest. Memories of war, family, life's hardships slowly began to release me from their wicked grip. I felt myself drifting off. I didn't resist. It didn't seem to matter that my body wasn't working. I was floating, floating away. Bliss, I felt as I left this world.

roadtrip.

We three sat at the Crab & Apple pub downtown. Silence. The experience with the old soldier left us in a funk. Barely knew the man, but mortality had a way of tapping on your window of consciousness. Of course, we were mournful that he was on his way out. But it was more than that. He was dying without any family next to him. No friends to see him off. We might have been the last ones to see this man, and we really didn't know him. How would we go? Surrounded by loved ones, our grandchildren tickling our feet, we would drift off into nothingness? Was this what I wanted? Does this ever happen?

The deterioration leading up to the inevitable end was often ignored or unrealized by the living, but it seems it would be the stage that the reflective dead would wish to shorten. Even so, that Marine probably did not live a safe life. I imagined that he fought in battles, went on grand excursions to dangerous places, yet, in the end, it was his own body that betrayed him. I could not be sure what my two friends were thinking, but I was certain all our thoughts were swimming in the same current.

"Let's get outta here." I polished my beer and slammed the empty on the counter, signifying we should go home.

Kat and I paused. We looked at each other for a moment as if we telepathically just shared the same thought. We needed to take a hiatus from this town.

The sly grin that appeared on Kat's face opened up as she threw back her own beer. Slammed it on the counter. "Let's get the fuck out of here."

We both looked at Fred Briggs. He was the hometown boy. We were the travelers. We felt at home on the road but he was born and raised in Santa Labre. Fred would never admit that he was afraid of the outside world. Sure, he had been to New York once. He drove up to Portland with his family one time. He didn't look upon those times as pleasant memories.

> *Why the fuck would I leave this town? There aren't any better than right here.*

The wildman of Santa Labre would likely die here. But,

today was different. Fred Briggs looked down at his beer and shook his head. He tossed it back, belched loudly.

"I hate you people." He slammed his mug on the bar in concord. We tossed some cash at the barkeep, and headed out of the bar. Kat went home to grab some necessities, and Fred and I did the same. Fred called his shop on the way back to the house to give them a heads up.

"Yeah, I'll be gone a few days," Fred Briggs said to his cell, driving with one hand. "How long? Good question… Hey Leo, how many days are we going to be gone?"

"No idea, man. At least a few."

"What? Come on, I gotta give them something!"

"What do you want me to say? I don't know. Do you have anything coming up at the shop?"

"Hey Raul, let's say a three days. I'll give you a call if I end up being longer. Thanks." He hung up. "How will we know what to pack? Where are we going? Which car are we taking? Or are we all just going to pile onto your little bike?"

Fred Briggs' Chevelle was the natural choice for the trip. It had seen some years, but was still the least likely to break down. We herded Donnie into the back seat. I bounded inside the house and grabbed my pack. I always kept it packed and ready so I could be on the road in seconds. Fred grabbed a sleeping bag, some blankets, a loaf of bread, two bottles of wine, and a fifth of Jack Daniels. We headed off to pick up Kat.

I missed the road. When you are constantly trying to find where you are going to sleep, where your next meal is coming from, where you are going, life is simple. Everyday life becomes complicated. Complacency allows us to overthink.

On the way to Kat's I sent a text to the captain of the fishing crew to let him know I'll be out of town for a few days.

> *No problem, Leo. Let me know when you are back in town.*

I was reading his reply as we pulled up to Kat's. I got out and helped Kat load her bags in the trunk.

"Go ahead, take the front," I offered to her.

"Nah," she slammed the trunk closed with a half-empty wine bottle in her hand. She gripped the cork with her teeth and took a pull. "I gotta take care of this."

"Give me some of that," I grabbed the bottle from Kat

and took a gulp. "So, when's your next obligation, Miss Kat Scindo?" I returned her bottle after she was settled in in the back seat.

"I got nothin' until next weekend! Fuckin' free. Andiamo."

"Alright, let's do it." I said.

"Let's get outta here, gypsies!" Fred Briggs peeled out of Kat's driveway.

East, we went.

thin air tastes better.

On the road, again. I wrote.

Serenity.

Overwhelmed with emotion, eyes struggle to keep up with the textures, the colors laid out before me. Soft green pines jut from the brown soil. Grand domes of granite rise from the sea of emerald, islands of solidarity warming their bald faces in the morning sun.

Crisp.

A quick inhale. Morning mist sneaks in through nostrils, racing down and delivering a taste of the world abound. Almost bites. A deeper breath, slow intake. The pine and redwood stretches itself on tongue, throat, nostrils. Fills lungs, travels through veins to arm, fingertips, legs, toes.

Incapacitated.

Relief.

Cool granite gripping rubber soles of boots. Boots wrapping around sore feet. Sore feet and legs supporting aching body. Barely. Back tender. Unclip waist strap, sternum strap. Pack slumps on the granite, grateful for the break. And reprieve flushes through. Through back, through legs, through feet. The appreciation of that moment reaches the granite. The granite smiles. The granite exists without a glimmer of tribute from the lowly life forms that rest upon it.

But still. The granite smiles.

the Major's memoire.

Fred Briggs in the back seat.

I loved driving and I loved this car, but tired is tired. Kat took the driver's seat, Leo as co-pilot, and I stretched out in back with the ice chest. I popped the top off a Negro Modelo, and relaxed, soaking in the desert scenery. Some hated these drives It stretched for miles, ending in ominous mountains far in the distance. Freckled with brown-green shrubs and the occasional cactus; this was the land of the horizon. We passed what looked to be an old abandoned Air Force base and landing strip.

The military establishment led my wandering mind back to the Major. Before he left us, he stole a brief moment of privacy between him and me. He had me take his journal in the hospital, and I put it in my jacket pocket, hidden from Leo and Kat. I'm not exactly sure why I hid it from them, but the Major seemed to choose that specific time to offer that to me.

As Leo and Kat chatted on in the front seat, I pulled out the brown, aged leather wrapped around its yellowed pages. I ran my fingers along the spine, wondering where it had been, what it had seen. I opened to the first page. It had a flower sketched in the corner, and a name – "Major Thomas Calhoun." I flipped to a random page, and found the beginning of an entry.

> *My Memoire – The Oldest Brother - July 4th, 1975*
>
> *I grew up in a poor farming town in the heat of the Southern Californian desert, a small collection of farms that called themselves Niland, nestled in the Imperial Valley. I spent my youth working in the strawberry fields with my four brothers, while my sister helped my mother in the house. My father owned the farm, and hired a crew of migrant workers, and my brothers and I grew close to them. Doris, a 50-something year woman, would sing beautiful hymns in Spanish as we picked berries or ploughed rows. We had no fucking idea what she was saying, but I used to repeat the sounds she made as I worked. Her dark eyes were comforting to me, and the slight creases*

on the corners of her eyes created a permanent smile.

The brothers' alliance would work hard under the harsh supervision of our father, but we were as mischievous as hell. We would play fight, wrestling in the dirt, ride our 50cc's over the dunes, or shoot lizards with pellet guns. My oldest brother was Harry, I was the second oldest boy, the twins Rex and Blackie were next, followed by the youngest Bruce. Our sister Sue was by far the oldest, by 9 years.

We brothers were constantly competing but Harry always seemed to be our father's second set of eyes. Although he played, we all sensed a greater aura of responsibility around him. Maybe that is why our father passed his .22 rifle to Harry on his 15th birthday. It was a small rifle and dwarfed all of our pellet guns in comparison. I remember riding behind our dirt bikes, with Harry in front of me, and I would see the piece slung tightly over his shoulder. Sun glinted off the black blue steel barrel, wrapped with the beautiful marble-grained wood stock. At 13, I was able to understand why Harry was the recipient of this gift even though the pang of envy still brewed inside me. The twins were much more openly resentful, while young Bruce, strangely, did not exhibit any outward angst against the gun. I summed that up to his youth. That is, until one morning, 3 months after Harry's 15th birthday.

I shared a room with the twins, and Harry shared a room with Bruce. I sleep like a fucking rock, always have, so I did not even stir when little Bruce came and awoke the twins at dawn. Today was supposed to be our day of rest, so I wanted to take advantage of it. What did wake me was the cracked yell of a boy just in the throes of puberty.

"Where's my gun!" The still desert morning somehow got more still.

Before opening my eyes, a smile sneaked onto my face, as I knew one of the brothers took it. My subconscious mind put that together when the three youngest were up and about before the rest of the family. Harry burst through my bedroom door and I held up an empty palm without lifting an eyelash. Harry seemed to outrun the sound of his hurried steps; I swear he was outside yelling before I heard the sound of his feet hitting the squeaky bottom stair. A frantic scene. I got up from the bed, and leaned against the window.

In the dim waxing light of the morning, a movie scene unfolded. On one end of the yard were the twins, running in circles around Bruce standing on a chair, waving the rifle, posed like a goddamn action hero. He was smoking a giant air cigar, holding his finger in a hook shape, and moving it from his face and away from it, over exaggerating his lips, showing his smoke ring skills. A giant, stupid smile was splattered all over his stupid, fat face.

By now, Harry was bounding over to the trio. Doris aimed her usual early morning stroll toward the spectacle. Harry stopped just short of Bruce, yelling as Bruce proceeded to hold the rifle and point his imaginary cigar at the twins, both howling with laughter. Harry's voice cracked, sending the twins' shrieks to greater heights. I looked down on my brothers fondly, each of them playing their specific roles. Each of them fit so well together. Harry learning responsibility by looking out for all of us youngsters, the twins learning to support their younger brother while having fun, and Bruce glowing in the attention of it all. Amid the new waves of laughter, Harry decided he had enough, and grabbed the barrel of the rifle. Bruce, eyes changing from smug joy to stubborn, immature outrage, pulled the stock away from Harry. The crack of the rifle rang out, running in every direction.

The twins stopped running. Bruce dropped the rifle, and it flopped on the ground, now a useless stick. Doris put her hand to her mouth, eyes wide with shock. Harry dropped to his knees, then flopped backward, next to the rifle. From where I was standing, I saw Harry's face. Stoic, mouth closed, at least one of his eyes were open. A steady stream of blood ran from his right eye. I stared at his face from where I stood on the balcony. Doris let loose a blood curdling scream.

I looked at Bruce. His smile had vanished and hid deep within him well into his 20s.

That was the day I became the eldest brother.

I closed the notebook, and took a deep breath. I wasn't sure what I was looking for when I opened that book. I thought about Harry, the Major's brother, and his early end. I tried to wrap my head around Major Thomas

Calhoun living for decades as the oldest, but not oldest brother. Yet, even Thomas, the survivor, still faced his own humanity.

I tipped the beer bottle and finished it off. I belched, and Leo laughed.

"How dare you belch in front of a lady," Kat said. She returned the belch before refocusing on the road. I smiled, and tried to enjoy that precise moment, with those two wandering people, in that desert.

distract.

There is a haven for those weary travelers, wandering through the desert of life. An oasis for the monotony of a suit-and-tie day. A place that was designed to tickle the animalistic side of human beings. An anti-Socratic place where your senses are fed with physical pleasures and sporadic gratification and gluttony. A place where, but for a moment, the cubicle-stranded allow their debaucheristic inner demons to claw and rip their way out of business suits and corporate shackles. There is a place where addicts and their sorted baggage are welcome. There is a place called Las Vegas.

The 15 was a lone highway leading through the scorching American Southwest, leading to that strange oasis of lights and money. Like weary, thirsty vagrants wandering the desert, we were relieved to see the glowing city appear on the horizon, interrupting the stillness of the night. We chose a cheap motel that straddled the border between the touristy Fremont area and the decrepit North Vegas.

The room stank of cigarettes and pine air freshener. A terrible pastel-colored print of a ship at sea was nailed to the wall above the bed. The lights shone a white fluorescence. And the bed itself. Well. It was a cheap motel in Las Vegas. We didn't spend much time there.

We unloaded our things into the shithole of a room, and caught a shuttle that took people to the Strip, the heart of Vegas. We found three empty seats on the bus amongst the crowd of tourists, dolled-up young people reeking of terrible cologne. Separate, but at least there were three. Fred Briggs grabbed a seat directly across from me, face-to-face. Kat snagged a window seat next to an old Korean woman with an absurd, golden-yellow, wide-brim visor. Throughout the thirty minute ride, Kat kept her eyes glued on every casino, every light. She absorbed the environment to its fullest, with a slight smile plastered on her face. I watched her from across the bus, watched that glazed-over look, and wondered what was going through her mind. Hypnotized.

After jumping off at the northern end of the Strip, we headed straight for the nearest restaurant, a cheesy

50's-style diner. Buddy Holly waiters and Lucille Ball hostesses mingled with customers, balancing vanilla Cokes and burgers on red plastic trays serving families seated on red plastic benches. The plastic happiness had infected even the imposter James Dean rebel rockers in this world of manufactured reality. We three took a booth. Kat sat next to me and Fred Briggs stretched out on the opposite side, enjoying the extra space.

Fred Briggs and I ordered burgers with fries. Kat, a club sandwich. We joked and laughed and ate. The hyper-happy atmosphere was almost eerie. But, to be honest, I was OK with it. This happiness was surely fleeting, but isn't that the nature of it?

Check came. I pulled out my wallet, checking the inventory of its contents. Fred sluggishly did the same, and I could see the contents from across the table. Sparse bills, all single digit.

"Don't worry, fellas. I'll get this one." We both looked at Kat with raised eyebrows. Fred Briggs stopped fumbling, but I still pulled out a twenty. I wasn't too keen on taking handouts.

In response, Kat revealed a medium-sized manila envelope. Out of it, she drew a hundred dollar bill, placing it on the table. I caught a glance at the inside of the envelope: a hefty wad of cash.

"Whoa there, rich girl. Where'd that come from?" I nudged Kat in the ribs playfully. A grin stretched across her face.

"Photography and gigs. I guess people like to have their wedding pictures taken and listen to my shitty music. Chumps."

"How much?" Fred Briggs bluntly.

"Fuck if I know. Around eight grand? Nine?"

"Damn!" We both responded in unison. Conceding to her generosity, we let Kat pay for the meal.

Tab paid, we took high spirits to the streets. Las Vegas Boulevard under our feet, neon lights burned our retinas. Girls in club dresses and heels waddled down the street like newborn fawn. Guys in collared shirts and rolled-up sleeves followed the herd of girls, hoping for a lay at the end of the night.

Although I'm not usually one for these type of scenes, I could not help but be swept into the euphoria of this ridiculous world.

We walked into Treasure Island.

"What's your game?" Fred asked us as we walked through slot machines jing-jangling.

"I guess black jack." I never really got into gambling. I was always able to do all right at the tables. I just didn't like losing. Fuck that. I looked back at Kat. She had dropped back a few steps, and I saw a glint in her eyes, reflecting the flashing and spinning lights. Her mouth was slightly agape. Her right hand was in her front jean jacket pocket. Gripping her earnings, probably. She still had that odd look in her eyes. Hypnotized.

"Hey, why don't we...Let's...Where's the bar?" She stammered, tearing her gaze from the machines and tables and wheels and chips. We found a bar in the middle of the floor.

A shot of Patron apiece, and a Long Island Iced Tea apiece. We rarely indulged in these sweet concoctions, but Kat ordered, paid, and provided. We clinked shot glasses together, threw it down. Ordered another round, sending them down the hatch. We took our sweet blue drinks to the floor.

Free drinks at the blackjack tables may seem like an irresistible perk. And they are. We drank and played slots and played blackjack and played craps and drank. Freddy ended up winning $150, I came out even, and Kat told *distract.*

us she lost about $100. We moved on, along the strip. A liquor store stumbled into our view. Fred Briggs, the winner so far, bought the cheap bottle. I also grabbed three cigars and shoved them in my inner jacket pocket.

Eventually, our journey led us to the Cosmopolitan. Tall, clad in glass windows, this hotel casino was adorned with chandeliers that dangled over countless tables and machines.

"Wanna check out the club?" I saw a group of stunning girls head up the escalator. From the second floor, the Marquee sign shined down on us. This was a popular club, and there were 200 or so suits and dresses waiting for a chance to get in. Fred Briggs and I slowed, reluctant to wait in a line Kat continued to the front.

"Is there cover for this place?" I aimed my question in the general direction of a skinny blonde girl in a backless black dress. Sometimes you can instantly sense that you do not like a person. Almost a stench. The girl turned to me lazily, and her blue eyes scanned me up and down in a split second. Her lips curled into the slightest of snarls.

She exhaled. "Uh, yeah."

"Do you know how much?"

"Well, a promoter invited us here, so we are getting

221

like half off, so…"

Just then, Kat came and hooked her arm around mine. She looked the blonde girl in the eye, read the situation, and overplayed to send a message to the girl. "Come on, babe. We are going in now."

"Thanks for your help, anyway," I left the smug girl and her smug friends.

Kat slipped the man at the velvet rope three hundreds. As we passed through the entrance, I looked back at the line. The blonde threw her hands up in the air. We briefly made eye contact, and I smiled.

Cocktail dresses. Flashy suits. Colorful drinks. Music blasting. Terrible music. And bodies. Bodies everywhere. Elbows and shoulders and butts and sweat flew everywhere as drunk party-goers acted like they could dance. And it was exciting. I was swept up by the nonsense, and soon I was joining the mayhem.

The three of us soon separated, unintentionally. We could have been only feet from each other but walls of humans blocked us. I was heading to the bar when a hand with manicured fingernails grabbed my shoulder and spun me around. It was the blonde girl from the line. The music boomed, much louder than either of us could talk. She took my hand and led me the rest of the way to the bar. She was really trying to be graceful, stumbling on her stiletto heels. I wanted her to stop walking; she seemed on the brink of snapping her ankles. We eventually made it to the bar. She leaned over, said something into the bartender's ear, and he returned with two colorful drinks that tasted like sugar and sour and perfume. I brought out my wallet, but the woman stayed my hand. She took two twenty's out of her clutch and handed them to the bar keep. He held out a hand with five fingers extended, and mouthed something over the loud music. She shelled out another twenty, and she again dragged me through the crowd. Not keen on handouts.

We found a seat slightly away from the music, allowing us to talk in raised tones. Maybe it was the shrooms, but I could only focus on how much fucking makeup she had on. Oh, right. Kat apparently thought it was wise to bring some mushrooms on our road trip. The Kat slipped me a handful back at the motel, and we ate them at the diner. I ate mine with my burger.

Anyway, back in the club, I was looking at the painting that was this girl's face. Blues, reds, and peach-colored smudges streaked across her face, highlighting the features she wanted highlighted. My mind wandered and I wondered when it became acceptable for women to wear face paint, but men could not. Fuck, my eyebrows are god damn gorgeous. Why would I not paint them purple? I wondered what she looked like without her mask. I didn't fault her for wearing the mask, the heels, her act. She carried herself like a confident person would, and maybe this whole act helped her do so. Then, I realized the mask was talking to me.

"How do you think I look?" Came through the noise.

"You look great." She was beautiful, or at least her mask was. I made eye contact and I wondered if she knew that there were rainbows shooting from her ears.

"This is Louie V," she pointed to her clutch. Then she motioned toward her shoes. "But these, these are custom designed in a small Italian design studio. You probably wouldn't know who it is."

I humored her. "Yeah, you're probably right."

We were sitting in the lounge area, adjacent to the outdoor dance floor. There were a few tables on the opposite side. Roulette, poker, blackjack, and a few other card games I couldn't quite make out. I wondered who would pay to get in a club, and then go straight to the tables. Then, I saw a little girl with glasses hanging from her neck. She jumped up and yelled, raising her arms. Kat. I watched her from across the club, and the dance floor. The woman sitting next to me, the dragons flying through the air, all quieted for a moment.

I wanted to go over to Kat but just sat and stared. Ripping me from my trance, skinny fingers wrapped around my forearm. The woman mouthed something to me with furrowed eyebrows. She didn't seem so graceful as her ear rainbows turned to ear flames. I lifted my glass, thanking her for the drink, and stood up. Her grip pulled me back, and she mouthed something else.

I smiled and pointed across the crowd. Raised my glass to thank her for the drink, and melted into the masses.

Elbows and shoulders and butts and sweat lay between me and the tables. I would never make it in that condition. I felt my world start to spiral, when a hand grabbed my shoulder and turned me around, pulling me back from my downward descent. Fred Briggs. He shoved his fucking beard in my ear as he tried to communicate over the chaos.

"Let's get the fuck outta here, gypsy!" He shouted. I barely heard him.

I repositioned so my mouth was close to his ear.

"Where's Kat?"

"Just got a text from her, she left." She said she would meet us back at the room.

I was confused because I thought I just saw her at the tables. I pushed my way the rest of the way to the gambling area. Kat was nowhere to be found. I guessed psilocybin molded my brain. Fred and I made our way to the exit. We explored the hotel a bit. Away from the casino floor and the club, the hotel was relatively quiet. There were empty ballrooms, empty hallways. We wandered, and I was glad to be away from the noise and in a place where I could hallucinate in peace.

We continued to stroll down the empty hallway, red and gold patterned carpets mirrored by the reflection on the ceiling. We came to the end of the hallway where a staircase led down to a large, heavy double door.

"EMERGENCY EXIT: ALARM WILL SOUND"

Fred Briggs hopped down the stairs, and rested a fist on the push bar.

"Don't you do it."

He looked up at me. I stood on the top step. "We gotta get outta here, gypsy."

"Don't do it."

He examined the door, read the signs. Knocked on the door, testing its structural integrity. Then he rested his palm on the push bar again. He looked me straight in the eyes with a mischievous glint in his eyes. I knew what he was thinking, but I was particularly alarmed that he seemed to be morphing into a sphinx.

I took another step down the stairs. "OK. Really don't do it. If you do it, we are going to have to run. I will run but I don't want to. These shoes don't fit me."

He considered my statement, looked at my shoes, then back up at me. Then, he turned toward the door.

"Shit, here we go," I mumbled as I kicked my shoes off and jumped to the bottom of the stairs, just as the alarm started to sound.

RHEEEEE. RHEEEEE. RHEEEEE.

Sometimes it's good to have an escape plan. Have an exit, have a backup, keep a Plan B. But there is something to be said about that moment when you are thrust into the unexpected. It tests you. Either you react now or you will die or go to jail or your friends will be hurt. A voice whispers to you. Some will freeze. Others rise to the occasion, reaching levels they never knew possible. If you know there is a safety net, you won't be afraid of falling. It is that fear that can drive you to creative desperation. Ideas fly through your mind, fueled by adrenaline, trying to grasp at something that will allow you to survive.

That something - for me - that night, was this casino hotel's elaborate waterfall and fountain garden. After bursting outside, Fred shot to the right and I ran left. After a few minutes of running, I came upon the beautifully artificial waterfall that tumbled into a series of pools and fountains. Walkways above the pool bridged the gaps as the water gently bubbled along. I could hear yelling from security but couldn't tell from which direction. I hopped the fence and fell about six feet into the shallow pool. I waded to a darker part of the pool, and hid under a walkway. I was still, quiet for a countless amount of time. I heard nothing.

It occurred to me that the fungi shrooms were probably hearing those voices.

vice.

From the dither of Kat Scindo.

Truth is, I was terrified. I was drawn toward the flash-ing lights and ringing bells. When we went into the club in the Cosmo, I hoped that the loud music, alcohol, and sweaty bodies would distract me. I was wrong.

The envelope of cash was so heavy in my pocket that I couldn't get the thought of winning out of my mind. It tickled some deep-down, fucking visceral desire I had in me. Maybe addiction was engrained in my DNA. Thanks, Mom and Dad. I had largely avoided temptations toward addiction. Sure, I was kind of in a heavy-drinking spell right now but that was just because of my new-found friends, Leo and Fred Briggs. I at least had some control over that addiction. Sure, drugs made an appearance once in a while, but I had a handle on that, too. Like now as the shrooms had started to kick in. I liked the feeling.

My mind raced as I tried to guess the odds of losing, thinking the big win was right around the corner. It drew me inexorably. I knew how dangerous it was, and I knew my own demons in the past. But I always thought that I was on the upside of the learning curve.

I found myself at a table next to the dance floor. I pulled out a single hundred dollar bill and the dealer gave me a small stack of chips. Doubled-down, won. Won again. Within 10 hands, I had transformed my hundred into three. Hook, line, sinker. I blinked my eyes to moisten them; I had forgotten to blink. I sat out a hand, and looked out to the dance floor.   Strobe lights, lasers, sweaty bodies bounced around to the shitty club music. I didn't see Fred anywhere, but I saw Leo sitting on a couch placed on the outer edge of the dance floor. He was sitting with a beautiful blonde girl, and sipping some pansy drink. Deep down in the pit of my soul, there was a pang of jealousy but I shoved it down as I imagined how hard he must be tripping at this point. I had the highest tolerance to drugs of the three of them, and Leo took just as much as I did. Well, he did at first. I took a few extra when they weren't looking.

I returned my attention to the table. I played a few more hands. 10 more hands, and I added a couple more hundred to my winnings. Know when to walk away. I got up, gave the dealer a hefty tip, and walked across the dance floor. At the bar, I grabbed an over-priced seven-seven, and headed back to the dance floor. I was out of place in my jean jacket and tattoo'd arms, but it wasn't long before a guy started dancing with me. I humored him for a bit then eventually felt too out of place. I slammed the rest of my whiskey drink, tapped the rim of the empty glass, nodded to him, and gave him my best seductive smile. The idiot took my glass and headed off to the bar. I headed toward the exit. Fuck this club.

I stopped short of the door. That goddamn envelope was so heavy in my pocket. I'm on a winning streak. I can afford to play some games. Roulette, put 100 on black. Lost it. 100 on black again, won. One of the booty-bearing waitresses came around and asked what I wanted.

"Bourbon straight, three fingers." She looked surprised but wrote down my order and waddled away in her ridiculous heels. I turned back to the table.

I watched the roulette wheel spin, the ball bouncing around the black-and-red colored wedges. I saw the table swell, and I thought the chips were going to fall off. I put more chips on the table just in case mine fell off. I wasn't sure whether I was winning or losing so I continued to put chips on and randomly take them off the table. I re-alized that I was slouching, staring at the spinning wheel when a voice pulled me out of this strange world.

"Honey, here's your bourbon." The waitress had re-turned. I pulled out a chip and put it on her serving tray. She raised her eyebrows and thanked me but I didn't re-ally know how much I gave her. I slammed that bourbon like a fucking lady.

The shrooms made the rest of the night a mix of terri-fying interactions with strange people, flashing strobes, alcohol, walking the streets, trying to make sense of this bizarre world filled with sphinxes, the Statue of Liberty, roller coasters, and gambling. I vaguely remember some-one offering to sell me an eight ball. I turned it down. Goddamn, am I good at avoiding temptation, or what? I remember thinking to myself.

At some point, I sent a text to Fred, telling him that I would meet them back at the motel. I was enjoying my-self too much to leave this place. And I was starting to get used to lugging this envelope around. I walked the strip with the bundle of cash as my close friend, follow-ing me everywhere. Oh, wow, the Venetian? I've never been to Italy! My homeland! I have to at least check out what it's like inside. I saw nothing of the fake Italy. I went straight to the tables. And again at Treasure Island. And the Wynn. And a thousand other fucking casinos in that fucking city.

At some point, I realized that the eastern horizon was rapidly getting lighter. I hailed a cab, and climbed in. The cabbie was a middle-aged man with a heavy African accent. I don't claim to know the African languages, but I knew it was African. He chatted on about how much coyotes in the States freaked him out and how he would have to kill elephants for food for his town. I would have been entranced with his stories, had I not pulled out the envelope. Only four hundreds, a few twenty dollar bills, and a handful of ones remained. I started with over ten grand. I felt like I was going to puke, then die. We arrived at the motel, and I gave the cabbie a couple twenties to cover the fare. I climbed the stairs to our room, opened the door. Leo was passed out, face down on the floor. Fred was asleep on the disgusting bed. Donnie wagged his tail as he greeted me on my return.

The sun was just starting to shed some light on Las Vegas, and I watched the sunlight climb up walls and buildings throughout the city, spreading like an infection. I watched each of the neon casino lights turn off, and they rested, waiting for night to lure in people like me.

wild.

"I'm going to die," Fred Briggs' voice rang out and woke me.

"Uhh...." was all I could manage in response.

I forced my eyes open. I was on the floor of our shitty motel room, staring up at the stucco ceiling. I was still for a few moments, trying to collect strength, and while recharging, I tried to find patterns in the bumps and ridges created by the stucco. I turned my head, and saw Kat sitting in a chair facing the window. It was open, and sunlight was pouring in. She was staring out the window. I started moving and Donnie came over and licked my face. He put a heavy paw on my chest and stuck his tongue in my nose.

"Damn it, Donnie!" His affection did wake me up. I sat up, gave him a hug and scratched behind his ears.

He smiled at me.

I turned toward the direction of Fred's voice. He was the only one that made it to the bed, and laid sprawled out there. He pushed himself up on one arm, assessed the room for a second, then looked at me and Donnie on the floor.

"Let's get the fuck out of here, gypsies."

Kat moved for the first time, turned and stood up. "Fuck yes, andiamo." She looked a little tired, and her eyes were a little red but she was not nearly as bad as Fred Briggs or me.

"I'll drive," she said. We packed up the few things we had, and we all climbed into Fred's car and escaped that godforsaken haven for the godforsaken.

* * * * *

East. Kat drove, said nothing. We blasted some folky-blues music from a band called Devil Makes Three. Fred was obsessed with these guys, and his passion for them spread to us. They talked about drinking and dancing and lost loved ones. That music struck us at the right time. The music coming from the speakers allowed us to comfortably sit in silence, each of us recovering from the night before. The 15 took us from Nevada into Utah as the scenery changed from stretching expanses of brown-red desert to dramatic, rocky cliffs and monoliths.

Fred Briggs broke the silence. "So when'd you get back last night, Kat?"

"Probably around 5 or 6."

"Any luck?"

A long pause. Kat shifted uncomfortably in the driver's seat. She put her hand in her jacket pocket where she kept her envelope of cash. Fred couldn't see Kat's face from the backseat but I saw her eyes from the passenger seat. She was blinking back tears.

I had to interrupt the uncomfortable pause. "Fuck the city, we need some nature. You guys down for Zion?"

Fred Briggs leaned back and scratched Donnie's ears in the back seat. "The fuck is Zion?"

"It's a national park. We're heading in that direction. We can find a nice spot away from people."

"Let's do that," Kat finally spoke. We continued east toward our new destination as Devil Makes Three echoed off the canyon walls.

We pulled into the visitor center a couple hours later,

and grabbed a park map. We talked to the uptight visitor center guide after waiting behind a swarm of Chinese tourists. I'm not sure if they were a large family but they certainly clung to each other like they were sharing organs. The visitor guide was a little short with us, and scoffed at our appearance. Being the most experienced backpacker of the three of us, I did most of the talking but the fucking guide still talked down to us.

"Can you at least tell me where would be a good place to start if we are just doing a short back-and-out for the night?"

"So are you…prepared?" he said as he peered down at Kat's tattered Converse.

"Look man, can you just tell us where a good spot would be?"

"Well, I know you can't do the Narrows, you're clearly not geared for that…"

"OK, thanks for the help." I yanked the map out of his hands and the three of us headed for the door. A huge man with worn boots and a dirty backpack held the door open for us.

"Y'all looking for a trail?" He looked to be about 50, and greeted us with a huge smile with missing two teeth.

"Yeah, we are. We tried to get some help, but that asshole over there didn't seem to want us here," I responded.

The seasoned hiker let loose a hearty laugh that made his giant belly jiggle. "Yeah, they can be a little pissy when they get tourists all day. Know what I'm sayin'?" He elbowed Fred who couldn't help but grin a bit at the giant.

"Well, I'd say you should try the East Rim. You'll be hard pressed to see anyone, and it's goddamn gorgeous. I just got back from there, and didn't see a soul. Did see bear shit though."

"Bear? I didn't know Zion had any bears."

"Yeah, there's a few blackies running around these hills. Probably gone by now, anyway. Better a phantom bear than these annoying fucking tourists, ey?"

"Yeah, that's true," I said. "Thanks for the tips. How cold did it get last night?"

"Bring a jacket," at that, he howled with laughter and slapped me on the back with a giant hand, knocking the map out of my hands. He went into the visitor center, and we climbed back in the Chevelle to head to the East Rim trailhead.

We only had two backpacks but mine was big enough

to carry most of the gear. I carried the sleeping bags and tent, Kat took the cans of chili and some water we picked up at a general store before we went in the visitor center. Fred, without a pack, put Donnie on a leash. The hike was just 6.3 miles. Not the most strenuous hike which was a relief to our unprepared little troop. I leveraged my pack on my back as the other two prepared. My pack hugged my back, and I felt its firm embrace as I buckled in. It was comforting to have my long-time buddy on my back, and I felt a surge of energy as we started down the trail. I led the way.

Left, right, left, right. Breathe in, out. The rhythmic nature of backpacking was soothing, hypnotic. I would count my paces up to 20 and then start over again. One, two, three, four, five, six… The waist straps helped to evenly distribute the strain of the weight on my back. The high altitude stole oxygen, and I breathed heavy with exertion. Sweat collected on my hairline and beneath my eyes, raced down my face, dripped off my chin, and landed on the ground, leaving a trail of me behind us. My knees hurt, my legs were sore, and my feet ached. My mind wandered. With so much pained stimuli, I forced my mind to focus on anything, everything.

We walked for breaks. No matter what kind of shape I

was in, stopping to sit, stretch, and take off my pack was euphoria unmatched by any drug. Especially when those breaks coincided with our arrival at beautiful overlooks. Kat was in decent shape, but Fred, even without a pack, struggled up and down the hills. He wore work boots, not ideal for hiking, and often lagged far behind Kat and me. Donnie pulled Fred forward, licking his hands in encouragement when Fred bent over to rest his hands on his knees. But it was the alcohol from last night was what weighed him down the most, and he puked at the top of a particularly strenuous climb.

Kat was the map holder, and she had circled a small area where backpackers camped. It was the middle of nowhere and appeared to sit near a cliff with a view of the valley. Unfortunately we reached the camp about an hour after sunset, and the dusk enveloping the valley was just beginning to turn into night. Didn't matter. We, especially Fred, were relieved to be at our destination and off the trail for the night. Fred and Kat set up our single tent, and I set out to collect firewood.

I returned to find Kat, Fred, and Donnie sprawled out at camp, all three munching on beef jerky. Kat pulled a strip out, threw it to me. I dropped the firewood in order to catch the snack. Goddamn was it tasty. Kat and Donnie *wild.*

were sitting half-in-half-out of the tent, while Fred sat on a log that he rolled over to our area. Fred rummaged through Kat's pack and re-emerged, munching on a bag of Fritos.

I crouched, hunched over a circle of rocks with charred ashes and remains of a fire from the previous night. I thought back on the man that told us of this place and wondered if this was his fire. I started stacking the wood in my favorite configuration for building a fire: I leaned a few sticks against each other, like a tiny teepee, and, surrounding the teepee, stacked wood planks log-cabin style. Kat scooted over to watch my technique. I'm sure she had her own, as everyone has their own opinion on how to best build a fire in the wilderness. She just wanted to see how I did it. Donnie trotted over and sat next to Kat so I had an audience as I tore a bit of toilet paper to use a fire starter. A lighter made short work of my construction, and we soon had a small fire going. It expelled much needed warmth, and I drew closer to take full advantage.

Kat leaned back, face toward the sky. "Space." She shielded her eyes from the light to see starholes pin light through the sheet of black sky. Fred Briggs and I joined her.

We three, shoulder-to-shoulder, absorbed the night,

far from any worries or cities or troubles. Sat for a long stretch, only interrupted by the occasional sit up for a bite of chili. Silent, until it wasn't.

A long sigh from Fred Briggs. Then, "That was a crazy thing. With that old man."

"Yeah, man." Kat also sighed.

"Do you think his family came?" I added.

"Who knows?" Fred. "Do you remember what he was saying? 'Yes, yes.' Over and over. I can't get that outta my head. Shit."

"People die. Shit happens," Kat tried to be tough and push feelings down, but realized she stepped too far. "Here's to him." She raised her can of chili. We joined in a strange toast for the stranger.

"He seemed like a good dude," Fred Briggs again.

"What do you mean? We didn't know him. Not really. Not trying to be shitty. Just sayin'." Blunt Kat.

"Well. Actually, he seemed like an alright dude from his journal."

"What?" I looked over at Fred Briggs.

"Yeah, dude. This journal; he gave it to me. Pretty

interesting. I read a little in the car before Vegas. I left it back in the car but I'll show you once we get off this mountain."

I sat back, wondering why Fred hadn't mentioned it before.

More silence. Again broken by Fred Briggs. "Beautiful out here. I don't think I've ever seen this many stars."

"Ye," Kat said.

I responded with a few more words, happy to share this experience with others. "This is what I live for. Out here. Simple. Free. Sometimes cities and all that make you feel trapped, ya know? I miss this. Fresh air. Pines. Fire. Road. Road. Road. I missed you."

I realized I had drifted a bit, and expected a witty retort from Kat. I was surprised to hear a soft, "Yeah, I do too." She cleared her throat before continuing. "I could get used to this." She stretched out, then retracted. When she did, she was a little closer to me.

"Gotta keep movin', ya know?" I said to break the awkwardness. "Forward, onward. Too much to see, too much to do."

"I know, Leo. I know. The only thing is," she stood up,

spun in a circle and yelled. "Who the fuck will I play my stupid music for out here!" Her voice echoed for miles. The following silence was even more intense after her outcry. The crickets quieted to listen.

"Don't you get homesick?" Fred suddenly asked.

Kat and I fell silent. For me the road was my home. I wasn't sure what Kat was thinking.

Finally, Kat leaned on her arm to address Fred's question. "Well, for me..." Kat stopped mid-sentence as she turned and to look at Fred, who was still munching on junk food.

Donnie gave a low-throated growl, and I grabbed his collar. The hair on the back of his neck bristled and I felt every muscle in his body tense.

"What's wrong with you people?" Fred said. The words had barely left his lips when he looked over his right shoulder, and jumped up at the same time, screaming like my little sister. The Frito bag flew and barbecue-flavored corn chips rained down on our campsite.

The flickering fire revealed the outline of a bear just within our campsite.

Kat had her own way. She stood, waving her hands

and clapping in the air and started yelling at the bear, trying to scare it away. Egged on by the commotion, Donnie started barking and straining against the collar. I had to pull him back with all my strength to keep him from running at the bear. Or maybe Donnie was all talk. Probably best for his dignity that someone held him back.

The bear wasn't huge, maybe 300 pounds or so, and three or four feet at the shoulder. Big enough to do some damage to any one of us but not nearly big enough to risk taking us all on. I could not help but admire the bold beast. His muscles tightened and released beneath is dark brown fur-covered hide. I looked into the bear's eyes. He moved purposeful, wary of us, but without fear. He sensed our own fear in the breeze. He heard our hearts beating out of our chests. His grunt was a laugh at our sad attempts to scare him. Trudging along, now ignoring our shouts of protest, he grazed on the fallen Fritos, keeping a cautious eye on Kat and Donnie, but not giving any ground. I pulled my knife out from its holster on my belt. Just in case. Cityboy Fred Briggs stood frozen by the fire, too scared to do anything. I could tell he wanted to run but didn't want to leave the protective light of the flame.

"FRED! Here, take Donnie," I felt helpless as I struggled against the strength of our German Shepard buddy.

Fred awoke from his trance and hopped over to me. "Do NOT let him go, man!"

"Yeah, I got him," Fred grabbed Donnie's collar as he continued to bark and strain. I stood up and grabbed the small log I was sitting on when I was building the fire. I threw it in the bear's direction, forcing him to take a step back but he didn't run. Instead, he strolled over to our packs near the tent.

"HEY BEAR!! NO! GET OUT OF HERE!" Kat was shrieking, and I joined her. The bear paused for a second and looked at me, as if assessing how much of a threat I was, stuck his muscular black-brown head into my pack.

I had heard of bears stealing packs in national parks but that was in Yosemite, back in California. I didn't know there were bears in Utah, much less how they acted. This bear was by far the boldest wild animal I had come across. It barely seemed wild. I saw the bear with its head in my pack and pawing at it with its huge claws, and I thought about all the times I had with that pack. All the memories alone on the road, with only my pack to comfort me. I imagined the bear bounding off, laughing at me, as it carried away my pack. Carried away my life.

I looked around wildly for anything to scare away the bear. I still had my knife in my hand, but I really did not want to get that close to the bear nor did I want to hurt it. He was just trying to get some food. Not mine, not today. My hands landed on a fallen branch that I had collected for the fire. It was sturdy enough and was long enough to allow me to stay at out of the bear's reach. Branch in my right hand and knife in my left, I yelled and advanced on the bear.

"HEY! GET THE FUCK OUT OF HERE! GET OUT!!" I yelled as I got closer. The bear pulled his head out of the pack and looked me straight in the eye. Not aggressive. Not angry. Not even scared. He looked at me as if calculating what I was doing, and if he was willing to find out. I jabbed near the bear's head, and he took a single step back while dodging and shucking his head to avoid the threatening tree branch. I was now so close to the bear that I could smell him. A rotting smell, almost like old barbecue that you threw out two weeks ago. I pulled the branch high, slammed it on a log next to the bear. The dry branch splintered in an ear-shattering crack and the bear finally lumbered off into the darkness.

The calm returned. Kat stopped screaming. Donnie gave a few extra barks that echoed briefly off the canyon walls, then cuddled up to Fred Briggs, as if to make sure that he was safe. My hand, still gripping the broken branch, trembled with adrenaline. I didn't feel it yet, but splinters punctured my palm like a pincushion. The fire crackled and popped in the silent dark.

"What the fuck, man!" Fred broke the hush.

"Ha! Yeah, that was pretty crazy," Kat said in a strange, high pitched voice. She laughed in an awkward way that seemed both forced and sincere at the same time.

"Fucking bold," I said, looking down at the remaining Fritos littering the dirt of our campsite. The bear clearly connected people with a food source on some level, and probably smelled the chips and snacks that we were munching on. First off, we had to get rid of that smell. "Donnie, here boy."

Donnie trotted over and made quick work of the spilled foodstuff.

"Alright, here's what I propose," I took a seat, cross-legged, turned to the two people. Donnie rested his head on my knee after finishing up his task. "Let's save the other chili for tomorrow morning, and just finish up all the food that we opened, especially that beef jerky. Just so our friend doesn't come back."

"Yeah, that's probably the best idea," Kat said. "What about the trash?"

wild.

"Normally, we would want to put it in a bear locker but there definitely aren't any of those around. We can hang it," I walked over to my pack and grabbed a stuff sack and some paracord. I collected the trash we already had, and set the sack by the fire for any of the remaining trash.

"I'm still hungry," whined Fred the diva. I tossed him the bag of jerky.

"Well, there is one more thing," Kat stood and sauntered over to her pack. "Are bears attracted to whiskey?" She pulled out a near-full bottle of Jim Bean. But she also pulled out something else. The firelight reflected off something metal, but I couldn't quite make out what it was. She slid it in her jacket pocket.

"Oh, they absolutely are," I grinned. "We have to get rid of that. It's just safe."

We fed the fire, and we passed that bottle around. Taking swigs, talking story, laughing at Fred for being such a wimp with the bear. We even poured some out in a mess kit bowl so Donnie could lap the fiery liquid with his tongue.

Nice and toasty from fire and fire, I finally asked Kat. "What's that in your pocket?" I pointed to her jacket pocket.

Her eyes went wide with surprise then subsided to a mischievous, proud grin. Like the grin Donnie had when he brought back a dead bird as a gift. She opened her jacket and pulled out a revolver, a .38 special with wood handle. She held it flat in her palm, displaying it for both of us.

"Let me see that thing," Fred moved to grab for it but Kat pulled it back.

"Not now, maybe another time I'll show you."

"Fuck you, Kat," Fred Briggs slurred jokingly as he slumped down to his resting position. I was equally curious about Kat's gun but I knew we were far too drunk to handle it. We would have time to talk about it later. Protected from the cold wilderness, in our own little glowing bubble of warmth, we finished the snacks and crawled into the tent. It was fucking freezing but the whiskey and the close quarters company kept us warm through the night.

* * * * *

I woke first, closely followed by Donnie who romped over Kat and Fred Briggs to greet me.

"Alright, man, take it easy," I whispered. I unzipped the tent, and Donnie and I went outside to pee together.

Viscous cold bit at my face, and squeezed the oxygen from my lungs. The relative warmth provided by the tent was a hard contrast from the slap in the face from the lightening terrain outside. Donnie bounded about, peeing on trees unaffected, but I could hardly move. I ended up peeing close to the entrance to the tent and forced myself to move legs and feet over to the firepit. Even though the coals were still warm from the night before, I still had to rebuild the teepee to get it started. My shaking hands and frozen fingers were barely able to flick the lighter. The heat immediately rejuvenated me. My joints loosened and the gears of my mind started to turn. Donnie sat next to me to join in the glory of the fire. The other two remained asleep, and I heard Fred's gentle snores escaping the tent.

I wrote.

> *I stand here alone,*
> *Snow and ice surrounding my feet.*
> *My warm body warms this world,*
> *Little by little.*
> *Maybe, my lone existence*
> *Will thaw this tundra to paradise.*
> *Would be faster with another next to me.*

"Ye, fire!" exclaimed Kat as she unzipped the tent. As she stepped out, felt the cold, and followed up with,

"FUCK! THIS! SHIT!" She ran over and cuddled up next to me, grabbing my arm, trying to steal my warmth. Donnie greeted Kat with a smile and wagging tail. I closed my notebook and stared into the flames with Kat's head resting on my shoulder.

Only a few minutes went by before we heard a stirring in the tent. Fred unzipped the tent and stepped out.

"NOPE!" He said as he retreated back into the tent only to come back out bundled up in his sleeping bag. He waddled over to the fire, trying to keep the sleeping bag out of the dirt and failing miserably. "I'm fucking starving."

"Chili!" Kat yelped and jumped up. She ran back to the tent and reemerged with her pack. She produced three cans of chili as she returned to the fire.

"How are we going to do this?" Fred said as he turned the can around. I responded by plunging my knife into the top of the can of chili, and cutting the top in a circle. I placed the can at the edge of the fire to warm it up.

"Do mine" Kat tossed her can my way, and Fred did the same. It wasn't long before we each sat eating out hot chili straight out of the cans. We took turns using the knife to scoop out the red beans and meat, warming our mouths and throats as it fell down to our stomach and filled the pit of our soul with warming energy. Even with the faint taste of steel, it was one of the most delicious cans of chili I had ever had. I ate most of mine then dumped the rest out on a rock so Donnie could enjoy it. The sun had now breached the tops of the canyon and started to warm the forest around us.

Bellies filled with food, we packed up camp and the trash, put out the fire, and headed out. Downhill back to the car. It felt good going downhill.

Not one of us struggled as we jaunted down toward our car. We reached the Chevelle, threw down our packs, and stretched to rest a moment before jumping in the car. Kat drove. We had barely left Zion when Kat yelled and pointed ahead.

"PIZZA! BEER!" She pulled the steering wheel toward a shanty restaurant on the side of the road. She was like a child hankering for a toy. I admit I shared her enthusiasm for a real meal.

"Alright, fucking calm down!" Fred said as we pulled into a spot, and we climbed out. We left a window open for Donnie and headed inside to demolish an extra large pepperoni and a pitcher of beer without effort. Satisfied, we grabbed some gas at the stop before hitting the road again.

those fucking deer.

Back on the road, I thought about the wild we had left. The ecosystem and each organism had its own place in that world. I wrote.

> *My trunk is wrinkled but strong with years passed. My branches are crooked but support birds and their nests. My leaves fall every year but during the spring they give shade to rabbits and forest dwellers. I stand next to my brothers, sisters, family all. The breeze rolls through, and we together dance.*
>
> *But those fucking deer.*
>
> *We drop our Children acorns on the forest floor. Some grow into saplings, young and green. We smile down at those that will provide the landscape far after we have passed.*

Until those fucking deer.

Insatiable appetites devour our young. We stand by, helpless as they trod on our Toddler saplings, chomp down on our Infant acorns. Their black hooves and gnashing teeth destroy our future.

Those fucking deer.

Their numbers overwhelm us. We plant more acorns, more deer appear. As the older trees die off, the forest Family thins. More and more sunlight is shed on the forest floor.

Those fucking deer.

Until one day. Our savior. A man, a human, and his son. We cheer and celebrate as the Father and Son creep between us with stealth, sneaking up on the enemy deer. We hide the pair with our trunks and use our branches to shade their eyes from the glare of the sun. Our smiles are reflected in the glint of their boomsticks . CRACK! The silence is broken and a deer falls and we all cheer with glee. They did not take all the deer. Just a few. Just enough so our young can grow. Those young grow old, and that Boy hunter now walks through us, protecting us.

Fuck those deer.

amigos nuevos.

It was clear: we had no destination. But we drove. We drove and drove. We switched off driving, played music loud, rolled and smoked cigarettes, stopped to pee and fill gas and coffee and snacks. We probably smelled like grime and sweat but no matter. Funny how others can't smell your musk if their musk matches yours. We had been passing signs for the Grand Canyon all day, and it called to us. It was late afternoon when we reached the turnoff to the park.

"What do you guys think?" Fred Briggs was driving at the time, and he pulled off to the side of the road at a turn off.

"Yeah, I'm down." I said. I was ready for a place to stretch and sleep. I looked in the back and Kat and Donnie were both asleep, supporting each other in an awkward but comforting position. I couldn't help but smile.

Fred Briggs pulled into the national park.

As we drove along the southern rim, I peered down into the great crevasse. This park was typically packed full of tourists but it didn't seem too bad today. In that moment, I remembered why people from around the world came to this mecca. The sun was setting behind us and the shadow of the rim created a distinct line, a barrier between the warmth of day and the cold of night.

Before picking a campsite, we stopped off to enjoy the sunset. We chose a spot away from the selfie-taking tourists. We hopped the guardrail and sat with our feet dangling in the Grand Canyon, Donnie laid down next to us. We watched the shadows lengthen, darken, and the sky change hues. We sat in silence as the arid heat cooled to a more comfortable crisp.

Fortunately, we had a few choices for campsites, we chose one that was fairly isolated. We stopped by the general store to grab some hot dogs, buns, water, beer, and a few bundles of firewood before finding our campsite.

Darkness was spreading across the park as we pulled into the parking spot next to our site. Kat and Fred set up the tent, and I started building the fire in the firepit barbeque in the center of our camp. Donnie supervised. Before long, we had a steady fire going, and we each pulled up a log to sit on. Kat used a stick to turn the hot dogs. Fred stared, entranced by the fire, absentmindedly scratching Donnie's neckfur. I busied myself rolling a slew of cigarettes. We were quiet. In the distance, we heard voices in Spanish. We heard drums beating, some kind of stringed instrument, and singing. Kat perked up, lifting an ear to the music.

"Watch those hot dogs, Leo. I'll be back."

"Wait, Kat, I'm coming, too." I didn't want to let her venture into the darkness to see some strangers alone.

"So I guess I'll watch the god damn hot dogs then," Fred Briggs complained sarcastically. "Donnie won't leave me though, right buddy?" We ignored him and walked toward the voices.

As Kat and I walked, we saw some campfires in scattered throughout the camping area. Glowing bubbles of light flickered and illuminated people's faces. We eventually found the source of the music. Four people, two men and two women, were passing around an enormous jug of tequila, laughing, and talking loudly in Spanish. My Spanish was certainly limited. Kat, fortunately, picked up my slack.

"Buenos noches, amigos! Que pasan?"

amigos nuevos.

"Oi!!!!" The group all shouted in unison. One of the girls had her legs crossed and rested a djembe drum in her lap, and one of the guys had a little travel-sized guitar. Kat proceeded to talk with them, and I just stood there and grinned like an idiot. I did like being in that group, though. Their drunkenness made me comfortable. After some conversation, they all stood up. Kat had invited them to join us. They followed us back to our campfire.

"Hola, mi llamo es Carina," the girl carrying the drum grabbed my arm to catch my attention.

"Hi, Carina. Mi llamo es Leo. Como esta, err...tonight?" I tried to use my best Spanish and failed miserably. Carina laughed. Kat turned around and interrupted. "Disculpen mi amigo. Es un cerebro de burro." I didn't understand what she said, but I knew it was something negative. Carina turned back to her friends.

Donnie was stretched out in the dirt near the fire and Fred Briggs was enjoying a hot dog and a beer when our crew finally reached the campsite. He perked up, stood, and offered a big smile and warm embrace for all of them. Fred always was hospitable. He grabbed beers and handed them out to everyone.

Since there was a language barrier , Kat took the lead in bridging the gap. She facilitated introductions, and we all took a toast of tequila at our newfound friendship. Donnie welcomed them too, and slumped down, half leaning on Carina's lap. She spoiled him with affection. We all ate hot dogs with our beer and tequila.

Eventually, Kat brought out her ukulele and I dug out my mouth harp from my backpack. She started playing some standard chords, and I knew enough by ear to play along. Carina adjusted Donnie off of her so she could beat her djembe. The guy with the guitar started plucking and playing a beautiful single note walking melody while simultaneously trying to find the key that Kat was playing in. He found it, and started strumming a harmonic chord pairing to Kat's. Luckily, Kat picked a key that I would match my harmonica, and I blew it rhythmically to match the simple beat that our group created. Those without instruments used their knees as percussion instruments until we crescendoed into a point where they stood up and danced, occasionally stopping to sloppily pour tequila and beer into open mouths. Fred danced with Carina. I was happy to see him interacting with a girl. He hadn't gotten to close to anyone since Nicole left. Well, I guess Kat, too. But Kat was different.

Kat began to sing:

> *"Ain't got much money,*

amigos nuevos.

Ain't got much time.
I spend all my days,
Paying back the banker's dime.
Good thing they gave me
These shoes on my feet.
Might be kinda weird,
but we'll still dance off-beat!
Feet all beat, from dancing off beat
Must sit to rest, just gettin' too old
So I sit next to my baby, this man so sweet
Then I find him with his new babe, a guy named Harold
I cry all night,
Because I liked what I had.
But can't help but laugh
Because Harold now has my crabs!
Thanks be to the gods!
Who's feelin' kinda odd?
Feelin' kinda odd!
Thanks be to the gods!"

We sang and laughed and drank and danced and fell and drank.

Suddenly another figure appeared in our circle. A middle-aged woman with a motherly look about her interrupted us with a furrowed brow and stern tone.

"Excuse me, I'm sorry to interrupt your band but it's one in the morning. My family is trying to sleep. Thank you." She left us in silence.

A few moments went by. Then, Kat leaned in, and in a loud whisper, said, "She thinks we're a band!"

Fred and I burst into a roar of laughter. Kat repeated what she said to our friends, and they joined us in our laughter. We quieted down, as we were all tired and drunk at that point We embraced each other and said our farewells. It was as if we were saying goodbye to long time friends. We waved and watched them walk down the road back to their camp. Just before they disappeared into the darkness, Carina came running back. She went up to Fred, grabbed his face, pulled it down to hers and gave him a kiss. She pulled back and pulled a beard hair off her tongue. They both laughed.

"Adiós, Fred!"

"Adiós, Carina." And she ran off to catch up to her party.

We slept well that night.

edge.

I woke up early, before Leo and Kat. When I stirred, Donnie crawled over the other two to lick my face. He and I got up and walked outside into the biting cold. Donnie pissed on a tree, and I chose a tree next to him. *No hangover today, or at least not yet. Today, I feel pretty great.* I thought that tequila was a sure road to a painful morning, but I seemed alright. I stirred the embers of last night's fire, still warm. I knelt down on one knee and blew on it, breathing life into it, and I saw the coals glow orange, then fade back to the black-gray. I looked up through the evergreens towering over our camp, and saw the sky was starting to get lighter. Sunrise at the Grand Canyon? Yes, sir. I walked back to the tent to wake the others. Leo was snoring like a fucking bear, and Kat was cuddled up in her sleeping bag. I shook the tent to wake them.

"Oi! Gypsies!" I said when they didn't move. "Sun's arising! Let's go."

"Go fuck yourself, then kill yourself," Kat said quietly. She curled up deeper in her sleeping bag.

Leo started to sit up, then was pulled back down to the comfort of his own sleeping bag. "Nope." He drifted back to sleep.

Alright, I tried. I opened my car door, letting Donnie jump into the passenger seat. We drove down the road, looking for a place to watch the sun rise.

We came to sign reading Yaki Point with an arrow pointing left.

"What do ya think, Dontron 3000?" Donnie sat up with an excited look on his face. I opened his window so he could stick his head out.

We drove to this Yaki Point, and pulled into a parking spot. There were a few other cars there, and a number of people bundled up in sweatshirts and jackets. We took the short walk to the edge of the canyon. I was tempted to hop the guardrail, but instead, grabbed an open bench with Donnie at my feet. We probably had about 20 minutes before the sun peaked over the eastern horizon.

While waiting, I watched the tourists roaming around the lookout. One family with Southern accents leaned against the railing. A few kids ran around, yelling and playing. The dad drank from some kind of silver can, either an energy drink or a beer. He polished it off, set it at the bottom of the rail then kicked it into the canyon. Asshole. A group of younger folks, probably college kids, were clad in beanies and jackets and carried blankets to stay warm. I noticed that they reeked of alcohol as they passed, and at least two of them appeared drunk.

"I'm going to yack…" one of the guys said, then fake-puked over the railing into the canyon.

"The Grandest of Pukes!!" one of the girls said, a little too loudly.

Their rowdiness was a sharp contrast from the serenity of the morning, and I turned back to the canyon to prepare for the sunrise. I thought about the friends we made last night. The language barrier was a hurdle but words weren't necessary for the experience we had. And that experience. It was so different from what I was used to. Back home Santa Labre, I talked to the same people, listened to the same music, ate the same food. It was safe. When Kat ventured out into the darkness to meet the loud strangers, I didn't quite get it. I thought she was ruining a perfectly fine evening between three friends and our pup. I had no idea that bringing these new people into our circle could be so uplifting. We danced and sang. I never danced, sang. Not like that. And Carina. She was a beautiful girl from Mexico, who could barely speak a lick of English. If Kat didn't take a chance to meet those people, I would have never met her. Sure, I would probably never see Carina again. But did that make my short time with her any less significant? In a way, it made it more significant. We all enjoyed each other's company, and, knowing it was temporary, we just enjoyed the moment. The fleeting moment allowed us to enjoy it to its full extent. It was a moment I would not soon forget. And to think that moment would have never happened, had we not taken this spontaneous, wandering trip into the desert.

I looked east just as the sun was peeking over the horizon. I scratched Donnie's neck, and he sat up. I watched the colors change and the light start to illuminate the layered stone walls of the Grand Canyon.

I thought to myself. *Those two silly gypsies. They are missing out on this. And for what? Just for the warmth and comfort of their fucking sleeping bags? It's not even that cold. They don't even know what they're missing.*

* * * * *

edge.

Donnie and I returned to the still campsite.. There was plenty of heat in the coals to restart the fireso I relit the fire with a piece of cardboard . I added a couple logs and sat by the fire, Donnie at my feet, until our two friends awoke. Kat came out first, looking groggy, and Leo followed her. Kat brought her sleeping bag out, and took a seat by the fire. Leo went straight to the edge of the campsite behind the tent, and I heard him puking. I was surprised I wasn't hungover at all. I threw him a water bottle when he joined us around the fire.

"What's the plan?" I posed to the dying folk.

"Let's head west," Kat murmured.

"West, ey? Want to head home?" I was a little disappointed, but it was probably wise given our abrupt departure from Santa Labre.

"I'm down. I should be back at the docks on Monday. Just give me 20 minutes and I'll be road ready." I said getting up. I took a gulp of water leaned over and drenched my hair in the freezing liquid.

I did most of the packing up as the other two recovered, with Kat attempting to help fold the tent. We were in the car and out of there in the promised 20 minutes. I drove, Kat as co-pilot and Leo asleep in the back with Donnie.

We drove through the desert in the general direction of Santa Labre. And I fucking drove. Those long, straight roads allowed the speedometer to stay right around 100 miles per hour for long stretches. Kat cracked her window and smoked a rolled cigarette, leaving a thin trail of smoke all through that god damn desert.

Along the way, we saw a sign:

JOSHUA TREE NATIONAL PARK

97 miles

Kat was awake but Leo and Donnie were both fast asleep.

"OK. I'm just putting this out there," Kat said as she put her cashed cigarette in an empty beer bottle. She then reached into her jacket pocket, and produced a sandwich bag packed with mushrooms. Stems and caps bulged the plastic baggy as if trying to escape the invisible force field. Kat set the baggy on the dashboard, just above the radio.

At first I said nothing. I hardly even looked at the baggy. My eyes were glued to the road. I was never one for psychedelics in large amounts. But I thought about our road trip so far. I handled myself just fine in Vegas. Sure, we were hammered but the shrooms didn't seem to affect

Kat and Leo too much. They seemed to have a good time. I thought about the bear experience in Zion. I was scared shitless, for sure, but I was already excited to tell that story when we got back home. I thought about our friends around the campfire, and wondered if they would try this funky fungus. Then, I thought about the sunrise at the Grand Canyon rim. I thought about the wonderment and joy I got from experiencing something new. I had avoided psyche drugs for what? Was I scared of what would happen? Or was I scared because they would show me a part of myself that I had been suppressing? I mulled these questions around my mind, and realized my curiosity was overwhelming. I couldn't not try them. I couldn't afford to miss out.

"Joshua Tree?" I said after a long silence.

"Ye." Kat responded.

I floored the Chevelle, and we zoomed through the desert toward something new.

dive.

We pulled down the 177 toward Joshua Tree, headed slightly south and more west. I leaned forward when Fred Briggs pushed the Chevelle further and further into triple digits. From the backseat, I was just an observer to that Tarantino-esque scene in the front seat. Looked left, saw Fred Briggs' eyes glued to the asphalt, intensity plastered on his face. His hands and arms were loose though, one hand gripping the steering wheel, the other the shifter. I looked right. Contrasting Fred Briggs' stoic expression, Kat had a maniacal grin on her face, and was drumming on the dash. She stuck her head out into the hot, dry world outside.

"FUCK YOOOOOOOOUUUU!!" Her rebellious cry ricocheted off the faraway mountains; they cringed a bit at the sound of her voice. I noticed a sizeable baggy of stems and caps plumped on the dash. Just as it was about to be blown out the window during Kat's outcry, her hand snatched the baggy and it was stuffed safely in her denim jacket pocket. I leaned back. Donnie, tongue lolling, licked my face and seemed to sense the excitement from the roar of the car engine. I threw an arm around his thick neck.

"This is it, buddy. This is how we die." He responded by jumping on my lap and tasting my face with his big, stupid tongue.

We continued at those blitzing speeds for half an hour or so before Kat yelled something over the growling engine and ferocious wind.

In a way that only a refined woman trained in the Cotillion art of grace and proper etiquette, Kat screamed, "I GOTTA FUCKIN' PEE!!!!"

"Hold on," Fred Briggs said way too quietly. I grabbed a hold of Donnie just as Fred slammed on the brakes, pulled the emergency brake, and we slid sideways to until we were facing the wrong way on the side of the road. That crazy fuck cracked a little smile. Kat popped the door open, and went to the back of the car to pop a squat and relieve herself like a lady. Fred Briggs and I stayed in the car with Donnie and discussed our next move.

"Thought: maybe we shouldn't do these drugs in a national park. Tourists, rangers, and glampers seem non-ideal, ya know?" I said.

"Yeah, I agree," he responded. He leaned over and opened the glove box. He pushed aside the car registration and receipts and condoms before producing a Thomas Guide.

"Who the fuck has a Thomas Guide?" I said to the empty air as Fred Briggs thumbed through the pages of maps and maps and maps. He stopped on one page, tracing a road with his finger. Kat jumped back in the car, just as he stopped on a darker streak in the center of the lighter patch of the map.

"Wiregrass Canyon." He pushed the tattered book of directions toward Donnie and me in the back. The destination looked tiny in the middle of the desert but it did look nearby. Kat took the book and found the spot.

"Let's do it," I said.

"Sure, I'm down." Kat tossed the book on the floor and sat back in her seat. "Andiamo."

Without a word, Fred fired up the Chevelle, floored the sedan in reverse, then jerked the car and its inhabitants in a violent J-turn before speeding down the road.

dive.

We drove for about 45 minutes before Kat picked up the Thomas Guide to make sure we didn't miss the turn-off. Fred Briggs finally slowed down at a dirt road. The car rattled over a cattle grate as we headed down the road through the increasingly-hilly landscape. We turned a corner and found a stream cutting through the desert. The water crossed our path, muddying the road, making it impassible to our rear-wheel-drive muscle car. We stopped and got out to look at our options.

We had been standing there for no more than five minutes before we heard a low grumble, a mechanical roar, a metallic clanking. From the other side of the stream, a bulldozer lumbered around a knoll, and came upon our crew.

"You kids lost?" The driver of the giant piece of machinery yelled down at us from his high perch, a friendly grin on his sunburnt face.

"Yeah, we are trying to get to Wiregrass Canyon for a hike," Kat spoke for us.

"Way out there, what for?"

"We've heard good things."

"Well, you ain't getting across in that beauty you got there. How about I flatten this stream a bit for ya?"

"Wow, that would be amazing! You sure?"

"Yeah, young lady! I need to keep up the maintenance on this road, anyway."

"Much appreciated! You're a hero!" Kat bounded back to the car, and we followed. We watched the man and his metal beast flatten the stream, dumping a huge mound of dirt on the river before stomping it flat with their tank treads.

He crossed the stream and looked down at us from his high seat. "Make sure you get a little speed as you're going across, and you'll be fine. Don't get too crazy, son," he added as he saw Fred's grin from behind the wheel.

"Thanks again!" Kat leaned out the window and waved at the man of construction and salvation. We made it across with no problems at all, and continued lumbering down the dirt road toward this place called Wiregrass, somewhere in this Southwest desert.

We saw a sign.

Wiregrass Trail

Pulled over. The three of us got out to stretch our legs, and Donnie was eager to explore this new place. I walked over to the sign to survey what lay ahead of us. The trail immediately dove down into a rocky crevasse. The steep ravine looked like a snake that cut into the mostly flat landscape. Almost underground.

I turned back to the crew. Fred Briggs was stretched out on the dirt road, photosynthesizing in the warm sunlight. He was completely still, aside from his right hand, which was scratching Donnie behind the ears. Kat was fiddling with something on the trunk of the Chevelle, so I walked over to check out what she was doing.

"You see this place?" I put my hand on her shoulder and looked around, scanning the faraway ridgeline of the mountains. "Crazy."

"What? Yeah, nuts." She didn't even look up. She had dumped all of the dried brown mushrooms on the trunk of the car, and was now splitting them into three equal piles.

"We really doing this?"

She stopped and smiled at me. Picked up a pile, grabbed my shirt, and emptied the handful into my front shirt pocket. "You decide." Then she walked over to Fred Briggs and placed his share in the same spot. She put her share in the front pocket of her denim jacket. The trunk now clear, she opened it and grabbed three beers and the bottle of Jack Daniels. Kat and I shared the open trunk as a bench, and Fred ambled over. We shared a few swigs of the whiskey, and cracked open the beers.

"So, when do we start?" Fred Briggs poked at a cap in his palm.

"Now," Kat took a couple caps and a stem and threw them down the hatch, chased by beer. She grabbed her backpack, threw in a big water bottle, and gave bottles to Fred and me.

"Andiamo," she said as she headed off down toward the trailhead.

Fred Briggs tossed his single cap down, took a swig of beer, took a few steps toward the trailhead, stopped, then grabbed about half a dozen more pieces. He crumpled his face as he tried to drown the terrible taste with alcohol.

Fred Briggs looked back at me. "If you're going get wet, might as well go swimming." A smile.

I leashed Donnie, grabbed my beer and water bottle, and slammed the Chevelle trunk closed. I pulled a couple pieces out of my front pocket.

"Well, here we go." I looked at Donnie. He looked at me, encouraging me to do it. I tossed them down and

dive.

followed Kat and Fred Briggs' example and chased it with beer. Down we went into the ravine.

To this point in life, I had not tried many hallucinogens. At the beginning of this day, I hadn't even thought about hallucinogens, much less expect that I would be partaking in them. I wasn't conscious of my depression. I didn't know the turmoil that was now tumbling in my subconscious washing machine. Because I didn't know, I wasn't looking for a cure, wasn't aware a cure was needed, and didn't know a cure existed. But I somehow knew. I woke up, I left that bar in Santa Labre, I left my home years ago, and I knew. I was walking along a road that led to this moment. I was ready.

The four of us walked together for a while, silent. Our footsteps barely made any sound, shuffling through the soft, light-colored dirt on the bottom of the winding ravine. We could hear the sound of our breathing bouncing off the stonewalls. In some places, the canyon was narrow enough to touch both rock walls with outstretched arms. In other places, the walls opened up to cathedral-like openings wide enough to fit a semi-truck. I wasn't feeling much, just captivated by the layered rocks walls, the rock pillars rising from the canyon floor, the tiny rocks beneath our feet. We paused in one of the cathedrals near the wall to rest in the shade.

We drank from our water bottles, still silent, but a calm peace exuded from us. Suddenly, a raven flapped through the canyon, the first sign of life we had seen. Its wings beat the air violently, and the sound was like a series of explosions that broke the quiet. It was incredible. Fred unhooked Donnie's leash to let him run free as we continued down the path. I was in front, Fred Briggs and Donnie in the rear, and Kat between us as we walked single file down a narrow part of the ravine. Suddenly, a voice.

"I think I'm going to stay here for a bit, I'll catch up." It was Fred Briggs. Kat and I said nothing as we continued forward but we heard Donnie's panting grow quieter as we walked further away. Donnie stayed with Fred. In a cathedral larger than any we had seen thus far, Kat whispered to me.

"I like this place." Kat in awe.

I stopped, looked around, and continued on. After a few minutes, I realized could not hear Kat nor Fred nor Donnie behind me. I rested for a moment in the shade to take in my surroundings. There was a small cave perched about 20 feet above my head with a fairly easy climb up the rock face. Putting my water bottle and empty beer

dive.

bottle on the ground, I headed up the rock face to a ledge sheltered by an overhang. I pulled myself up and sat cross-legged on the ledge. I dipped my fingers in the soft dirt, lifting it up to watch it fall through my fingers to return its brethren back to the ground. I pulled out a ciga- rette I had rolled, lit, and inhaled. That was the jumpstart that my consciousness was waiting for.

Not a sudden drop into dimensional abyss. A cold wa- ter wade, calm waves rising against your skin as steps are taken toward the inevitable drop. A look left. Some friends are ahead, slightly deeper than you. You see the water level lapping slightly higher on their breast than yours. You can see them as a warning, a glimpse into your own future that is only steps away. You look right. You see other friends, slightly behind. You want to reach out to them. Some are scared. Some excited. You want to reach out and tell them, "It will be alright."

But your words are trapped. The water level rises above your mouth. In those few seconds, the water is high enough to cover your mouth, but not high enough to cov- er your nostrils. A few seconds of agonizing terror. Can't turn back. Can't help or be helped. On a journey with a set deadline, a required completion. Fear envelopes.

The water rises still. Nostrils now covered. Panic. On

the brink of an unknown world, you grasp desperately for the reality you just left. Lungs burn as you struggle to hold on to the last breath saved from the world you once knew. Power of will drives you on but nature pushes you ever forward. The last breath explodes out as you watch your stored reality rise up as bubbles. The bubbles of reality rush to join the rest of the reality. You wonder if those bubbles will tell the world of the piece they are missing. The panic that was you now transforms to a calm acceptance. You take a deep breath in, filling your body with the new world, expecting catastrophe.

It is not the next world that should be feared but the last breath that you hold onto. That last breath that you desperately keep is what brings you pain. The fear of change can be stronger than the pain of not. That last breath of reality burns fire in lungs, but a fire we know.

A fire we know burns us no less.

I don't want to give all credit to the drugs. It was the environment, the time of day, the days leading up to that point, my mood, the music I heard at that time, the people I was with. The people I was with. Goddamn I love these people.

* * * * *

dive.

The dragons were starting to subside from the farrows of our minds. We sought shelter from the heat at the foot of a large outcropping of slate rock. We spread a blanket at the corner where the sand met the foot of the rock. We said nothing. Donnie laid his head in Kat's lap.

"Oh, excuse us!"

A foreign voice rang out, echoing off the rock face behind us and into our heads. It shook us out of our trance but I welcomed the new presence. A man and his two sons had rounded the corner and were now walking in front of us, parallel to the rock wall. Donnie perked up, tail wagging. The trio carried a slew of climbing equipment: ropes, harnesses, carabiners, chalk bags. The eldest boy looked to be about twelve, and the other was about three years his younger. The man bore an old, faded Broncos hat and a dark gray-speckled. His eyes were friendly.

"Don't mind us, we will be out of your way," the dad offered.

"Let us know if we are in your way," I counter offered. "We can move, the wall can't." I placed a smile on face to appear friendly. Too much smile. I felt like a psycho so I pulled it back. Now I bore a strange half smile so I closed my lips. This inner struggle resulted in two things: an odd, pursed-lip smile and a realization that the mushrooms were still very much pulling at the strings of my mind.

"Much appreciated, young man, but the area is for everyone to share," he said amiably. I appreciated the sentiment. I looked over to our group and noticed that Fred Briggs had antlers and Kat's tattoos had escaped her arms and were now dancing on the ground in front of her. We were in no shape to move locations.

The trio moved up about 20 feet to our left so we watched them set up their harnesses as the dad briefed them on their upcoming challenge. The wall, easily exceeding 40 feet tall, reached straight up skyward from our side but there was a back way that made the top much more accessible without climbing rigs. Taking this easy way up, the dad set the anchor between two slabs of slate. Tested it. Solid. He lowered the now-anchored rope to his sons below. He hiked down the backside of the rock, the easy way.

Once at the bottom, he gave the rope a quick sharp tug. "It's ready." He turned to his sons. "You ready, Noah?"

Noah was the younger one. A brown haired, bright-eyed youngster, he bounded toward the rope and the monolith. His harness was tight on his legs and waist but his dad still checked it. Noah bore red and gray climbing shoes with the typical pointed toe and extreme arch designed for climbing. Noah's dad took his hat and hooked it on a carabiner on his belt loop. That's when I noticed a small device curling out of Noah's ear. It was a common device for elderly people but it looked out of place on a young boy. And by the size and complexity of the device, I knew that Noah must be near-deaf at best. Noah clipped his harness to the rope while Dad set himself up as ground anchor of the operation. I looked up and saw the tiny hook lodged in the rock and imagined how it would be used as a pulley. I was scared for Noah.

He was tiny but he appeared even smaller next to the stone monolith. It cast its shadow over him. The little warrior laid a single hand on the monolith as it glared down upon him. Then he placed another hand. Then a foot, then another. Six feet off the ground.

"Dad, I think I'm stuck."

The monolith grinned.

"OK, that's fine Noah. I can lower you down right now. Just take one more look for a way up."

Noah did. He looked and found. Left hand grasped edge. He pulled himself further. Fifteen feet off the ground.

"OK, Dad! I want to come down." Noah's little fingers clung to the rock face.

"Are you ok, Noah?"

"Yeah, I think I'm just stuck."

The monolith chuckled.

"OK, you're doing great son. Just take one more look."

Noah did. Craning his neck back, eyes scanning for a route, a lip, a grip. Gaze fell upon and locked on a crack. Fingers sought and found. Noah continued up.

"I can see all of Joshua Tree, Dad!" Noah had found a stable ledge and was now looking out toward the desert and the world behind him. Twenty-five feet up. The monolith grew jealous of this small creature that was now sharing its grand view.

"I know, Noah! Great job, son!" The father beamed with pride, eyes glistening, grin peaking from his beard. He held the anchor strong.

The other son, now entranced by his brother's progress, spoke to his father.

"Look at him, Dad! Noah's doing it!" He pointed upward and hopped around his dad. "You said he probably wouldn't be able to make it pass ten feet! What are you going to do if he makes it?"

"I...I don't know, Adrian. Just...I don't know." The father's voice faltered momentarily. The deep that I saw between sons and father put a lump in my throat. A tear leaked from the corner of my eye as Noah continued up.

"You fucking softie," Kat whispered as she tugged at my pant leg. I smiled and the lump subsided.

Noah, now well over thirty feet up, was on a roll. Adrian and father yelled instructions up to Noah, but in vain. The wind and distance, combined with Noah's auditory shortcomings, made communication impossible. The shouts from below fell short and drifted off into the warm desert breeze. Noah was on his own.

He climbed, his confidence solidifying. The monolith trembled, sensing its imminent defeat.

Finally, Noah slapped the steel anchor jutting out from the rock, a mile above the Earth.

"AHHHWHHHOOOO!!!!" The boy howled in triumph. The monolith shrunk, cowering in the shadow of this young warrior. The dad wiped a tear away before losing a shout of his own.

"YEAH, NOAH!!!"

"You did it!" Adrian shouted.

The lump I had been fighting off now pushed its way up to my eyes, spilling out over my eyelids and dribbling down my cheek. I wiped it away quickly.

"How fucking intense was that?" Fred said. I had forgotten he was there. I realized I was now standing. I looked down at Fred spooning with Donnie on our little blanket. Kat said nothing, but I saw what looked like a glisten in her eye. She turned away and sniffed and I said nothing.

Noah's father carefully slacked the rope, allowing Noah to scramble down the rock face. "Trust the rope, lean back, buddy. Push off with your feet." The father's words now reminded Noah and he squared off and re-pelled down the rock wall.

Finally, Noah's climbing shoes reached the dirt. Adrian ran over and high-fived his brother. The dad picked him up with a full embrace. The monolith nodded its respect.

I found myself walking toward Noah and his sup-port crew. I held out a closed fist, offering Noah knuck-les. I saw his eyes light up with the excitement of a stranger's approval but he quickly hid it in a confident, act-like-you-have-been-there smile.

"That was incredible, man." It was all the lump in my throat would allow me to muster. Noah beamed, meeting my knuckles with his own.

"Thank you."

* * * * *

I still think about Noah. I imagine him going back to school and showing his friends his scrapes and bruises from the climb. I imagine the disapproving look he got from other judgmental parents who eliminate risk, regardless of the benefit. I imagined how hard it must have been growing up deaf, how many days he must have come home crying from teasing and bullying. Kids can be cruel.

Talking about Noah's triumph still makes me choked up to this day. But I don't cry. I don't cry, nor do I ever, because I'm a fucking man.

Wherever you are, Noah, I hope I can climb like you someday.

digest.

Back in Santa Labre.

It's not that I was depressed going into the road trip. Fred wasn't depressed. Kat sure as hell wasn't depressed. But for me, that trip to the desert and back felt like a grand exhalation. Like I was holding my breath for so long that I forgot I was holding my breath. My return to Santa Labre, from the very moment that we crested the ridge into the city nestled in the valley, was a relief.

But if I had forgotten my breath was held, then Fred Briggs had never breathed fresh air in his life. I came home from the docks the next day to see a changed man. Backpacking magazines strewn on the coffee table and a hunched-over Fred scanning travel websites or online outdoor gear stores.

I jabbed this new man. "What is up, Mr. Adventure?"

In response, a middle finger rose from his sleeve as he lifted his arm, greeting me without words. His eyes smiled over the top of his laptop, front-lit by the bluish light.

"You been to Big Sur, Leo?"

"No. I was planning on going there next before my Jeep broke down in this town." A pang in my gut. I was glad Fred Briggs continued. A welcome distraction.

"Let's do it next weekend! I can't believe I've lived here my whole life and I haven't been there. What a fuckin' waste…"

The man was hooked.

Our conversations no longer revolved around the carrying-on of everyday life, but by plans for future trips. Like a new convert, Fred was the catalyst to these discussions, pushed forward by a fevered, newfound enthusiasm.

The now-happy-go-lucky Fred Briggs just laughed, even when Donnie got out of the yard once again.

"You seen Dontron 3000 today?" I asked him, striding around the house. I called out to the hidden shepherd.

"Yeah, haven't seen him for a while," Fred sipped his beer. "That garbage dog's a wanderer, he'll be alright." He barely paused before returning to his Outdoor magazine.

"What about Yosemite?"

"I love that place," I answered as Kat walked in the door and plopped on the couch.

"Little touristy for you, isn't it, Leo?" She said.

"On the valley floor, sure. But there are some beautiful spots on the north end that are away from the crowds. Look up Ten Lakes, Fred Briggs."

Without a response, Fred dove back into his laptop, typing with fury. Kat leaned forward, stared at him with a furrowed brow, then shot me a smile. I shrugged my shoulders and returned the smile.

The new energy in the group was refreshing to me. *Iyashi*, as my grandpa would say. As I sat on that couch, I reassessed my goals. I was always pushing forward, always pushing to see more. But the past few months had been easier because I could lean on these new friends. This last trip to the desert was one of the best trips I could remember although I had been to most of those places before. Was it the contrast between monotony of the job and the exuberance of the road? Or was the experience itself enriched by these other fools? I imagined what it would be like to make Santa Labre my home base. Home. For the first time, that thought did not terrify me.

adios.

A warm spring night in Santa Labre. Fred Briggs was out at the bars, celebrating one of his shopworker's birthdays. Probably enjoying a bit of beer or tequila or cocaine. Kat and I were both hungover from a previous night of debauchery, and stayed in for the night. The two of us sickly people melted into the couch while sharing a spliff. Pulp Fiction played on TV, and I was being sucked into the world of Marcellus Wallace and Vincent Vega in Tarantino's flick. Turning to Kat, I noticed that she was facing the TV but was not watching at all. She was in a trance, staring about 6 inches above the screen with her hand suspended in the air holding the spliff.

I cleared my throat to gently nudge her out of her waking coma. She blinked twice, looked at the spliff, and took a long draw.

Smoke cascaded from her mouth as she spoke.

"Where's Fred, again?"

"Shit if I know. Downtown somewhere."

She jutted her hand out, offering the burning-tipped cone to me. I plucked it from her hand. The silence was filled with unspoken thoughts and smoke. The comfortable bliss allowed us to deal with thoughts and silence without stress. The bliss lulled me to sleep.

I woke up, still glued to Kat's couch. She was nowhere to be seen so I assumed she was asleep in her room. Some infomercial about magical cleaning solution was playing on the TV, and I turned it off. Kat's wall clock read 7:47 AM. I looked around and didn't see Fred Briggs. I thought he would have to come over to Kat's place. Maybe he found a cute young lady to spend some quality time with. Maybe he was still partying now. Probably, he was asleep back at our apartment. I gathered my things and headed for the door. Out of the corner of my eye, a still-full shot of liquid caught my attention. I turned back, grabbed it, and threw it down. I had a few blocks to walk.

It was a brisk morning, and the cool air was refreshing. I fitted my cheap Ray-Ban knockoffs to my face to conceal my bloodshot eyes, and began the stroll to Fred Briggs' place on the other side of downtown. It was early as I trudged down Higuera as people were just beginning to start their Sunday morning. A homeless man was feeding his dog some leftover breakfast burrito. His canine friend was sharing the bench with him and they both seemed content in their world at that moment. He laughed as the dog scarfed down bacon and eggs and tortilla. As I got closer, I saw a cardboard sign leaning against their bench.

"TODAY IS THE DAY OF THE REST OF YOUR LIFE. SMILE"

I chuckled inwardly. He was clearly referencing the cliché phrase, "Today is the FIRST day of the rest of your life." I knew what he meant. It was a charming mistake that lent the sign character. I imagined him gathering supplies for the sign, preparing to convey a worthwhile message. I imagined him remembering this phrase and, in an excited fervor, wrote the message as quickly as possible. I imagined him realizing the error in his message, and shrugging his shoulders. He probably showed his dog the sign, and I am sure the dog supported the man's disjointed creative attempt at spreading good will. It's the intent behind, not the words themselves.

There was a small cup with some change next to his sign, and I threw the contents of my pocket into it.

I went into a Black Horse Coffee, and grabbed a small cup of black and a poppy seed muffin. The caffeine and food now accompanied me on my journey home.

I arrived with high spirits. The caffeine complemented the whiskey I took in at Kat's, and the combination of the homeless man, the happy puppy, and the encouraging sign made for great start to the day. I tossed my garbage from my breakfast toward the trashcan in the corner and walked into the living room. I poked my head down the hall, saw Fred Briggs' door was open, and peeked in. No one. After grabbing my black leather notebook, I turned on the stereo on in the living room, and sank into the couch. Jimi Hendrix blues wafted through the room, and I leaned back, closed my eyes, and absorbed the building, releasing, writhing, turning rifts for a few moments. Riding the high, I watched my wrist twist and dance with the black pen on the clean page. I wrote.

> *As the tips of my boots reached the edge of the plank, I began to recall the life that I led. Living in the moment was my goal, and that goal I reached. I glanced back at the swashbucklers behind me, then to the swirling depths below. Both I learned to love and fear. Both were dangerous, but I could not live without either. Regardless, I hadn't entered into this life to be safe.*
>
> *Amid rowdy shouts and rum-slurred yells, I*

*couldn't help but think that I was being released
from the arms of a loved one into the embrace of
another.*

A call from Kat. The phone rang a few times while I
finished my train of thought, but I grabbed it in time.

"What's up, Kat?"

Silence for a second, then I heard her breathe out
slowly.

"Fred Briggs is dead."

"What?" I must have misheard. "How? What happened? That's impossible..." Grabbing smoke.

More silence on her end.

"Kat? Kat!...I'm coming over." Dial tone.

Little Wing was still playing as I ran out of the house.
Jumped on my motorcycle. Flipped the ignition, squeezed
gas. Zoomed down the street. Mind racing. Ran stop signs
and a red light. Two and a half minutes later, I pulled
onto Kat's street. Cop car parked out front. Hopped off
my bike. Jumped stairs upward to Kat's number 22. I
wasn't sure what to expect as I reached Kat's open door.

Inside, Kat sat straight up on her couch, and she

actually shot me a smile as I entered. I wish I could have said her gesture gave me relief. Two cops were standing near her, and they turned to me. One cop immediately looked to the floor. The other took a step toward me.

"Why don't you take a seat...I assume you are Leo Mas?"

I took the seat next to Kat, and threw a comforting arm around her. She leaned close to me, resting her head on my shoulder. A lead weight in my stomach.

"There's no easy way to put this," the cop's voice was soft as he tried to sound comforting. "Your friend, Fred Briggs, is dead."

The room went black and white. My throat closed tight. Palms started to sweat. The cop's mouth moved but made no sound. The room blurred. The lead weight in my stomach dropped 84 stories. I was aware of Kat, though. She began breathing a little faster, but she wasn't crying. In fact, aside from her breath, she revealed no emotion, not even acknowledging the cops' presence. She adjusted closer to me.

A jumble of words fell from my mouth, as I excused myself from that spinning room. I walked seven long steps to Kat's bathroom. Clutching her toilet, I released the contents of my stomach. It tasted like coffee and whiskey and poppyseed muffin. I pulled myself up, washed my face. In the mirror, I stared deeply into my own brown eyes. My face was pale, and the whites of my eyes were slashed and zigzagged with broken capillaries. I was staring at my eyes when the tears began to escape.

I cleared my throat, pulled myself together, washed my face again, and re-entered the scene. The cops were still standing in the living room, but Kat was now in the kitchen brewing some coffee. I sat down on the couch.

"What happened?"

The cops shot each other a quizzical glance, and non-verbally realized that I had not heard a word they said.

"Fred was struck by a car near Toro and Walnut. A nasty intersection." Two blocks away. He almost made it.

"The driver of the vehicle was intoxicated." It wasn't Fred Briggs' fault.

"This occurred as somewhere between 2AM and 3AM. He was declared dead on the scene." It wasn't his fault.

"Was he...messed up?" I wasn't sure how to ask the cops if Fred was drunk or high, but luckily the cop understood.

"Blood results detected some alcohol, but nothing else." He wasn't even on coke. It wasn't his fault.

Kat poked her head in the room to hear the cop's description, but she still bore a blank expression. I buried my head in my hands, searching for some protection from this strange world. My friend. Gone.

My mind wandered back to the homeless man's sign.

"TODAY IS THE DAY OF THE REST OF YOUR LIFE. SMILE"

fallout.

A fog enveloped Santa Labre. I walked around, saw blurred faces. People were carrying on, business-as-usual. I sat at a coffee shop in a seat that faced the street. I held a pen to paper, but produced nothing. Everything was cloaked in a sheet of gray mist. A couple of street musicians played for a small crowd that gathered on the sidewalk. They plucked and strummed and beat a bucket. People clapped and smiled. I couldn't hear.

I imagined him smiling and laughing at a party, a girl under his arm or a beer in his hand. I imagined him leaving the party. Crossing the street. Then a car zooms around the corner, crushing Fred Briggs. Did Fred die instantly? Did he lie there in the street alone, or was he pinned to a light pole? Did he know he was about to die?

My thoughts eventually led me to the driver. I tried to imagine his face. Was it a man? I imagined him as a man.

Drunk, sad, a piece of shit. He was probably a terrible person. No friends, no family. The world abandoned this man as he had abandoned the world. He probably lied frequently. He probably stole frequently. Or maybe he was just a dude.

The pen I was holding snapped in half. On my notebook page was a dark, jagged mark that I had made in my anger, unknowing and unwilling.

I called Kat as I left the coffee shop. No answer. I hadn't seen her since we found out about Fred, but we had exchanged a few texts. She said she was busy with some photography gigs.

I hopped on my motorcycle, and bumbled down Chorro, toward the house that I was living in. I had no idea what I was supposed to do. Lost. Was I a squatter now? I knew Fred Briggs' parents were gone, but what happened to the house if I left?

I slammed on the brakes as I skidded to a stop, just short of the rear bumper of a car, stopped at a stop sign. I waved my hand in apology, and the older driver accepted it with a single-finger salute. Reminded me of the Major, on the day we found him, lying in his driveway.

Goddamn, I was distracted. I refocused on the

immediate task at hand, and eventually got back to Fred Briggs' house. There was a blue BMW 7-series parked in the driveway. Who is this? I suspected it was a member of Fred Briggs' family. I parked my bike on the street and walked across the lawn. I paused for a second, considering whether I should knock on the door or not. I decided not to. I opened the door and stepped into the living room. Heard crinkling of paper and saw a fifty-something year old woman packing glassware into boxes.

"Hi, I'm Leo Mas." I said as she looked up. She seemed a bit startled, so I followed up, "I'm...was...am a friend of Fred."

Her face softened, and she leaned against one knee, pushing herself up. She wiped off a dusty hand before clutching mine.

"Hello, Leo. I'm Fred's aunt, May." She had a comforting warmth about her, but her sad eyes stood front and center.

"I'm so sorry about Fred," I offered. It was hollow. I didn't know how to act in those situations. I felt like I was giving a bandaid to a person with a broken leg. Useless, but all I had were fucking bandaids.

"Me too, Leo."

"Fred was nice enough to let me stay here over the past few months."

"He was always so generous…"

"Would you like something to drink?" I offered a second token, and it was received by a smile.

"A beer would be lovely, Leo."

So, we had a few beers in the living room where I had done the same so many times with Fred Briggs and Kat and Donnie.

I told her stories. How I came to Santa Labre. The day we found the Major. Our trip to the desert.

"I haven't seen Kat in a few days," I said, almost under my breath. Non-sequitur. Not sure why I threw it out there. Then, I heard a scratching at the backdoor. Donnie.

"Excuse me, Auntie May," She smiled as I left. I don't quite know why I called her Auntie. But it somehow felt right.

I walked to the backdoor, opened it. Donnie greeted me with a wet tongue as I took a knee next to him. I hugged him close, and he kissed my cheek.

"That's adorable."

fallout.

I turned to see Auntie May leaning against the hallway wall. "He loves you."

A sadness struck me as I realized this pup had lost a friend, too. "Donnie is actually Fred's."

"Oh dear…" Auntie sniffed, then sneezed. "I'm not sure what I'm going to do with him then. I can't take him, and there really isn't anyone else. Do you know of any of Fred's friends that would take him?"

Just then, a phone rang. Auntie May retreated back to the living room. I heard her talking about funeral arrangements. Sounded like Fred Briggs was going to be cremated. I returned my attention to Donnie to push down these damn feelings.

* * * * *

That night, I sat on the back porch with Donnie. May was asleep on the couch. Fred Briggs' bed, behind closed doors, was empty. Of course it was. Donnie had been acting strange since the passing of his owner. He paced between rooms, he sat outside of Fred Briggs' bedroom. He looked up at me with confused and concerned eyes. He knew. He somehow knew. I hugged Donnie close to offer comfort to him.

So Donnie and I sat there, staring up at star-filled night

303

sky, me smoking a joint that I rolled, Donnie smoking nothing because he is a dog. At joint's end, Donnie and I went inside. We huddled together in my bed in this once strange house.

Rustling in the living room woke me up. Donnie had already left to check it out. A fresh pot of coffee already made, and I poured myself a cup before strolling to the living room. Auntie May had been busy. Fred didn't have many belongings, but they all seemed collected in cardboard boxes in the living room.

Deep within Cardboard City, a voice. "Good morning, Leo. Help yourself to some coffee."

"Thank you, Auntie. Already did." I opened a box and looked inside. Mechanics books. "So, what is going to happen to the house? Are you going to live here?"

The rustling stopped. "No, Leo. This house is to be sold." She must have read some surprise on my face, because she followed it up quickly. "The sale will be happening sometime in the next few weeks or months. You, of course can stay here for a while, but I can help you find a place."

I laughed for some reason. "No, no. I'll be fine." Then it was my turn for an untimely interruption, my phone vibrated in my pocket.

The first mate of the *Rascal* was calling. "Hey, bro. Can you come to the docks? We could use a hand with our last haul."

Paused for a moment before replying. "I'll be there."

I turned back to Auntie May. "Sorry, I have to head out for work."

"Of course, Leo. I am going to finish up here. We can talk later."

I put on some jeans and buttoned a work shirt. Grabbed my helmet as I headed for the door. May was back behind the boxes.

"Oh, by the way, May. I'll watch Donnie. I think that's what Fred would have wanted. Or would have expected."

She smiled, "I hoped you would say that. Donnie is best off following you."

I headed out.

* * * * *

I eventually returned from the docks. It was dark. May's car was gone from the driveway. Walked through the front door. The couch was still there, but everything else seemed to be gone. Stereo, gone. Toaster, gone.

Hang-towels, gone. Fucking gone. I peeked in Fred Briggs' room. Barren, wall-to-wall. Walked through the empty kitchen to the room I was staying in. I half-expected it to be empty, but it was not. It appeared to be mostly untouched, save for a single box, a manila envelope, and a folded letter with my name written in fine cursive. I reached down to pick up the letter.

> *Leo~*
>
> *Sorry I had to leave, but I have to tend to Fred's burial. We are doing it in Phoenix, near his brother, his uncle, and me. I'm sorry it's a bit far away, but we would love it if you came. Please reach out to me if you come - there are a few contact numbers on the fridge.*
>
> *I can tell you were a good friend to Fred. I will be back in Santa Labre within a couple months to assist with the sale of the house, but you are welcome to stay in the house. You are welcome to anything in the house, I cleaned and packed what I could.*
>
> *I hope you find what you are looking for, Leo.*
>
> *Love, Auntie May*

I folded the letter. I stood in the quiet solitude of that

house for years, staring at the letter. I finally took a knee, next to the envelope and box. I opened the box first. Shifted the contents around. A few automechanic books. An old jacket. A knife. And a notebook. It caught my eye because I didn't think Fred Briggs was a writer. I picked up the notebook, a fine, brown leatherbound notebook far older than mine. I flipped open to the first page. It had a flower sketch, and a name written below it: "Major Thomas Calhoun." I shifted to a more comfortable position, knocking the envelope to the floor. Its contents jingled a bit as it fell to the carpet. I put the notebook down, distracted by the tinkling sound. I turned the envelope upside down, and a set of keys dumped out. One key that I presumed was a house key. The other key had "Chevrolet" embossed on the black plastic. I turned it over in my fingers, letting it fall between fingers, caught by another, legerdemain. This was clearly the key to the Chevelle that was sitting in the driveway.

My phone buzzed, bringing me out of my trance. Text from Kat.

Hi Leo. I'm outside. Got a minute?

I hopped to my feet and bounded outside.

"What's up, Kat?"

"Your neighbor just cut down a dead tree. They're giving away firewood. Let's go burn some shit at the beach. Down?"

She didn't explain why she appeared outside of Fred Briggs' house. I didn't ask. "Down. Let me grab a jacket."

She turned to her car, yelled over her shoulder. "I'm driving!"

I went back inside. Went for the first jacket I saw, the one that I unpacked from the box. I took a knee next to some of the Fred stuffs that she had left. Setting the envelope to the side, I repacked the rest of it into the box. Carried it outside to Kat's car, and put it in her back seat.

preserve.

From the delirium of Kat Scindo.

Lost. Each breath I took was a little too shallow. Each bite of food, a little too bland. But I used salt.

Fortunately and unfortunately, I was busy. I had several gigs, which was good timing since I lost that chunk back in Vegas. I picked out a convincing smile, placed it on my face, and danced like a monkey so rich people would pay me.

On a Friday, I was playing at a welcome home reception for some kid that had just finished his undergrad at Yale. Filled with prominent brows and prissy dresses, they asked me to play some jazz standards on guitar and piano. I got lost in the music. The notes flowed second nature from my fingers, and I could feel an extra push as I sang. When I was on stage, nothing mattered. I was enveloped in the performance. Didn't matter that I was playing background music. It didn't matter that no one was standing and watching me. It didn't matter that I was alone on stage. It didn't matter that no one noticed or cared to notice that extra ounce of emotion I was putting into the music. A wonderful distraction it was. I played for a few hours before I earned a break from the stage.

"Thanks, so much, young lady," a woman in a pants suit said to me, as she touched my forearm. "We are going to do some announcements and toasts, feel free to take a few minutes and help yourself to a drink."

"Thanks, I'll be back in fifteen." I smiled at the Hillary Clinton-look alike.

"OK, make sure it's just fifteen."

I walked to the open bar and asked for a glass of chardonnay. I would have preferred a tall cup of a red, or a shot of gin or whiskey, but I had to keep up appearances. I watched the rich people in their fancy dresses and suits meander, talking about fascinating topics like the weather and their boring fucking cubicle jobs. I swirled my wine, feeling as an outsider looking in, even though I could blend. I wore long black sleeves to cover my tattooed arms. I smiled as I thought about ripping my sleeves and screaming just to fuck with these richies' world. I needed an escape, so I decided to step outside.

I walked out of the banquet hall, grabbed my denim jacket from the coat check, and followed the walkway outside. Around the corner, I took a seat on a concrete bench overlooking a beautiful courtyard. I took a gulp of wine, a gulp large enough to be inappropriate had I been within the eyes of the people inside. Pulled the glass from my lips, tipping it up, and watched the pale liquid retreat down the sides of the glass. Out of nowhere, the tears came. They streamed down my face, smearing my make-up and dropping to the sidewalk underneath my feet. Even when I had company or family, and even though I had lived alone for most of my life, I had never felt more lonely.

I tried fighting back, but I was a victim of the moment. I was forced to ride this emotion outburst until it ran its course. I grieved for Fred. But there was something else gnawing at me, something that confused me and pushed me further into my sadness. Guilt. Feelings of guilt were brought on because the majority of thoughts swimming around my mind were not of Fred, his life, or his untimely death. My thoughts were of myself, and of Leo. I hadn't seen Leo much over recent days. We had only talked a bit, since we found out about Fred.

My break was almost up now. I threw back the rest of my wine, trying to push myself back into reality. Left the glass on the bench, strode quickly and quietly into the ladies' room. I was relieved to find it empty. I blotted the tears from my eyes and face with a paper towel. Reached into my jacket pocket to grab some eyeliner. I fucking hated makeup, but it helped me blend in with these sophisticated types. Tonight, it would help to cover up the fact that I was bawling five minutes ago. As I was returning the eyeliner to my jacket pocket, I felt something peculiar. It was a plastic baggy. I pulled it from my jacket, still unsure of its contents.

Mushrooms.

I had forgotten that I had them in my jacket in a pocket I rarely use. Although we ate some in Vegas and in Joshua tree, I still had a hefty stash left over. I cracked open the bag, and examined a few caps and stems in my palm. I rolled them over with my fingers, admiring their alien shapes. I was entranced for a moment. Suddenly, I heard the bathroom door creak open. Panicked, I hid them the fastest way that I could. I hid them in my mouth. They tasted terrible, and I chewed them and swallowed them as I stuffed the baggy back in my jacket. Another Hillary Clinton strode into the restroom and smiled at me.

preserve.

"You were marvelous, darling," she said, complimenting my music for the masses.

"Why, thank you, ma'am," I plastered a fake smile and a respectful demeanor to my posture as I hid my internal panic.

* * * * *

And a second act it was.

Singing.

Strumming.

Was I singing too loud?

Talking between songs.

Stupid jokes.

Scattered laughter.

Lizard people dining on rainbow steak filets.

I can see their thought bubbles.

More playing.

Music danced from my guitar and piano and tickled their ears or slapped them in their lizard faces.

These notes sure are colorful.

Fraternizing with the rich folk after my performance.

Plastered smile as I watched non-existent facial hair sway in the non-existent wind.

Was I smiling too much?

But it was in my mind. The Hillary in charge paid me five hundred in cash, and even gave me an extra one-fifty as a bonus. They bought it.

Took a cab home. Got back to my apartment. Put my gig bag in the corner, and slumped into my favorite armchair. Pulled out my phone, started to text Leo about my experience, but stopped short. As I put my phone in my jacket pocket, I felt the crinkling of the plastic baggy again. I was still riding my impromptu trip. I smiled.

Fuck it. I poured a few more pieces of funky fungi into my hand and tossed them in my mouth. The bad taste hit me harder this time around, so I walked to my kitchen and took a pull from my bottle of gin.

A quick visit to another dimension was a welcome distraction.

I always had a fondness of psychadelics. I had a generous supply, and could not resist. I always thought of psyches as a restart button. A way to look at yourself

introspectively and objectively. A way to improve yourself as a person and see passed roadblocks that you would
otherwise be unable to see. But, damn. They were also a
lot of fucking fun.

I took a couple in the mornings, just enough to help
me enjoy vibrant colors or the cool breeze. I would take
taxis to my gigs. Usually. I drove a few times if I was late.
I was able to pull the gigs off just fine. Mostly because the
sets were vanilla, walks through a park. Actually, I had
more gigs than usual. Instead of putting my earnings in
the bank, I came straight home and tossed the cash in my
kitchen drawer that usually just contained spatulas and
ladles and rolling pins.

Sometimes, often, the shrooms would drive me deep
into my thoughts and introspection. That's where the gin
came in. It would allow me to trip through bliss. A wandering through a world of music you can see and colors
you could hear. The colors were actually kind of blue, but
still fascinating distraction.

On one such day, I started digging through a shoebox
labeled *"Favorites."* Inside were old photos and photos
and photos. I came upon a photo from our recent road trip.
It showed me, Leo, Fred, and Donnie slumped against a
tree after our backpacking trip in Zion. I remember that

moment so vividly. I had set my camera on a timer, and placed it carefully on the hood of Fred's Chevelle. Leo was stern-faced, trying to act tough after our trip. I was grinning like an idiot, holding a peace sign, and hugging the tongue-lolling Donnie. Fred blinked with perfectly imperfect timing. A huge grin shined through his thick beard. I laughed as tears cascaded down my cheeks. Then, my tears of fond memories turned to tears of desperate heartache. Maybe it was the hallucinogens or the gin, but I realized that I couldn't remember the color of Fred's eyes. I did everything. I imagined him looking at me. I took out my colored pencils set, and scattered them on the floor of my bedroom, searching for the correct shade. Blue? Gray? Light brown? Grasped at smoke. I searched through all my photos on my computer and saved in my camera. No clear photos of Fred's eyes.

Wallowing in despair, I stretched out on my back in the middle of my living room. Maybe that piece of Fred Briggs was gone. What if no one remembered the color of his eyes? If his eye color is never remembered, did it ever really exist? What else had the world forgotten of Fred, never to be recovered?

I crawled over to my phone to text Leo. I want to reach out. Grabbed the phone, returned to my sprawled position in the middle of the room. Searching for answers. Searching, but not finding. I felt my world spinning. At least partly due to the shrooms. I lifted my phone above my face to start a message to Leo. In the reflection of my phone, I saw me. Bloodshot eyes, red faced, dilated eyes, scraggly hair. I brought up the camera on my phone. But I didn't want to be remembered like this. Not like this.

SNAP. Oops. I took a photo with a twitch of my thumb. I dared not look at it, but I also didn't delete it.

I can deliver a better me to the future.

reunion.

Back in the house of Fred Briggs, Leo.

My phone buzzed, bringing me out of my trance. Text from Kat.

"Hi Leo. I'm outside. Got a minute?"

First text from Kat, since we found out about Fred Briggs. I hopped to my feet and bounded outside.

"What's up, Kat?"

"Your neighbor just cut down a dead tree. They're giving away firewood. Let's go burn some shit at the beach. Down?"

She didn't explain why she appeared outside of Fred Briggs' house, but I didn't ask. "Down. Let me grab a jacket."

She turned to her car, yelled over her shoulder. "I'm driving!"

reunion.

I went back inside. Went for the first jacket I saw, which was the one I had unpacked from the box that Auntie May had left. I took a knee next to some of the Fred stuffs that she had left. Setting the envelope to the side, I repacked the rest of it into the box. Carried it outside to Kat's car, and put it in her back seat.

Kat was across the street, standing amid the pile of lumber in front of Fred's neighbor's house. She stood on top of a stump, staring at me as I approached. The wood she stood on was oak. The neighbors felled an old oak tree, and it was now discarded, chopped into sections, waiting for someone or some trash truck to take it away. Kat stood on one leg, balancing.

"You gonna help?" I bent over to pick up a couple of the smaller logs.

She twirled on the stump. "I'm busy!" She hopped off, tried to pick up her stage, realized it was too heavy, then moved on to more manageable chunks. We put a half dozen logs in Kat's trunk.

Hopped in her car.

Headed beachward.

Windows down.

Music by Chicago blaring.

Kat sang along with *Make Me Smile*, barely above the music and wind.

I smiled. I missed this feeling this. Felt like it had been years. For a moment, I allowed myself to enjoy the smell, the wind, the feeling. Feeling.

We reached Avila Beach.

It was a weekday, so that sleepy beach town was quiet. A few couples strolled at the edge of the unfurling sheets that spread across the sand. We parked at the far end of the beach. The sun was an hour or so from set.

"How you been?" I broke the conversation drought.

Kat put her red Honda in park. "Busy as fuck, man."

"Yeah? Gigs?"

"Yeah. The money is hard to turn down." She opened the driver door and stepped out. "And a good distraction."

"Let's burn this wood. You got any tobacco?"

"Ye."

"I'll roll a couple doobies. You unload this wood, mister."

"Don't fuck up those rolls, Kat. I'm trusting you with my life."

"I learned from the best."

I carried the logs, two at a time to a spot away from the meandering couples. Kat leaned against her front bumper, using the hood as a flat surface to roll her smoking tools. She finished up and jaunted over.

"Two cigs and a spliff," holding them out proudly.

"Three, ey?"

"One for Fred Briggs."

"Good call."

Start with the spliff. "To Fred." Kat lit the tip and inhaled deep.

She passed it to me.

"We love you, Fred Briggs." I inhaled, held it in, eyes closed.

"Fucking crazy." I finally released, staring at the horizon. I passed back to Kat.

"Yeah, Crazy." She inhaled. "Just like that. Gone. Why? He was so happy. For sure happier than you, you sad fuck."

"Speak for yourself, you fucking sunshine-on-a-daisy downer."

Laughs. "Fuck you, Leo." She turned to the wood. "We burning this shit, or what?

"You do it. I carried it over here. Let's see how your fire building technique is."

"I'll burn this fucking beach down. I'm going to build a log cabin starter."

"Whatever the fuck you want."

She started digging a small pit.

"I'm gonna grab something." I left her to her work.

"I'm busy!" She shouted.

I went to Kat's car, opened the back door, and pulled out the box of Fred's belongings. I leaned it against my hip, and closed the door. Returned to Kat's project.

"How's it going over there, Kat?"

"Shut the fuck up, Leo. What do you have there?"

"Box that Fred Briggs' aunt left at the house. Bunch of Fred's junk."

She stopped, kneeled next to the box and peered inside.

"Anything good?"

I unfolded the top. Kat peered in, poked at the contents, lifted up the automechanic books.

"Junk. What's this notebook?"

"I'm not sure, I was just starting to look through it when you texted me. I didn't know Fred Briggs had a notebook."

"Yeah I didn't think he did." She thumbed through a few pages. "This is old, man." A few more pages. "Shit! I think this is the old man's notebook!"

"Fred's dad?"

"No, no. I think this belonged to the old dude that we found on that driveway. The military guy. It looks like he was a Major. I think this notebook was his while he was in the service."

"Oh yeah ... I kind of remember Fred Briggs mentioning that when we were in Zion. Definitely something I wanted to check out, but completely forgot about it. May must have left it thinking it was one of ours."

"May?"

"Yeah, Fred's aunt came by and cleaned up a bunch of

stuff. This is pretty much the only box that she left."

"Ah, that's who's BMW was in the driveway."

"Wait, you came by the house?"

"Yeah." She started digging in the box, and quickly changed the subject. "Anything worth anything in here? Ah, this is a sweet knife." She snapped it open, ran her fingers along the sharpened blade. The wood grip was worn from the inside of many pockets.

I watched her as she twirled the knife through her fingers. "What are we going to do with this stuff?"

"Let's burn it."

"What? Why?"

"Do you want this junk? We came here to burn shit, so let's burn some shit. Fred Briggs wouldn't care. And, I don't know...it might be a good way to see him off."

"Hm ... alright, let's make a deal. Let's each choose one of Fred's things to keep. The rest of it, we will burn."

"Fair enough, Leo." She smiled and pointed to my chest. "I want that jacket."

The navy blue canvas jacket was keeping me warm, and I noticed Kat's bare shoulders. I wasn't sure if she wanted the jacket in memoriam of Fred Briggs, or if she was just cold. Either way, I didn't fight it and handed it over. She snatched the jacket from my hand and put it on. She ran two fingers along the embroidered name on the left breast. Freddy.

"Where's your denim jacket?" I asked her.

"Left it at home. I'm nice and warm now, though." She grinned. "Sucks to be you."

I leaned over and grabbed the notebook, but called her out as I opened it. "So are you going to start this fire or what?"

Kat didn't budge. "Is that what you're choosing?"

"Huh? Yeah, I guess so. I feel fucked up burning this notebook."

"But it's not even Fred Briggs'."

"Yeah, but a deal's a deal. We said one thing each."

"You made that rule, dummy." Kat folded the knife at her feet, stood, and tossed it at my feet. "Keep that. We can't burn it, anyway." She walked over to the fire, and continued prepping. She pulled out the contents of the box and started placing them amongst the firewood.

"Alright, fair enough."

Kat sat up, almost finished prepping the fire. "I want to add one more thing."

"Yeah? What is it?"

Kat leaned to one side, and pulled out and unfolded a photo from her back pocket. She handed it to me. It was a picture Kat, me, Donnie, and Fred Briggs at the end of our camping experience in Zion Canyon. A lump expanded in my throat, and I tried to swallow it. It only grew, and I felt drops climbing up the inside of my cheeks toward my eyelids. A desperate struggle to keep control.

"It's yours." That was all I could muster.

"I know it is." She took a knee, next to the fire again. She set the photo at the edge of the kindling.

"One more thing." She ran back to her car. There was something different about Kat. I couldn't put my finger on it, but she was changed. Her face, her eyes, her demeanor. Almost like she had spent days with windows drawn in a deep, dark cave, and she was still adjusting to the light of the real world. Kat returned with a red gas canister.

"What the fuck?"

reunion.

"What? There's just a little in it." She started drizzling the fuel on the pile of flammables. "If you're gonna get wet, you might as well drown."

I sat in the sand, uneasy. I watched Kat.

burn.

From Hades within Kat Scindo.

I licked my lips as I carefully made a small log-cabin style firestarter with sticks, some paper, and some dryer lint. The mounds of books and junk and memories were stacked around the little cabin. I paused, imagining the cabin was a home nestled in the valley within a great mountain range. Perhaps it was a mountain retreat for a suburban family. I wish I could just live in that comfy little house. A little haven from the outside world. Poking out from the pile was a photo of us three: Leo, Fred Briggs, and me. And Donnie. We looked exhausted after our backpacking trip in Zion. We looked too tired to be anything but happy.

I remembered back on how I felt in Zion. Exhaustion, for sure, but there was a simplicity in that. Leo sometimes talked about being comfortable while being uncomfortable, and I had always made fun of him for it. But, I kinda got it. That feeling that I got when I dropped my pack to make camp. That feeling that I got when I left my camp to end the hike. True relief. That's what I saw in our faces in that picture.

I blinked to refresh my dry eyes as they stayed glued on that little log-cabin fire-starter surrounded by my friend's belongings. I didn't take my eyes away from that photo, but my fingers stayed focused on the task at hand. They snapped a single match, and shoved the tiny flame into that little home.

The fire breathed life. The little sticks I collected caught almost immediately, licking the gas-soaked books and logs. It was almost as if the flames came from within the pages, as if a closed book simply prevented the inferno from escaping. I could feel the glowing orange warmth rising against my face. With each passing second, the flames danced and swirled around the fuel pile, elevating higher. Each second passed injected the pyre with new enthusiasm. Each second passed gave the fire new confidence until it was a roaring inferno.

The culmination of my tedious work, fueled by a strange, disconnected emotion, manifested itself in the burning of these books. Raised my head up from the pyre, my lips curled involuntarily toward the night sky. A smile, I guess. In my mind, I stepped back from the scene; I was watching myself in action. I saw me standing there upright, matchbook still in hand. I saw my stone face, licked by the fire. I saw Leo standing next to me. His gaze pierced me. But I could not look at him. He did not reach out to me. He did not speak. He did not move at all. I watched the two of us stand there, motionless as the flame danced on top of our friend's past. Our past.

detach.

The golden amber flames shucked and jived in the reflection of Kat's eyes. It was clear something was changed. I wanted to stop her. I wanted to stamp out the flame. I wanted to yell out my anger. I wanted to cry. I wanted to reach out and hold Kat and let her cry in my shoulder.

But I did nothing.

I stood there.

Kat walked over. Stood motionless, staring into the pyre. Then she gave me a hard shoulder bump and headed off down the beach. She thought she was tough. I followed her into the darkness, running my bare feet through the sand as we strode down the beach away from the fire.

Kat paused for a second, turned on her heel, and suddenly sprinted back to the fire. I watched as she leaned down and plucked something from the edge of the flames. She threw some sand on it, extinguishing the edges that glowed with heat. She stuffed it in her coat pocket. I never asked her what it was that she had kept.

We went straight from the beach to Kat's apartment. On the way there, I thought how strange it was that we had not seen each other in the past week. Now that we were together, there was a stiff energy between us, and there was a part of me that wanted to break it. I wanted to hug her and cry and let her cry. I wanted to run from her and go back to my bed and hide from Kat and the world. I wasn't sure if I felt like going into Kat's apartment, wasn't sure if I wanted to talk or try to move on without Fred Briggs. But his departure was inescapable. Kat, on the other hand, was still here, and I couldn't leave her alone. Like a zombie, I followed her into her apartment, and closed the door behind me.

She had three bottles on the counter. One, a red wine. Cheap and still corked. Two, a bottle of Jack Daniels. The square body showed the bottle was about two-thirds full. The third was a bottle of Beef Eater, also about two-thirds full. Kat went to her cupboard, grabbed two straight-sided glasses in one hand, and grabbed the bottle of Old Number 7 in the other. She set them on the kitchen table, and we took seats opposite each other.

We drank. We polished off the whiskey with ease before moving on to the gin. The power of the liquids was inexorable and melted down our sadness. We laughed, told stories of times passed, sang songs, and made fun of him as if he was sitting with us at the table. The moment of bliss was a pleasant distraction from the darkness of our own thoughts.

"I missed this," Kat said after taking a sip from her glass.

"What, you haven't had whiskey?" I joked.

"Hah, yeah. I missed whiskey."

I was happy to be with Kat. My main connection with her of late had been indirect, through the random text and the Instagram photos she posted. Being an artsy-type photographer, she was constantly posting photos of scenery or objects, never herself. However, I had noticed a trend in the past week. Not only were there more photos than usual but all the photos she posted were of herself. Sometimes an artificial smile decorated her face, other times her expression was stern and stoic. I wasn't sure which was more haunting.

"So, I've seen some of your posts on Instagram," I

casually lofted toward Kat. In response, she gulped down some gin. She stared at the empty glass, and I could tell that she had a mind full of grinding thoughts and theories, and she was mentally organizing themin a presentable way.

She spoke. "So, I've been thinking. I was looking up photos of Fred on Facebook. He posted some here and there, but you know how he was. Least photogenic person I've met. The few photos he did have were far away, or showed the back of his head or his car. So I Googled his name. A few more photos, but still not much. When someone looks up Fred in the future, they won't be able to see too many great photos of him. That goes for everyone. When you look up someone from your past, you know that that impression of them is just that: an impression. Not close to complete. Nowhere fucking close."

I swished my glass around before shooting my own glass. I grabbed the bottle and refilled both our glasses. I said nothing, but wondered where she was going with this.

Kat continued, "What will people see when they Google 'Leo Mas' 100 years from now? Will they see your crazy adventures? Will they see you on the day that you got poison oak and your eye was swollen shut? Will they see how you looked on June 16th, 2014? What about June

15th? 14th?" She paused to take just a sip from her glass. "No. No matter what you do, who you are and who you were will be lost forever. Lost, at the mercy of interpretation. Well, not me. I'm not gonna leave my impression up to the judgment of some fucking internet nerd 150 years from now. No, sir, not me." She set the glass on the table. For the first time, she had held direct eye contact with me for more than a few seconds. Our eyes were locked during her entire rambling.

I said nothing. Is there anything I could say? It was a valid point. I thought about the past week, and how her spiraling mind went down this wormhole, landing on this island of her final conclusion.

I said nothing about how we had just come from a bonfire where we burned books, photos, and other mementos of Fred. To me, it was a memorial, and a way to see Fred off to the next world. But, in the light of her most recent tirade of theories, what did the burning mean to Kat?

I remembered her running back to the fire and collecting a single artifact before it was engulfed in flames. I didn't ask what it was. As one of the road, I didn't like holding on to physical pieces. Took up space, both physically in its weight and volumes, but mentally in its weight. Still, I wondered what it was she took. But I said nothing.

Alcohol and music allowed the serious moment to quickly be shuffled off into the corner of our minds, and we continued on with the night.

Those bottles weren't full when we started, but they ended empty. I went outside for a moment, to get some fresh air and smoke a rolled cigarette. My knees wobbled as they adjusted to the equilibrium of the moving earth, and I found support by leaning against the wall. I looked out. Night still dominated Santa Labre, but the eastern horizon was just starting to tire of holding back the daylight. The blackness of night was not so black in the east.

I returned inside. A huge, drunken, mischievous grin spread itself beneath Kat's slightly drooping eyes. Both her palms were laid flat on the table, and the single overhead light shone down on her like an interrogation scene. Between her flattened palms were two objects. First, her shot glass, filled to the brim with gin. Next to the glass of poison was her .38 special revolver.

I froze. I felt the hairs on the back of my neck bristle. Then, my legs moved. They led me back to the seat opposite Kat. My face strained, forming some interpretation of a smile.

"What you got there?" I tired to sound as playful as possible.

336

detach.

"I like this gun," Kat responded. She didn't appear overtly angry or sad. She didn't seem maniacal. She talked with a level tone. Well, as level as one can speak after hours of whiskey and gin.

"Alright, Leo. *Andiamo.*"

I had no idea what she was talking about. Our eyes locked. She lifted the pistol, ejected the revolving carriage, gave a handy spin, flicked her wrist to close the carriage, and pulled back the hammer all with one hand. She then carefully placed the pistol in front of her, handle facing her, and the barrel facing slightly to my right.

"You're not down," she said coolly. Her face was joking, but her voice was serious. And her eyes. Her eyes pierced through me.

"Nah, not tonight, Kat," I tried to be cool, but my uneasiness was rising. I joked. "I'm not that old. It's too early to die."

"Are you?" Kat said. "Everyone dies. Some die young. Is it possible to die too early? Or does everyone die at exactly the right time?"

I said nothing. She was clearly wrestling with Fred Briggs' death inside her, and I just happened to be the object to which she was speaking.

337

She said something, though. "You're a fucking pussy."

She lifted the pistol, and examined the barrel. She ran her fingers along the Smith and Wesson engraving on the chrome-plated revolver.

Then, she lifted, pressed it against her temple.

Words were taken from me. Was she serious? Was this just her coping? Was she trying to shame me into her fucking game?

"What the fuck are you doing, Kat?"

"Come on, man. No quiero jugar?"

"No I don't want to fucking play!" My composure was starting falter. "Stop fucking around, Kat!"

"Why? I told you we were going to play someday. Why not tonight? Whether you like it or not, you're going to play someday. You're just putting it off." The smile now faded, replaced by a matter-of-fact tone, raised eyebrows, and wide eyes.

Oddly, perhaps as a matter of habit, Kat kept her finger off the trigger. Cold sweat drops gathered on my brow before joining together and racing down my face. I tried to stay calm, collected. I tried to control my breathing as Kat and I remained eye-locked, unblinking. The rotation of the Earth slowed, then stopped. The world outside that apartment hushed in anticipation, waiting for the moment to follow. I thought of lunging for the little revolver, but I was afraid the sudden movement would cause her to pull the trigger. I tried to grasp at the right words to talk Kat out of this. Comfort, logic seemed petty and useless. I suddenly noticed that tears were streaming down my face. Never had I felt so helpless.

Kat moved her finger so it rested on the trigger.

"Kat..." was all I could muster. Her face was like a marble wall, cold and unmoving.

Then, a slight curl of her mouth upward. Her lip quivered ever so slightly. Her dark, deep eyes glistened, but she did not cry. Her tendons in her forearm tightened, hand shifted slightly, and her finger began to tighten along the thin strip of metal that was the trigger. I wanted to tell her how I felt. But I didn't.

I said nothing.

She pulled the trigger.

Click.

The tension in the room immediately released. The colors returned to the walls and couches. I heard cars driving by outside, and the Earth restarted its spin.

"Relax, dude!" Kat burst out laughing. She threw back the shot of gin. "You seriously think I am just going to play fucking roulette? You are so gullible."

I breathed a real breath of air for the first time since re-entering the room. "Damn it, Kat! Fuck you!"

Kat set the gun on the table as she poured me another shot. I threw it down. A satisfying shot.

"Alright, that does it for me. Don't drive, you silly little bitch," Kat said as she was walked to her bedroom.

"I can fucking drive right now!" I called after her. I flopped down on the couch, and tried to allow the alcohol to soothe my thoughts after the fucking prankster pulled a fast one on me. I decided a glass of water would help, so I stood and walked to the sink. The alcohol had apparently affected me as I wobbled my way back to the couch. I walked over to the light switch to turn off the light that illuminated the dining table. In the corner of my eye, I saw the glint of the revolver. I picked it up, admiring the heft and solid construction of the chromed steel. I popped open the revolving chamber. A single bullet fell out.

realization.

I put in extra hours at the docks. I found it easier to ignore and see through the gray mist when I occupied my mind with menial tasks. I talked to no one. Just continued working. I tossed fish into ice chests. Prepped them with my knife. Chopped and slid them back into the chest. Chopped and slid. Chop and slide. Chop. Slide.

"Whoa! Easy there, Mas," Tom Carter, Jr. threw a friendly hand on my shoulder. I had been slamming the blade against the cutting board over and over. I had been chopping the same fish over and over, leaving the fish in a bloody mush of slivers and cubes of scales and flesh. I snapped out of my trance, wiped my brow, and turned to CJ. His normal smile melted away as he looked into my dark eyes. I felt a lump form in my throat and fought it down, shoving it deep into the fathomless pit where I hid the rest of my woes.

"What's up?" CJ offered. "Take a seat, man."

We sat on the side of the dock, dangling our feet over the edge. CJ pulled out a flask of a mystery liquid and handed it to me. I took a long pull of the strong stuff. Wiped my mouth. Handed it back to him.

"So what the fuck's going on?" He asked after a few moments of silence.

I sighed to stall. Outside, I was mostly stoic. A serious stone wall. I built that wall from the inside out with droves of masons working tirelessly to pile stones high, separating the outside world from my thoughts inside. Separating passersby from the writhing mess inside, protecting the mess. But, the protection was not absolute. Through the windows of my eyes, I knew the keen observer could see a swirling darkness within. Once in awhile, the darkness would overflow and leak out through my eyes. My horde of masons within were quick to patch the crack.

I pulled it together so I could look CJ in the eye. I only held it for a second before I started feeling a crack forming in the wall. I looked down, struggling to maintain the wall. As I answered him, the words felt foreign as they left me. It was as if someone else assembled them and pushed them through my mouth.

"It's my friend. He's gone." I told him just enough about Fred's accident. I didn't want to talk. I didn't even think I wanted to be around anyone. But, somehow, I did feel better saying it aloud to the fisherman. I realized I hadn't said anything at all for a few days. I would come home, and drink. Donnie lay next to me on the couch. Sometimes he would go into Fred's empty room, then come back and give me a confused look. I couldn't tell him that Fred was gone. Mostly because I had such a hard time saying it out loud.

Breaking my thoughts, CJ's voice, "What are you doing here? Get the fuck outta here!!"

I looked up at him, puzzled. He was yelling at a seagull that was trying to sneak and steal a fish. Although his message wasn't aimed at me, it found its home at the forefront at my mind.

"Yeah, this was just supposed to be a stop for me. Wasn't even supposed to be a stop. It's a mistake that I'm here." I stared off toward the ocean, watching the gull fly off in search of easier food.

"Well, what's really keeping you here?"

Silence for a stretch. "I don't know, man," I finally assembled some words. "Maybe I'm just getting lazy? Or complacent? This is the longest I've stopped in a few years. It's just...I don't know."

"Get the...fucking beat it!" CJ yelled at another gull, creeping toward our catch. There was a small flock circling us above. "When are you going to settle down, Mas? I can tell ya, we can use your hand here."

I chewed on it a bit, thinking of a way to word without offending. "Not really my thing, ya know? I want to see more. Being tied down gives me anxiety."

"Don't tell any ladies that, Mas!" laughed CJ.

"Maybe I need someone who is as adventurous as me…" I drifted.

"Good fucking luck with that, my friend." CJ stood and stretched his back. "Sorry for your loss. I'm sure your buddy is in a better place now."

"Thanks, CJ."

"You can take the rest of the day. I'll finish up here."

"Much appreciated, thanks."

CJ slapped a hand to my shoulder. "Take care of yourself, Leo. Get some rest, you look like shit. The Cap left your cut downstairs." He disappeared down below deck and reappeared with an envelope. "Here ya go."

"Sweet. Have a good one, CJ."

"Ride safe."

* * * * *

Strapped my helmet, slung a leg over my bike. Flipped the ignition, thumbed the starter and the motorcycle grumbled to life. Squeezed clutch, eased gas, shifted to first. Zoomed toward what I knew was a still house. Fred Briggs'-not-Fred Briggs' home. At least Donnie was waiting.

I reached the Santa Labre exit. I felt a little sick after my talk with CJ, and, although I couldn't put my finger on it, I had a general idea of where this uneasiness came from. I leaned into a turn and headed toward Kat's.

Jumped up the stairs to her apartment. Apprehension. I was anxious to address the gun incident, but there was also another fluttering in my gut.

Kat's door was unlocked.

An opaque quietude greeted me.

"Hello? Kat? Just wanted to say what's up. It's been a few days."

The still stiffened. I tiptoed through her apartment. Not sure why I was tiptoeing.

Kitchen. Looked like someone had emptied the kitchen cupboards of food. Dishes were still in the cabinets and in the dish rack. One drawer was pulled out of the wall, and dumped on the floor. Spatulas and serving spoons sprawled across the linoleum.

Living room. Messy, but not in bad shape. Stray tobacco and marijuana crumbs were scattered on the tabletop.

Kat's bedroom. The sick feeling in my stomach was growing. Dressers pulled out. One shoe here, another near the closet door. Sweaters, scarves, dresses in a pile.

Boxes were pulled from the closet and their contents were now spilled across the floor. I didn't see any art supplies. Unusual. In-progress art projects were a constant at Kat's place. Seemed like some of that should have been strewn about, but no.

Still no sign of Kat when something caught my eye. A bundle wrapped in a red bandana was placed on Kat's made bed. The neatly folded comforter contrasted the disarray that surrounded it. I shimmied through debris to the bedside. Took a seat on her bed. I picked up the bandana, rolled it around a couple times in my hands. Untied it.

Flattened it out on the bed to reveal the bundle's guts.

First. A .38 Special. Kat's little chrome revolver was the first thing I noticed. The silver barrel glinted in the afternoon light of her room. I picked it up, feeling the warmth of the wood grip. I thumbed the latch, and flipped open the cylinder. Six bullets loaded. There were only a few times that I had seen that .38.

Thoughts raced. The first time I glimpsed it was on the road trip with Kat, Fred Briggs, and Donnie. Just after the bear lumbered away into the bush, Kat slipped the gun from her pack into her jacket pocket for protection. She promised that she would let us shoot it when we sobered up, but that never happened. Shot it, I mean, not sobered up. The next time I saw it was a few days ago when Kat and I were sitting in her living room, drinking. Fucking Russian roulette. I still didn't understand what happened. I remembered the fear that stabbed my guts as she held the gun to her temple and pulled the trigger, and the flood of relief that washed over my body when she laughed and said she was joking. And then the disemboweling confusion that filled me when I saw there actually was one bullet in the cylinder. I never asked if she knew it was there.

Second in the bandana bundle. A bag of mushrooms.

The same bag that Kat had brought to the desert. The plastic bag was worn and strained, and lighter than last time I had seen it. Someone had been busy consuming these magic beings. Very busy. Or maybe they were lost in some other way. I pushed them around in the bag, then unzipped it and placed a single cap in my palm.

I thought about our time in Vegas. Wandering around clubs and casinos. Colors spinning and music throbbing. Wandering, but also searching for Kat. My thoughts meandered to *Wiregrass*. The dive deep into another realm. The emotions that engulfed me, magnified our surroundings. Noah, the deaf boy who climbed to the clouds with his dad's encouragement and guidance. I remembered Fred's boyish glee, unrealized by Fred Briggs of the past. I remembered Kat's glow in the desert heat.

Third, last, item in the bandana bundle. A photo paper clipped to a note. The photo was burnt on the lower left hand corner, charred and black. Ran my fingers along the crisp edge. This was the reason Kat ran back to the funeral pyre that we had for Fred on the beach. The picture was from our road trip to the desert. Fred Briggs, Donnie, me, and Kat. Fred Briggs' eyes were closed. We looked so tired, and so content.

A cement lump formed in my throat, and I struggled

to swallow. When I did, a couple involuntary abrupt breaths pinched air and delivered it to my struggling lungs. I regained control of my respiratory system, and took a single deep breath. Set the picture to the side, and directed my attention to the note. It was from Kat.

> *Leo -*
>
> *I assume you will be the one who first gets this letter. If you're reading this, I have left Santa Labre. Our trip to the desert reminded me what I was missing. And after all that's happened, I don't think I can stay in this city.*
>
> *It's been a rough few days. I'm sorry we haven't talked much since Fred's death. I wasn't sure why I was acting how I was, but I am sorry I wasn't there for you. I still can't believe what happened…*
>
> *I'll never forget my time with Fred Briggs and with you, Leo. I am sorry if I put you through anything, I just don't know how to act. I didn't want to hold you back. I'm afraid. Just know that I cherished the time we had together. I hope you don't forget me. I hope you find what you are looking for. I won't forget you.*
>
> *Love, Kat*
>
> *PS - I'm heading north.*

Tears ran down my cheek, dripped off my jaw, landed in my lap, followed by others, And others. A vice gripped my rib cage and crushed it into dust. I left the unfolded bundle, the letter, the photo, the mushrooms, the revolver on the bed, and dragged myself out through the debris in her room back to the living room. I slumped down on the couch.

Alone. The quiet pierced, and my ragged breath cut the silence. I stared at the ceiling, on the couch, in that apartment, in that town. In this world, alone. A rare close friend died. But I didn't have any control over that. I was devastated by that loss, and somehow this new one sent me reeling. My vision wobbled and spun and went black and white. As I drifted off into dark dimensions, four words ran through my mind.

I let her go.

continue.

I woke slow. It was mostly dark outside, but the fingers of dawn were just starting to reach up into the sky. The brisk morning air infiltrated Kat's apartment, and I welcomed the first waking moment of the day. Then, as my vision adjusted to my surroundings, the paraphernalia-littered coffee table, the stillness of Kat's living room, the events of the previous day crept back into my mind. I sat up, rubbed my eyes, hoping to awake from a nightmare. Hoping Kat was asleep in her room. Hoping Fred Briggs would call me, wondering if I was going to come home. Of course. None.

Out of habit, and to give my mind an escape the already overwhelming reality of the day, I started rolling a cigarette. The materials were conveniently presented on the table in front of me, and my mind devoured the menial task. Pinched tobacco, lined it up neat on the thin rectangle of rolling paper. Held the parcel between my fingers, rolling it into a tight, gradual cone, just as I had hundreds of times before. Put the cigarette in my mouth, leaned forward to the center of the table, grabbed a book of matches. Plucked one and snapped it, watched as it burned down, then brought the tiny dancing flame to the tip of the cigarette. Deep inhale. It was in that moment that I realized I did not like the taste of tobacco. The dry, sharp, spicy taste was not enjoyable. It was familiar. The ritual of rolling the cigarette was the true joy, escape. That little task. What a wonderful distraction. Exhaled.

I wanted to leave this place, Kat's apartment. I walked back in Kat's disaster of a bedroom, skipped over the mess to the bed. Placed the revolver, mushrooms, photo, and letter in the center of the bandana. Folded them into a compact bundle, small enough to fit in my jacket pocket. It stuck out a bit, but was good enough for a short ride. I was headed back to the only place I could: back to Fred Briggs' house.

The brisk morning air bit my cheeks, and I focused on the ride. Leaning, braking, accelerating. Accelerating a little extra. A bandaid distraction on the disintegration of the world that was happening around me. But it ended; I arrived at an empty house in an empty town in an empty world.

Except for Donnie.

He had escaped the backyard; Donnie bounded toward me as I pulled up on my bike. He was upon me before I dismounted, and rejoiced in my return to the still house.

"What's up, buddy!" I embraced him and scratched the loose scruff of his neck. His excitement wound up and sprung him off his hind legs. The full seventy-some-thing pounds fell on me, and I went down to the ground.

"I know, it's been so long, right?" It had only been a day or so. His tongue unraveled and lathered my face. I let it happen. "Alright, Donnie. Let's go inside."

My spirits were lifted momentarily, another band aid, although the one that Donnie provided was stronger. As we walked through the front door, the Still sucked the oxygen out of the air. Even Donnie fell quiet. I laid down, sprawled in the middle of the empty living room. Closed my eyes on that morning. Thought about the last few months.

Bumbling into Santa Labre in my old Jeep.

That Jeep breaking down.

Meeting Kat Scindo in that bar.

Meeting Fred Briggs and Donnie.

Reuniting with Kat Scindo.

Bonding with new friends.

The old Marine and the consequential roadtrip.

Fred Briggs' death.

Kat's disappearance.

Here. Here. Here.

Words sound strange when you repeat them over and over and over.

I thought about how Kat and Fred Briggs and Donnie were before I came along. They seemed like they were doing fine. Was I the domino that led to the events of the past week? Was I to blame?

Donnie licked my forehead, snapped me out of my trance. Snuggled close to me.

"What's going to happen to us, buddy?"

Us. I said it out loud, and I couldn't let Donnie down. We were in it together. I thought about the house and all that I had. Took inventory.

My pack and its contents. All that I came to Santa Labre with.

Some cash. Actually, a decent amount of cash. Between my hours at the docks, my share of the chunk that Fred Briggs and I got from fixing Dorothy's fence next door, and the envelope that I had from before coming to Santa Labre, I had a sizable reserve. In fact, for once, I wasn't strapped for cash. There was one critical aspect that this chunk bought me: time.

I continued to lie in the middle of the living room, in the middle of that empty house. I thought about my possessions. I had Kat's package. The shrooms, the photo, the gun, and the note. I sat up and took off my jacket. I took out the bundle and unwrapped it on the floor. Gun. Shrooms. Photo. Note.

I stood. Went to the other room. Grabbed my pack. Returned to the living room, and upended its contents next to the unwrapped Kat bundle. Sleeping bag, tent, stove, knife, a few envelopes of cash, and some other necessities were strewn about in the middle of the living room in the middle of that empty house in that little town by the sea. I stood above my belongings in this world. Donnie sat next to me, also looking down at the collection.

"You know what we have to do, Donnie."

355

He looked up at me, and we locked eyes.

"Leo. We have to pack your shit. We have to take the Chevelle. Aunt May left the keys and registration for a reason. We have to go. I'm torn apart about Fred. I don't know what to do either. But we can't stay here. Neither of us are meant for this place. We live on the road. Road is home. I'm sorry what happened to Kat, too, but I think it's a sign. You have to chase her, Leo. You haven't been this close to anyone in years. You've been wandering, but you may have found something. It slipped, but it's not lost. Let's go home, Leo."

I exhaled.

North.

Homecoming.

"No man steps in the same river twice, for it's not the same river and he is not the same man."-Heraclitus

I wish I could say I wasn't lonely. Miles ahead, miles behind. Didn't know where I was going, but definitely not lost. A chase? An escape? Or was I just discontent? Bored? All that mattered was a direction. Forward. I had little, but I was grateful to have that.

I thought about my recent past. My heart tightened. A feeling unfamiliar to me, so I fell back on something I was accustomed to.

I stretched over and grabbed my notebook. I flipped through full pages gone past, and stopped on one. I read.

A man looks back on his past. He finds shelter in the only home he knows. It sprawls ahead, as far as his weary eyes can reach, and, as the colors bleed into a gradual dark hue, he finds comfort in the nothingness. He sees what others do not see. He walks where others do not walk. The sun soaked rock faces offer a warmth without caveat, without judgment, without wish for restitution.

He breathes deeply, slowly. The warm air fills his lungs, lifting his spirits as hills crawl over the horizon ahead, then retreat beyond the horizon behind. His world is packed on his back, yet his past is what weighs him down.

In his exodus from the world he once knew, he came upon the world he was meant to love. With a guardian protecting his steps, a man walks forward into abyss.

Donnie, the brown-black shepard, trotted over, and took a seat by my feet. He had wandered away, exploring in the bush, maybe chasing a rabbit. But he came back. He always came back. He rested on his powerful haunches, breathing in and out, his tongue gently lolling in the morning air. I reached down and scratched behind his ears. He angled his head up toward me. Gray hairs speckled his muzzle, but he was only about five years young. He must have lived a heavy life, I thought.

I stood up and walked a few steps from my transportation, a '69 Chevelle. I stood in the middle of the road. I had pulled over late the previous night. Had to get at least some sleep. I took in the seductive curves of the classic car, reflecting the morning sun that was just starting to peek through the trees.

Circled to the back of the car, opened the trunk. I took inventory of what Donnie and I had. A couple jugs of water. Some beef jerky, Cheetos from a gas station. Some oranges that I had plucked from a grove that I passed a couple days back. My pack. A weathered, black-and-grey Osprey internal-frame pack. Light, but it contained most of my life. I grabbed the bottom, and dumped the contents on the floor of the trunk. Gave it a shake as I watched the contents spill out. The normal backpacking stuff: waterproof matches, kindling, toilet paper, first aid kit, flashlight and headlamp, a Gerber fixed-blade knife. I left my old tent and sleeping bag in the pack. Then a small bundle wrapped up in a red bandana tumbled out of my pack. I knew my gear in and out, yet this bundle felt like a new addition to my gear list.

I grabbed the bandana, and unfolded it. The bundle contained a photo with a notepaper clipped to the back. I noticed the charred edges, saved from licking flames, but

I didn't spend the time to study the photo or the attached note. I knew who this bundle was from, and I would have plenty of time to look over it later. I walked around to the driver's side and put it in the glove compartment. There was another item in that bundle, and I held it now, still partially wrapped in the bandana. I looked out at the empty road as I gripped the handle tight. The wood grip was soothing, and the cold steel bit at my fingers. After a few seconds, the steel warmed, as if getting use to its new owner. It was small, but I knew the power it had, and what it meant to be carrying this. I tucked the item in my front jacket pocket. I circled back to the open trunk, repacked all my gear as efficiently as possible.

I breathed in, allowing the frigid air to enter my lungs. Holding it in for a second, I slowly let the now-warm air slip out of my nostrils and into the world. Wishful thinking led me to believe I was warming my environment, but I knew the reality. The little heat that I added to the world was insignificant, a miniscule blip on the world-wide thermometer. The effort and energy put out was much more of a hardship on my own body than it was a benefit for the world. I took another breath.

Made in the USA
San Bernardino, CA
20 July 2019